Praise for the Sloan Krause mystery series

"Fans of Kate Carlisle and Ellery Adams will love Alexander's latest . . . enjoy with a cold beer."
—*Library Journal* on *The Cure for What Ales You*

"Distinctive characters and fun anecdotes about beer and brewing help make this a winner. Readers will want to keep coming back for more."
—*Publishers Weekly* on *Beyond a Reasonable Stout*

"Exciting and irresistible . . . This absorbing mystery will not let you leave it unfinished. Ellie Alexander is a formidable mystery novel writer."
—*Washington Book Review* on *Death on Tap*

"With its beautifully described small-town setting and seamlessly entwined details about brewing beer, this cozy will appeal to beer lovers everywhere as well as readers who enjoy mysteries highlighting family relationships and independent female main characters."
—*Booklist*

"Likeable characters, an atmospheric small-town setting, and a quirky adversary for the amateur sleuth. The engaging premise and pairings of beer and food should appeal to fans of Avery Aames's 'Cheese Shop' titles."
—*Library Journal*

"A delight for foodies, craft beer fans, and lovers of twisty mysteries with a bit of humor
—*Ki*

"Charming . . . featuring a clever protagonist and a talented brewer whose knowledge of the science and art of brewing beer is both fascinating and fun. The cozy village and the quirky characters who inhabit it are a delight, and the intriguing mystery will keep readers enthralled to the very end."

—Kate Carlisle, *New York Times* bestselling author of the Bibliophile and the Fixer Upper Mysteries

"Ellie Alexander's prose bubbles like the craft beers her protagonist Sloan Krause brews—a sparkling start to a new series."

—Sheila Connolly, *New York Times* bestselling author of the Orchard Mysteries and the Cork County Mysteries

"A concoction containing a charming setting, sympathetic characters, and a compelling heroine that kept me turning pages way past my bedtime."

—Barbara Ross, author of the Maine Clambake Mysteries

"*Death on Tap* is an entertaining sip of the world of brewpubs and tourist towns. Sloan, a foster child turned chef, brewer, and mother, is an intriguing protagonist. Pour me another!"

—Leslie Budewitz, two-time Agatha Award winning author of the Food Lovers' Village Mysteries

"A 'hopping' good cozy mystery . . . Readers will enjoy listening to local gossip and tracking a killer along with her in the charming German-style 'Beervaria' setting of Leavenworth, Washington."

—Meg Macy, author of *Bearly Departed*

THE CURE
FOR WHAT
ALES YOU

ELLIE ALEXANDER

St. Martin's Paperbacks

This is a work of fiction. All of the characters, organizations, and events portrayed in this novel are either products of the author's imagination or are used fictitiously.

Published in the United States by St. Martin's Paperbacks, an imprint of St. Martin's Publishing Group

THE CURE FOR WHAT ALES YOU

Copyright © 2021 by Kate Dyer-Seeley.

For information, address St. Martin's Publishing Group, 120 Broadway, New York, NY 10271.

www.stmartins.com

Library of Congress Catalog Card Number: 2021016065

ISBN: 978-1-250-78147-5

Our books may be purchased in bulk for promotional, educational, or business use. Please contact your local bookseller or the Macmillan Corporate and Premium Sales Department at 1-800-221-7945, ext. 5442, or by email at MacmillanSpecialMarkets@macmillan.com.

Printed in the United States of America

Minotaur hardcover edition published 2021
St. Martin's Paperbacks edition / November 2022

10 9 8 7 6 5 4 3 2 1

This book is dedicated to the very real community of Leavenworth, Washington. Thank you for welcoming me to your village and allowing me to take inspiration from the place you are lucky enough to call home.

CHAPTER
ONE

THE SCENT OF CITRUS enveloped the brewery as I dumped a bucket of Lemondrop hops into the brew. The new hop varietal had become an overnight sensation, with its notes of lemon, mint, melon, and green tea. Garrett Strong, my brewing partner, and I were using the new style of hop to enhance the fruit profile of one of our spring ales—the Lemon Kiss. Our first batch of the light and refreshing beer had been a huge hit. It was unlike anything we had brewed to date, thanks to the unique hop profiles. In addition to the Lemondrop hops, we had added two of the most popular varietals in the region—Calypso and Lotus—along with lemon zest and fresh squeezed lemon juice. The result was a bright and tangy IPA that reminded me of sipping iced lemonade on the back porch. It was perfect for spring. The only problem was keeping it on tap.

Luckily we had planned ahead for this weekend's Maifest and brewed enough for the tourist crowds that would pack into the village for the traditional Maipole dance, Sip and Stroll, chainsaw carving, fun run, and outdoor spring markets. I knew that I was biased, but there really wasn't a bad season to visit Leavenworth, Washington. Our charming version of Bavaria tucked into the northern Cascade Mountains was worth the trek through the Snoqualmie Pass in the dead of winter when everything was draped with a crystalline blanket of white. The trip through the winding narrow passage with spring in full bloom was the stuff of dreams.

I had recently moved into town after years living in a farmhouse with a small hop field on the outskirts of the village. Not a day passed that I didn't feel a deep sense of gratitude for my decision to move. My "commute" to work now involved a short walk past the miniature golf course and rows of German-inspired buildings with their sand and limestone walls, tiled rooflines, half-timber framing, and balconies with window boxes overflowing with vibrant trailing geraniums, petunias, and ivy. No restaurant, delicatessen, shop, or hotel spared any expense when it came to colorful floral displays for Maifest. The abundant blooms dripped like a cascading waterfall from one story to the next.

Nitro, the nanobrewery where I had been working for nearly a year, sat just off Front Street, the main thoroughfare. I loved the scent of boiling grains and working up a sweat on brew days. Today was no exception. Garrett and I had gotten an early start. Maifest activities kicked off later, which meant the tasting room would be buzzing with activity by early afternoon.

With that deadline in mind, I turned my attention to the brew and used a large metal paddle to stir the hops.

Garrett tugged off a pair of rubber boots, placing them on

a shoe rack next to the stainless steel tanks. He had finished hosing down the equipment. Prior to learning the trade myself, I had always thought brewing was simply like baking or cooking, where you mixed a few ingredients together. But I had come to understand it was so much more. At least 75 percent of our time in the brewery involved cleaning. "Man, it smells amazing, Sloan. I think this batch is going to be even better than our first round," he said with a crooked grin.

That tended to be true. Garrett, like many brewmasters, took meticulous notes during each stage of the brewing process, from how long to steep the grains to ratios of hops and yeast. There was no way to identically craft the exact same beer each time. Often in second and third iterations of a beer, we would make minor adjustments to pull out specific flavors or reduce the bitterness. It was a constant tweaking and one of the reasons that brewing had turned into my dream job. It might be hard, physical labor, but it was never boring.

Garrett mopped sweat from his brow and removed his chemistry goggles. "I think that's it. Not bad for an early start. Now I need a coffee—or a pot of coffee."

I smiled. Garrett and I had opposite rhythms, which worked well in our professional relationship. We had recently transformed the upper floor of the building he had inherited from his great-aunt Tess into "beercation" suites. Four guest rooms, themed after the four elements of beer—water, yeast, hops, and grains—offered visitors a unique immersive experience that included a beer-infused breakfast, brewery tours, and complimentary tastings. We had officially opened for guests in January and had seen steady bookings ever since. There wasn't a weekend between now and Oktoberfest that we weren't sold out. Garrett had wisely decided that it was time for another set of hands at Nitro and had hired two college students who were home for summer vacation, Casey and Jack, to help pour pints, wait tables, prep pub fare, and wash dishes. Our permanent hire, Kat, had taken on a larger role building out our social media presence, managing guest reservations, and being our go-to person in the taproom. She had mastered how to pour a perfect pint and the subtle nuances of each of our beer profiles in a short amount of time.

I finished stirring the hops and climbed down the stainless steel ladder. "I wouldn't turn down a coffee. Kat should be done with breakfast cleanup. Then she and I are going to review the special Maifest weekend menu and make sure Casey and Jack are ready for the onslaught of beer enthusiasts."

"Sounds good. I'll go wash up and get ready to open the tasting room." Garrett tossed his chemistry goggles into a bucket of cleaning solution. "After I down a cup of coffee."

"I'm right behind you." I chuckled, kicking off my boots. Then I wiped the paddle with cleaning solution and hung it on the rack on the far wall. I stopped in the bathroom to douse my face with water. My olive-toned cheeks were pink from exertion. I cooled them with a splash of cold water and retied my long dark hair into a high ponytail. I found myself staring in the mirror a minute too long.

I knew why. I was hoping that my reflection might hold the key to who I was.

Everything I had thought I knew about my past and my family here in Leavenworth had come into question recently.

I had grown up in the foster care system. Being bounced from house to house had come with challenges, but it had also made me the strong, independent woman I was today. When I met Mac, my soon-to-be ex-husband, the experience of feeling like it was me against the world had shifted. His family—Otto, Ursula, and his younger brother, Hans—had welcomed me without judgment or expectation. For the last two decades, I had been a Krause. Otto and Ursula had become my surrogate parents and doting grandparents to my son, Alex. Then everything fell apart. I caught Mac cheating on me with the beer wench at Der Keller, the Krause family brewery and Leavenworth's largest employer. The shock of Mac's infidelity was nothing compared with what I had learned about Otto and Ursula. The sweet German couple who adopted me as one of their own and taught me their brewing legacy had been living a lie.

Sally, my caseworker from my foster care days, had uncovered information that linked the Krauses with Nazi war criminals and flagged them as potential Nazi sympathizers. She had been convinced that Otto and Ursula had been funneling funds from Der Keller to Ernst, Otto's uncle and one of the last living members of the Nazi regime who had escaped to America after the war. I had confronted them immediately. They admitted that they had changed their names when they fled Germany in the 1970s. However, they insisted their move to Leavenworth wasn't because of any Nazi ties. The exact opposite. Otto's uncle shared an unfortunate connection—the same name as a former member of the regime wanted for atrocities so dark it was impossible to fathom. I had wanted to believe them, but I had lost trust.

Fortunately, thanks to Sally and a friend of hers in the FBI, the Krauses had been exonerated. It had been a huge relief when Sally called a few weeks after my heart-to-heart with the Krauses to tell me the news.

"Sloan, I have an update for you," she had said, her voice

breathless and rushed on the call. "I was mistaken. We've been able to track down a cousin of Otto's who is still living in Germany. The Krauses are telling the truth. Ernst, who has since passed away, was cleared of any misdoings. He did not fight with the Nazis. He had the misfortune of sharing a name identical to a war criminal and nothing more."

I had told her it was a great relief to know that the surrogate parents who had taken me in and made me feel like one of them, and who had helped me raise Alex, were the people I believed them to be—kind, empathetic, and caring.

Sally had apologized profusely for her mistaken logic. I didn't blame her. Her theory had been solid. The Krauses were connected to my personal past. Ursula had received a letter from a woman named Marianne, who had visited Leavenworth in the 1970s with a young girl who bore a strong resemblance to me. According to Ursula, Marianne and a man named Forest, claiming to be her brother, arrived in the village under the guise of buying Der Keller. At the time, the brewery was just getting off the ground. Forest offered them a lucrative cash buyout, something that Otto and Ursula considered strongly. Only the offer was a scam. Forest had no intention of purchasing Der Keller. He had a history of swindling people like the Krauses who were new to the country and still learning the lay of the land and the language.

Marianne had taken off with me and vanished. Shortly afterward, I was placed in the care of the state. Sally had found incomplete pieces of my old case files and discovered that an agent, whose name was redacted, had been responsible for putting me in care. She had theorized that Otto and Ursula's story about Forest was fake. That the real reason Marianne and Forest had been in Leavenworth was to provide surveillance on the Krauses. She had believed that Marianne was responsible for making sure I was protected.

Of course, none of that turned out to be true, which left me with a new mystery—who was Marianne?

On the night that Mac and I got married, Ursula discovered a note from Marianne on their front porch. It said that I was in danger, but I'd be safe in Leavenworth, and should Ursula ever need her help, she left a PO box number in Spokane.

Ever since, I had been writing weekly to the PO box with no response. Sally had tapped into her resources as well, with similar silence. It was a long shot. The letter had been written sixteen years ago; what were the odds that the PO box still belonged to Marianne? Lately, another thought had been creeping into my head. What were the odds that Marianne was even alive? If I hadn't heard from her after all these years, maybe there was a reason.

There was one looming problem. The Krauses still hadn't told Mac or Hans about their past or the fact that their family name wasn't even Krause. I had been stuck in the middle. Ursula had begged me for more time, and I agreed. Maybe it was the wrong choice, but it wasn't my story to tell.

Stop, Sloan. I splashed more water on my face and tried to center my thoughts.

For the past few weeks, I'd been starting to feel like I was losing it. I would wake up covered in sweat from nightmares I couldn't remember. My memories of my time before foster care were fuzzy at best, but that hadn't stopped me from trying to recall every tiny flash of a memory until my brain hurt. On more than one occasion, I had thought I had seen a woman who resembled Marianne around the village—near the gazebo, at Der Keller, on Blackbird Island. I had always prided myself on my ability to keep my emotions in check. Suddenly, that was in jeopardy, along with everything else.

I let out a long sigh and went to the kitchen. Garrett had left a coffee cup, a spoon, and carton of cream next to the pot. It was the simple things that made me wonder if perhaps our working relationship might turn into more at some point. Leaving the coffee ready for me, checking in on how my search for answers was going, always being game to try any of my brewing ideas, and listening, really listening to what I had to say. Or maybe I was interpreting his kindness differently because of my past with Mac. Not that Mac hadn't cared about me. His style was grander—big gestures, expensive gifts—and a tiny piece of his attention.

I poured myself a cup and took another moment to ground myself in reality.

"Hey, Sloan," Kat called, coming into the kitchen with a tray of breakfast dishes. "How did brewing go? I can't believe Garrett was up before nine. That must be a record."

"Good. We're done. Now we wait." I raised my cup of coffee. "How are the guests this morning?"

Kat set the tray next to the sink. Her bouncy curls bobbed as she plunged the dirty dishes into soapy water. "Easy. They loved the beer-battered breakfast potatoes and devoured the entire platter of apple strudel."

"That's what we like to see. Empty plates."

Kat grinned, revealing deep dimples. "Empty plates mean easier cleanup."

"Do you want coffee?" I took a sip of mine.

"No. I'm good. I'm saving myself because I have to meet April Ablin at Frühstück, remember?"

"Oh, that's right. Sorry." I grimaced. "Thanks for taking

8

one for the team." Poor Kat, she was due to get an earful at Frühstück, a popular breakfast spot known for its traditional morning spread of rye toast with marmalade, nougat cream, and thinly sliced meats and cheeses. April Ablin was Leavenworth's most annoying resident. She had a penchant for finding ways to showcase the tackiest Americanized versions of German culture, from her rotating collection of dirndls to cheap plastic flags, nutcrackers, and other kitsch that she insisted each business owner in town display. Garrett and I were thorns in her side. We refused to succumb to the pressure. Like the rest of the village, the exterior of Nitro resembled Bavarian architecture, but we preferred to keep the interior modern with exposed ceilings and a clean beer chemistry vibe. Visitors who came to town to join in the revelry at our rotating festivals often dressed in German attire, but those of us who lived in the village year-round (excepting April) rarely donned lederhosen or a barmaid's dress with a plunging neckline.

"Hopefully it will be quick," Kat said, rinsing the dishes before arranging them in our industrial dishwasher. "I just have to get our assignments for tomorrow's parade, and she said she had some extra 'materials' for us to put on display."

"That's code for something ridiculous," I replied. "I'm envisioning Maipole bobbleheads, don't you think?"

Kat laughed. "Yep. That sounds right. Don't worry. I won't bring back anything with ruffles or an apron for you."

"And that's why you'll keep your job," I kidded.

While Kat finished the dishes, I reviewed our menu for the weekend. Since Nitro is classified as a nanobrewery, we serve a very small bar menu including a daily soup, meat and cheese platters, and a beer-inspired dessert. When I had woken up with a nightmare the other night, I couldn't go back to sleep, so I'd tried to relax myself by flipping through a magazine. A recipe for a British trifle caught my eye and gave me a spark of creativity.

"Okay, you want to hear my crazy idea for this weekend's special dessert?" I asked Kat.

"Of course."

"I'm thinking a beer trifle. We'll make a lemon pound cake and soak it in our Lemon Kiss beer. Then we'll layer it with lemon custard, fresh strawberries, and whipped cream. What do you think?"

"Delish. Yeah, that sounds amazing."

I'd never made a beer trifle, but if a traditional trifle could be soaked in liquor, why not craft beer? It was worth a shot.

"I want to be like you when I grow up, Sloan." Kat finished loading the dishwasher. "You're so fearless."

Yeah, right. I wish. To Kat, I smiled. "Maybe outwardly. I promise, inside I'm a total mess."

She dried her hands on a dish towel. "No way. I don't believe it. You treat life the way you treat brewing and baking—fully diving in. Maybe I should tell April that you're my hero. How do you think that will go over?"

"Now, that is an idea I can get behind."

Kat grabbed her phone. "Wish me luck. I'll be back soon unless I can't escape April's clutches."

"Stay strong," I called after her.

I checked the clock. It was after ten. Garrett would open the tasting room in an hour. I had time to pop over to the market to get the ingredients for my beer trifle as well as for a spring soup I wanted to serve in honor of Maifest—a fresh pea with bacon.

Garrett came downstairs freshly showered. He wore a pair of khaki shorts, a Nitro T-shirt, and a pair of hiking sandals. We kept it casual in the pub. "That felt good." He returned his empty coffee cup to the sink. "I can't believe I'm going to say this out loud, but there is something rewarding about having a new batch of beer done before noon."

"Does this mean I'm going to convert your night owl tendencies?"

"No way. Not a chance, but with so much going on this weekend, it is a relief to have that done." He opened one of the cupboards and took out bags of pretzels and Doritos. "I'm going to get the front prepped. Casey and Jack will be here in about thirty. Let me know if you need either of them to help out in here."

"I could definitely use a hand, but first I need to run to the grocery store and grab a few items."

"Sounds like a plan," Garrett said as we walked to the front together. I left him at the long exposed-wood bar, and headed for the front door.

Warm air greeted me as I stepped outside. Blue sky stretched to the top of Wedge Mountain, and the Enchantment Plateau was streaked with the last remnants of winter's snow. Waxy green leaves rippled in the trees and pastel ribbons and banners hung from streetlamps and balconies. When I turned onto Front Street, I was greeted by the sight of dozens of vendors setting up tents in the park. The aroma of grilling brats and roasting nuts made me pause. Was it too early for lunch?

There was no denying Leavenworth's charm. Every shop and storefront was designed to resemble a quaint German village. The brightly colored buildings with balconies and exposed timber framing were painted with unique murals like a cascading waterfall and a goat farmer shepherding his flock. Nesting dolls, gorgeous cuckoo clocks, beer steins, and Hummel figurines in the storefront windows made it easy to forget this wasn't Rothenburg or Schiltach. A wooden gazebo flanked by a massive weeping willow tree had been adorned with more flowers than most wedding venues. Keg barrels lined both sides of the street. They had been repurposed to display even more spring blooms. Each overflowed with fragrant hyacinths, primroses, tulips, and camellias.

The giant blue and white Maipole stood upright in its post. Tomorrow it would take center stage in the Maifest parade, where dancers in colorful pinafores and lederhosen would perform the traditional Maipole dance. Beautiful silk ribbons would stretch from the top of the pole to each dancer's hands. They would weave around the pole in a seamless rhythm, ducking under ribbons and creating a magical pattern of rippling colors. It was the highlight of the parade.

I continued past the gazebo, which had been adorned with six-foot-wide flower baskets filled with deep purple and lilac blooms. Nearly every shop and restaurant had propped open their front doors to welcome in shoppers and hungry tourists. Der Keller, the Krause family brewery, sat at the far edge of Front Street. The building itself was a sight to behold, with its sloped A-frame roofline, hand-carved trim and wooden shutters, and iron accents. Der Keller's outdoor patio had been decked out for the festival with strands of twinkle lights, strings of baby blue-and-white-checkered flags, topiaries, and more hanging baskets. Staff wearing *Trachten* shirts placed menus on the outdoor tables while a German oompah band warmed up.

The Festhalle was directly across the street from Der

Keller. Throughout the busy weekend, a variety of bands and musicians would perform on the stage. An outdoor fruit and flower market took over the grounds next to the Festhalle. Rows and rows of long tables had been constructed where local farmers and artisans were selling hop starts, flowering currants, blueberry bushes, heirloom fruit trees, and fresh cut flower bunches.

The excitement was palpable. Plenty of tourists had already arrived. I enjoyed watching them delight at the sight of the bustling village and the sweeping alpine views. A couple was trying to take a selfie at the end of Front Street in order to get the view of the gazebo, village, and the jutting alps behind them and yellow balsamroot blooming on the building next to them.

"Would you like me to take your picture?" I asked. It was commonplace for those of us who called Leavenworth home to stop and offer to snap photos for tourists. It didn't take any extra effort on my part, and it was one simple way (unlike April's in-your-face style) to make our guests feel welcome.

"That would be great. Thank you so much." The young woman handed me her phone. I took a few shots, making sure the Maipole and snowcapped mountains were centered behind them.

After I returned her phone, I was about to cross the street toward the flower market when a flash of movement caught my eye. A woman sprinted out of a narrow alleyway between the coffeehouse and wine shop on the opposite side of the street. She caught my eye. Our gazes locked on one another.

I froze.

I knew her face. I'd been carrying around a picture of that same face for months. She looked exactly like Marianne. Her silver hair flapped in the breeze. Her dark brown eyes were wild with fear.

My legs wouldn't move. I stood in the middle of the town square, unable to make sense of what I was seeing.

She broke eye contact first. Her manic stare drifting behind me.

I started to move toward her, but she bolted back down the alleyway.

"Wait!" I called, running after her.

She vanished.

When I made it through the alleyway, there was no sign of her. Where could she have gone?

Or did I need to ask myself a different question?

Was she real?

I blinked hard. Were my eyes playing tricks on me? Or, worse, was I really losing it?

CHAPTER

TWO

"SLOAN, YOU HAVE GOT to get yourself together," I told myself. There was no sign of the woman, and nowhere for her to have gone. Maybe it was time for me to seek some professional help. I had thought that I was managing my stress, but if I was imagining Marianne skirting through alleyways, that couldn't be a good sign. I blinked and rubbed my eyes, trying to shake off the internal sense of mounting anxiety. Had I made it up? I let out a long sigh before continuing toward the grocery store.

My hands were clammy and my breathing shallow.

"Get it together," I repeated, hoping that if I said it enough, I might believe it.

Sounds of laughter and chatter muffled together as I half stumbled into the store, which like everything else in the village, looked as if it belonged on a postcard from the Alps. Its brocade façade and hand-painted picturesque mural of a farmers' market made it a popular spot for tourists to snap selfies.

I passed by bundles of firewood for riverside bonfires and a freezer stocked with bags of ice and headed inside. The smell of peppernut cookies (or *Pfeffernüsse* if you *sprechen Deutsch*) sent a rush of hunger to my stomach. No one in the village, except my mother-in-law, Ursula, made the spicy cookies infused with black pepper, cinnamon, nutmeg, and anise better than the bakery attached to the grocery store.

I resisted the temptation, kept my head down, and made a beeline for the baking aisle. The grocery store stocked vacation treats, like the packages of s'mores supplies and local German pastries on display near the front door. Tourists staying at local guesthouses flocked in for milk and cereal, deli sandwiches for day hikes and picnics on Blackbird Island, and cold drinks for floating the Wenatchee River. The store also imported a variety of goods directly from Germany. It was my go-to spot for German chocolates and rich, spicy mustards during the regular workweek. Most villagers avoided shopping during festival weekends. I gathered everything I needed for the trifle and soup and made my way to the register.

"Hey, Sloan." The grocery clerk greeted me with a wide grin. He was a friend of Alex's.

"How's it going? Are you ready for the rush?" I hoped that my voice sounded normal. I was still in a daze from my standoff in the middle of the street. The last thing I needed was for Alex to worry about me.

"Yeah. It's every staff member on deck this weekend. It's going to be busy, but my shifts fly by when it's packed."

"True." I paid for the groceries and promised to pass on a hello to Alex.

Alex was helping at Der Keller this weekend. It was his first official job. Sure, it was for the family business, but nonetheless it felt like a tectonic shift to have my son earning a wage and finding his own space in the world. Wasn't it just yesterday that I was squeezing his pudgy little hand on the first day of preschool and trying to reassure him (and myself) that everything would be okay?

After Mac and I split, Otto and Ursula offered me a percentage of their successful empire. I wasn't ready to return to day-to-day operations at Der Keller, but Hans and I agreed to remain partners and steer Mac in the right direction. Surprisingly, Mac thrived with his newfound responsibility. Maybe that was what he had needed. He had taken a backseat while his parents were at the helm of the successful brewery, but now, with them easing into retirement, he had begun to shine. Hans and I were equally stunned and relieved.

Mac had hired a very competent manager, who oversaw staffing needs so that he could focus on brew operations, including the transition from bottling to canning. I had been impressed with his resolve. It didn't change my feelings about our future, or lack thereof, but Mac was Alex's father. We would forever share our son, so despite my lingering anger and hurt over his choices, I didn't wish him ill. I wanted him to succeed for Alex's sake.

Alex had recently turned sixteen, which meant he could officially become a Der Keller team member, something that he had been talking about for at least five years. The brewery was his legacy. He had beamed with pride the first time he put on his uniform—a crisp blue and white *Trachten* shirt, suspenders, and black lederhosen. *This weekend should be a good test for him,* I thought as I left the store and retraced my steps to Nitro.

I found myself staring into storefronts in hopes that I might spot Marianne again, pausing at Father Christmas, a year-round holiday shop complete with paper snowflakes intermixed with hand-blown glass ornaments in the windows, and the outdoor store, which advertised rafting trips on the Wenatchee River. No luck. There was no sign of her.

Garrett was wiping down the outdoor bistro tables on Nitro's small enclosed patio when I rounded the corner. "Looks like you bought out the store," he said, noting my shopping bags.

"I had to stockpile before the tourists clean out the shelves. You know what it's like."

"Yeah, locusts." He scooted two tables apart. "The bar is ready. We've had three groups stop by and ask when we'll be open. I told them to come back in a half hour."

"I better get baking, then." I hurried to the kitchen to find Casey already slicing salami and cheese.

Casey and Jack were twins who had grown up in Leavenworth and now attended the University of Washington in Seattle. I had learned to tell them apart by the slight curl at the bridge of Casey's forehead. Otherwise the brothers were identical. They were both tall and skinny with a smattering of freckles, blond hair, and goofy grins. They had brought a new life to Nitro. Jack was a prankster, who hit it off immediately with customers, given his outgoing personality and ability to talk about anything from the best hidden backcountry trails to why soccer was the most popular sport in the world. Casey was more studious. He was an observer, who had taken great interest in the science of brewing, something Garrett appreciated.

"Hi, Sloan, Garrett put me to work on the lunch platters

and told me to check with you on what to do next." Casey fanned slices of cured salami onto plates.

"That's perfect. If you could finish those and then make sure the bar is stocked with pint glasses, that would be great. I'm going to whip up a quick spring pea soup and a trifle for dessert."

Casey chatted about his experience taking a culinary class at college while I creamed butter, sugar, eggs, lemon juice, flour, and buttermilk together. The base of my trifle would be a lemon pound cake that I would soak with our Lemon Kiss. Then I planned to layer the sponge cake with fresh strawberries and whipped cream with a touch of fresh lemon zest and vanilla. We could serve them in mason jars for a sweet bar treat.

The cake came together quickly, so I shifted my efforts to the pea soup. I chopped garlic and onions and sautéed them until they were translucent before adding fresh peas and chicken stock. Soon the kitchen churned out a melody of spring scents. Hopefully they would waft to the front and entice beer enthusiasts to order lunch.

By the time my soup was ready, the taproom was packed with thirsty travelers eager to try our Northwest style ales and lagers. Nitro had a completely different atmosphere compared with Der Keller. Garrett had spent the first half of his career working in high tech in Seattle and had designed our marketing materials with a nod to the chemistry of brewing. He had embraced his scientific roots with clean lines, exposed beam ceilings, and subtle nods to chemistry on our chalkboard menu, like our logo, which replaced atoms with hop cones, and our tagline: BEER HANDCRAFTED WITH SCIENCE SINCE 2017. A long barn-wood bar divided the brewery from the tasting room, where customers could pull up a barstool or gather at one of the many high-top tables.

When Garrett had hired me to help him brew as well as run the kitchen and tasting room, I had suggested adding a few subtle touches to soften the sterile white walls. One fact that many craft beer aficionados didn't understand was how much cleaning went into producing barrels of beer. The brewery's level of cleanliness was on par with any scientific lab. However, part of the experience of drinking a handcrafted ale is the atmosphere. It hadn't taken much convincing to get him to let me string soft golden twinkle lights from the ceiling and add black-and-white family photos and pictures of the building from the late 1800s to the walls. As time had gone on, we continued to bring in a few personal touches, with menus designed by Alex, fresh flowers in beer stein vases on the tables, and live guitar music on weekend nights.

I delivered a tray of soup and snack plates to a few of the tables. Nearly everyone in the dining room was dressed in pastel checkered dresses or felt German hats—a telltale sign that it was a festival weekend. After I dropped off food orders, I squeezed behind the bar where Garrett was pulling pints. Jack was cleaning tables outside, and Casey was taking lunch orders.

"Is Kat still gone?" I asked Garrett.

Jack answered first. "I haven't seen her since this morning."

Garrett topped off a pint of our signature Pucker Up IPA, a bright and hop-forward easy drinking pale ale that we kept on tap year-round, and handed it to a customer. "Yeah, come to think of it, I haven't seen her since breakfast."

"Oh no."

"What?" He shot me a concerned look. "Do you think something is wrong?"

"No, no. I'm sure she's fine." I set the tray on the bar. "It's just that she met April for breakfast."

"Ah. Got it." Garrett lined up a tasting tray to pour two-ounce samples of our spring line. "I hate to say this, but better her than us. She's young. She can brush off the April energy, right?"

I looked to the front door at that moment to see it open and Kat walk in wearing a fuchsia barmaid dress that barely covered her thighs. The neckline held no modesty either. It was cut low enough to reveal her belly button. She yanked the skirt down and scooted over to the bar. She dropped a box off on the counter and used her free hand to cover her chest.

"Do I even want to know?" I asked with a grimace.

"God, it's so embarrassing. April mentioned that she needed another dancer for the parade. I've always wanted to be part of the Maipole Dance." She paused and chomped on her bottom lip. "Big mistake. This is the dance costume she gave me. She said it was the only one left and from her personal collection."

The dress's satin fabric and ruffles were straight from the page of a 1980s prom yearbook photo.

"You look good," Jack said, giving her a lopsided grin. "I mean, you blend in with the crowd here, right?"

Kat rolled her eyes. "I'm *not* trying to look like a tourist."

Jack wisely ducked outside with a tray of beers for guests on the patio.

I couldn't stifle a chuckle. "Oh yeah, there is no doubt that dress is from April's collection. How did she convince you to wear it?"

"Don't ask. She insisted. She said it was my duty as one of Nitro's and Leavenworth's ambassadors this weekend. What am I going to do?" Kat moaned. She turned halfway around. "Can you see my underwear?"

"Only if you move."

She yanked the skirt down again. "I'm going to have to move tomorrow. That's the whole point of the dance, isn't it? So, basically I'm going to be flashing the entire town?"

I felt sorry for her. "Go change. I'll find something for you. Working at Der Keller for so many years means that my closet has a fair number of German costumes, too. I'll bring you a couple of options tomorrow."

"Thank you, Sloan. I'm dying right now." She wrapped her arms around her exposed chest and scooted upstairs.

"Only April can create this kind of havoc. I swear she does it just to bug me. Who would send a young staffer out in that getup?" I said to Garrett. "That dress definitely falls into the not safe for work category."

Garrett threw his hands in the air. "Don't look at me. I'm not about to touch this conversation with a ten-foot pole."

Poor Kat. I looked through the box that April had given her. It contained a stack of event brochures with maps and schedules of the weekend's festivities. I was more than willing to distribute these in the pub, but as for the rest of the contents, not so much. April had included a variety of German flag pins, felt caps, and fake flower crowns. The handwritten note attached read *Garrett and Sloan, it's imperative your staff embraces the German spirit, or as I like to say,* Spiritus *for Maifest. Please make sure every member of your staff has their Bavarian bling on in full spring bloom to welcome our guests to the village.*

As always April had butchered her German. *Spiritus* did indeed translate to spirits, but not the kind of spirit April was referencing. I knew the term well from Otto's bartending skills. He often created beer-inspired cocktails with his favorite spiritus, as in alcoholic spirits.

Garrett took one look at April's "bling" and shoved the box under the counter. "That's not happening. The only bling we need at Nitro is in the form of frothy beer."

"You're not going to get an argument from me, but I wouldn't put it past April to come by and inspect whether we're following her outlandish rules."

"Bring it on." Garrett motioned to his chest. "I would love for her to stop in. She and I can have some words." He turned his attention to a group waiting to order.

I did the same.

For the next few hours, we poured pint after pint and ran back and forth between the bar and the kitchen to keep up with food orders. Festival weekends were a lot of work, but they brought in serious cash. Over the next three days, we would likely quadruple our profits.

There was a late afternoon lull as customers headed to Front Street to watch the Bavarian Brass and Edelweiss dance troupe march to the gazebo, followed by a mini Maipole raising and the kickoff of the Sip and Stroll. Tomorrow the *Festzug* (or German march) would take place at noon. Nearly everyone in the village would participate in the festive parade. Tourists would line Front Street and watch the big Maipole raising and dance.

The Sip and Stroll was a new addition to the Maifest celebration this year. Makers of cider, wine, and beer, Nitro included, had been invited to set up tasting booths amongst the other vendors. Participants would receive souvenir tasting glasses that they would bring with them to each booth for delectable samples of pear cider and merlot.

Garrett flipped the sign on the door to SHUT as the last of our guests left to watch the action. "The twins should have everything set up for us. I just need to run upstairs and grab a sweatshirt in case it gets cold later. Otherwise, I think we should be set. Can you think of anything else we need?"

I picked up a handful of the glossy brochures April had given us. "I'll bring a few of these. People always seem to misplace their maps."

"Good idea. I'll meet you over there in a few."

"Sounds good." I took the brochures and headed outside. Instead of walking directly to Front Street, I went by the back route, knowing that the main thoroughfare would be impossible to navigate with the crowds.

The streets and sidewalks were nearly empty, since everyone was crammed into Front Street. I passed the hospital on my right. It was constructed with natural woods, a high slanted green metal roof to allow for snow accumulation, and large windows that offered patients calming, healing views of the mountains. Visitors often mistook it for a spa. Which in my opinion was a good thing for anyone needing medical care on vacation.

I continued on past the Gingerbread Cottage, where the sweet and spicy aromas of cinnamon and nutmeg from the gingerbread made me consider a quick stop for a hit of sugar. The cookie shop was known for its elaborate gingerbread designs and delicious flavors. A white picket fence housed a storybook cottage. Giant cardboard cutouts of gingerbread cookies dotted the front lawn. I was so distracted by the whimsical window display of a four-foot-tall gingerbread Maipole and gingerbread men and women dancers that I walked right into someone.

"Sorry." I looked up. Then I took a step back and gasped. The event brochures dropped from my hand and scattered on the sidewalk.

It was the woman I had seen earlier. This close-up made me even more convinced that she had to be Marianne. She had the same Greek features, long dark hair that had grayed with age, and doe-like eyes.

"Hey, I—" I started to speak, but she pressed her finger to her lips.

Her eyes were focused behind me. They were wide with fear. I half expected to turn and see one of Leavenworth's resident brown bears standing behind me.

I turned around to see what she was looking at.

There was nothing.

The streets were empty.

I turned back around just in time to see her run off again.

What the hell?

CHAPTER

THREE

THIS TIME I DIDN'T bother to chase her. I bent down to pick up the brochures. My heart pounded in my chest. Who was she, and why did she keep running off?

I pinched my forearm, just to make sure I wasn't dreaming.

The pinch sent a small wave of pain up my arm and left a red mark on my skin.

Okay, so you're not dreaming, Sloan.

That left two alternatives. I was either having some kind of a nervous breakdown, or the woman was real. Assuming the latter was true, and I hoped it was, why the strange behavior? Ducking into alleyways, acting like she was being chased, and running away. It didn't make sense.

I inhaled deeply, trying to steady my breathing, and continued on, checking the narrow alleyways between the shops and ducking into the bakery, a high-end shoe shop, and the butcher shop. She had vanished again. Once I rounded the corner and turned onto Front Street, I knew I had lost her. I found myself in the middle of the action. There were thousands of people packed onto the sidewalks and in Front Street Park, listening to the upbeat sounds of the German brass band and dancing on the street. Flags waved, the crowd clapped along to the rhythmic beat of the shiny tubas, and the smells of grilled onions and corn on the cob filled the air.

I kept my eyes open for any sight of the skittish woman as I squeezed through the crowds to the Nitro booth. It was easy to spot with our distinct hop-green logo in the shape of an atom. Casey and Jack had done a great job on setup. Our Nitro banner hung from a ten-foot table. Four kegs were hidden beneath the table with taps extending up to the top. There were stacks of the Sip and Stroll maps, along with our stamp—a hop wreath—and a matching green ink pad. They had also set out plenty of our coasters and menus for guests to take with them.

Our booth was located next to the park near my favorite bookshop, Das Buch. The bookstore was on the first floor with huge light-filled windows. Das Buch hosted author signings and events, and often partnered with us to provide beer samples. On quiet weekends, I would spend an entire Sunday afternoon perusing the store for new reads. Since Leavenworth was a tourist Mecca, the store stocked vacation reads—rom-coms, mysteries, popular fiction, along with an extensive collection of Pacific Northwest authors, literary fiction, and poetry.

Ten vendor tents for the festival had been set up on the cob-blestone square near Das Buch. Our fellow merchants for the Sip and Stroll included a winery, an organic cider company from Spokane, a cheesemonger, a soap maker, and a variety of brat and pretzel vendors from Leavenworth. The energy was palpable as artisans set up displays of blueberry, lemon, and thyme goat cheese and crystal bottles of pear cider.

Participants would wander throughout the village to find each of the ten tents with reusable tasting glasses. Our role was simply to fill their glasses with our spring line of beer and stamp their passports. It should be easy enough.

"Nice work, guys," I said to the twins, adding the extra passports I'd brought with me to the pile. "It looks great."

"We've already had people asking for samples," Casey replied. He was taller than Jack by a half inch. "We told them to come back at five."

The brass band stopped marching in front of the gazebo. The sound of the horns echoed through the streets as tourists clapped and danced along.

"That's right," I confirmed. "Since there isn't a ton of space, we figure we can take shifts. Two people at a time. Garrett and I can take the first shift to work out any kinks. Why don't you come back around six forty-five? Go enjoy yourselves and get some dinner."

"Cool, thanks." Jack shot me a grin. "I told Kat I would help her take photos for social media."

This was our first time doing an off-site tasting with a keg setup. We'd done a few house parties and small weddings with growlers, but with thousands of visitors in town for the weekend, we were definitely going to go through a few kegs, even just giving small tasting samples. Garrett and I had agreed it was worth the effort, not only to help get the word out about Nitro, but because we'd had time in the slower winter months to brew enough to manage the pub and an event like this. It should be a good test for the future. As of yet, Nitro hadn't had a presence at Oktoberfest or the holiday markets because of volume. We'd opened our doors last fall right before Oktoberfest. If the Sip and Stroll was a success, it could provide a roadmap for how we might be able to scale up our brewing efforts for the busy fall and holiday season.

Garrett showed up a few minutes later with a Nitro hoodie tied around his waist. "Did I miss anything? Has there been an April sighting?"

"No." I glanced around us. "Although I'd stay on your toes."

He chuckled and stretched a leg over a stack of supplies in the back of the booth. "We'll sling drinks from both sides, yeah? You take two taps, and I'll take the other two?"

"Yep. I told Jack and Casey to come back a little before seven. That way we can see how this goes. I have no sense of what sort of line and crowd we're going to get."

Garrett reviewed a set of safety protocols. "We have to check wristbands. One sample per stamp, and then the rest is boilerplate, stuff we already know and have drilled into our staff. Don't serve anyone who is intoxicated. No minors. The usual."

The brass band finished their set. They exited the gazebo stage and were replaced by none other than April Ablin. Her outfit wasn't much better than the one she'd given to Kat. Her carrot orange hair was tied in braids and twisted into a headband of yellow, pink, and white flowers. Her pink dress and yellow apron hit midthigh, with a revealing neckline and tightly cinched bodice. She had a goat on a leash standing next to her with a similar crown of flowers tied around its collar.

"Welcome, welcome, everyone, to our Maifest Frühjahrswiesn!"

I wasn't sure what she was trying to say, but whatever

word she was shooting for sounded ridiculous in her fake German accent.

"If this is your first time in our little Bavaria, you are going to be in for a treat! Next up, our very own Alpenfolk will serenade you with traditional folk songs. Be sure to get your passports and wristbands for the Sip and Stroll. The first section of our vendors is right here." She pointed in our direction. "Vendors are spread out over the entire village and in the Festhalle, so be sure to wander and stop in our authentic Bavarian shops."

I had to credit April with her enthusiasm. She and I might have drastically different styles, but I couldn't fault her for her relentless promotion of our town.

As soon as her welcome speech was finished, lines began to form at our tent. Garrett and I filled taster glass after taster glass. It was rewarding to see people savor our brews and to answer their questions about what they were tasting. Craft beer is meant to be sipped slowly. We spend weeks meticulously documenting and tweaking each stage of the brewing process. There's nothing worse than having a customer down a pint without taking the time to allow a beer to sit on their palate and bring out each nuanced flavor that we had intentionally crafted.

Shortly before my shift was over, Otto and Ursula wandered over to our booth. Ursula was walking without a cane for the first time in months, but I noticed that she still had a slight limp and that Otto kept a firm grasp on her forearm.

"Sloan, Garrett, Nitro has been ze talk of ze village tonight," Otto said with a wide grin. He wore a pair of black and red lederhosen, a white shirt, and suspenders. Ursula's black-and-red-checkered dress matched his outfit. I knew that their attire hadn't been mass produced and made from cheap cotton. These were the traditional clothes of their motherland sewn by Ursula. She was an expert seamstress. When Alex was young, I used to drop off bags of the clothes that he would quickly outgrow for her to let the seams out. Needlecraft was a hobby for her. Birthdays, Christmas, any holiday worth celebrating meant that Ursula would use her magical fingers to piece together a quilt, tablecloth, or delicately knitted shawl. I treasured every gift she had made for me.

Garrett poured them tastes of our Lemon Kiss. "Greetings, Krauses, I'm excited for you to try our new spring beer."

Otto studied the beer, holding it up to the light to inspect the color and clarity before taking a drink. It was a gorgeous pale yellow, the color of daffodils, with impeccable clarity. "Zis is very nice. I don't zink I recognize ze hops."

I exchanged a knowing look with Garrett. When it came to craft beer, no one knew more than Otto Krause. One of the things I appreciated most about my father-in-law (or whatever he would become to me once my divorce was final) was his generosity. He took it upon himself to share his wealth of beer knowledge with anyone who needed it. When Garrett had opened Nitro, Otto and Ursula were the first people to offer their support. At least once a week Otto stopped by Nitro to tinker in the brewery with Garrett. His years of experience building a brewing empire were invaluable. Otto also had a unique gift—he had a pristine palate. His taste buds could pick up every ingredient used in a beer. To watch him taste a beer was like watching Picasso put a brush to canvas.

When Mac and I had first gotten together, Otto had done the same thing with me. He had taken me under his wing, which drove Mac crazy. Otto claimed that I had "the nose," as he called it. I wasn't so sure. Not that I wasn't confident in my ability to brew and catch the nuance of flavors in a pint, but Otto was in a class of his own. He wasn't one for showmanship (that was Mac's domain). However, many years ago, shortly after Alex was born, an influential group of craft beer writers from the best magazines in the industry had been in town. Mac convinced Otto to showcase his incredible skill set for the journalists. He lined up a dozen tasting glasses with a variety of beer styles. Not just Der Keller beers, but beers produced throughout the region and even a German import tossed in. I had watched in awe, while bouncing baby Alex in my arms, as Mac blindfolded his father and Otto proceeded to correctly identify each beer set in front of him. He picked out the hops, grain style, yeast strands, and nearly every extra ingredient used to brew the sample beers—from crushed boysenberries to coffee. It was a sight to behold. That spontaneous blind tasting helped propel Der Keller onto the national stage. For months afterward, not a week went by when Otto's face didn't appear on the cover of a glossy magazine or newspaper.

Garrett's response brought me back to the present moment. "Yeah, those are a brand-new strand out of the Yakima Valley: Lemondrop. What do you think?"

"Very nice, *ja*." Otto let his eyelids fall heavy as he stuffed his nose into the tasting glass and inhaled the scent. "*Ja*. I love ziz. It is very subtle, but ze lemon and citrus come through so nicely. Ursula, do you agree?"

Ursula handed me her empty glass. "I liked it so much it is gone. I was going to ask for another taste."

I smiled and poured her a second sample. "Do you want to try anything else while you're at it?" I asked Otto. "We have our Pucker Up, of course, and a hibiscus rose, and a honey amber."

He finished his taste. "I zink I would like more of ze Lemon Kiss, too."

Hans came up behind them. "I thought I might find you two here." He bent down to kiss Ursula on the cheek. Hans was the tallest in the Krause family, with sandy hair and muscular forearms from time spent lifting heavy wood in his workshop. Tonight he was dressed in a pair of jeans and a thin Der Keller pullover. His tool belt was absent from his waist.

"How are things at Der Keller?" Garrett asked, glancing up Front Street, which was a sea of people.

"Busy." Hans took a glass from Garrett, then he turned to me. "I just checked in. Alex is doing well. Mac put him on bussing duty. He's not going to need to do any soccer training this weekend because his legs are going to be sore from running between tables inside and outside."

It was a relief to know that Hans, Otto, and Ursula were keeping an eye on Alex.

"This is a punch of citrus, whoa," Hans noted as he took a sip of his beer.

"Is that a good thing or bad thing?" Garrett braced himself for Hans's response.

"It's awesome." Hans gave him a thumbs-up. "Are you guys here for the rest of the evening, or do you want to grab a bite?"

As if we had scripted it, Jack and Casey showed up to take over.

"I guess that answers your question," I said, making room for Casey.

Jack wore one of our intentionally faded hop-green Nitro hats. He looked around. "Is Kat working the booth with us, too? I couldn't find her to help with pictures. It's like a frat party mosh pit out there."

"No, but she's around, so I'm sure she'll stop by," I replied, coming around to the front of the booth.

"Cool." He didn't say more, but I noticed Casey nudged him in the ribs.

"We are due to dance at ze Festhalle soon," Ursula said. "You should get some food and join us."

"Deal." Garrett gave Jack and Casey a quick reminder of how to swap out the keg if necessary and made sure they had both of our cell numbers. "Let's do it."

The three of us weaved between the vendor tents. Suddenly I was famished. Everything smelled fantastic.

"Sloan, what are you in the mood for?" Hans asked, pausing when he noticed me practically drooling over plates of pork schnitzel.

"Would it be wrong to say that I want to stop at each booth?"

Hans laughed. "Not by me. What do you say, Garrett? Should we grab a smorgasbord and meet at the Festhalle?"

"You two focus on food," Garrett suggested. "I'll go snag us a table and beer."

"How could I forget about beer?" I said to Hans.

He wrapped his arm around my shoulder as we crossed the street to wait in a line for giant pretzels served with beer cheese sauce and spicy mustard. "That's a mystery to me, sis. You must be distracted."

I knew he was kidding, but his words still gave me pause. "Yeah." I forced a laugh.

"So, how are you liking the new digs? Is it great to roll out of bed and walk to the pub?" Hans asked.

"You have no idea. It's a dream. I can't believe we didn't do it years ago. It's so great to be in the village. I've been getting up and taking early morning walks and runs through Blackbird Island. Then I stop for a coffee and pastry. It's pretty much perfection."

"Glad to hear it. Alex told me he's loving it, too."

"He did?" That news perked me up. When I had made the decision to move out of our family farmhouse, I had been worried about Alex. The property had been his child-hood home. It was hard enough that Mac and I were sepa-rated, and I hated the idea of forcing him to move, but the minute I laid eyes on the cottage, I knew I needed a change. Living out of town made it too easy for me to disappear and disconnect. I'd done that for my entire life. Mac's boisterous personality allowed me to take a backseat, a role I'd become intimately acquainted with in my years in foster care. I was ready to stretch. It was time to push out of my comfort zone and build new relationships.

Hans gave me a funny look. "Yeah, why?"

"You know teenage boys. They're not exactly quick to chat about their feelings."

"True, but Alex sounded genuinely excited about living in town. He talked about walking to friends' houses and school. Unless I was reading him completely wrong, he didn't seem like he was harboring any hidden angst."

"That's a relief." We inched closer in the line. "I'm sure you didn't read him wrong. Your emotional IQ is off the charts."

Hans smiled. "Thanks. I'll take that as high praise from you."

"I don't know, Hans. I'm kind of a mess right now."

"Are you?" He frowned and studied my face. "What's going on?"

"I think I might be having a midlife crisis," I confessed. Hans had become a true brother over the years. He was my most trusted confidant, and one of the only people I couldn't hide my emotions from.

"You?" He shook his head. "No. No way. I don't buy it. You've gone through a lot the last year, Sloan. Everything with Mac, a new job, a move, Alex becoming more and more independent. I know that you're a superwoman, but you're also human. If you weren't feeling some level of stress, I would have to wonder if you were a robot."

I smiled.

He squeezed my shoulder tighter, pulling me toward him. I caught a whiff of cedar and pine. "Seriously, Sloan. It's normal for you to be stressed. I don't think you're having a midlife crisis, but maybe it's time to talk to someone."

"Yeah."

We made it to the front of the line. Hans placed our order, buying me time to collect my thoughts. I appreciated Hans trying to normalize my fears, but I hadn't mentioned anything about how I'd been dreaming of Marianne and now was seeing her around town. He might change his tone if he knew I was seeing imaginary people. Maybe he was right. Maybe it was time to seek professional help.

He balanced a plate of pretzels. "Where to next? Brats?"

"Absolutely. It's not a Maifest without a brat."

"Look, I'm going to drop it for now, sis, but if you need a listening ear, I'm always available. You know that, right?" His voice was tender with emotion.

"I do. Thank you."

"Okay, I'm going to check in with you again in a few days, got it?"

"Got it." I moved toward the brat tent and changed the conversation. By the time Hans and I made it to the Festhalle, our arms were loaded with German delicacies. I tried to let thoughts of Marianne go as I took in the sight of rows and rows of wooden picnic tables in the ornate, cavernous ballroom. Giant iron chandeliers filled the ceiling, casting a golden light on the dance floor and stage. Revelers stood shoulder to shoulder, swinging their glass beer steins to the music. It was impossible to dwell on my worries in the midst of such joy and cheer.

Garrett waved from the end of a long picnic table. He raised a beer stein. "You're just in time. Otto and Ursula go on next."

Hans set the food on the table. I sat down and took a stein from Garrett. We watched the Krauses perform folk dances and listened to three bands. Their energy amazed me. I hoped to be like them in my seventies. Ursula didn't let her hip stop her. She lifted her skirts and sashayed across the stage.

Sometime after nine, Garrett went to check in on Jack and Casey. The Sip and Stroll was winding down for the evening, but the festivities would continue long into the night at the Festhalle.

"I think I'm going to head out," I said to Hans. "I have an early start at Nitro for our overnight guests, and tomorrow is going to be a whirlwind."

"Yeah. I'll duck into Der Keller on my way home and make sure everything's running well. See you at the parade?"

"For sure." I left him with a long hug.

Stars flitted overhead, and the moon loomed large over

the alpine peaks surrounding the village as I walked home. The crowds had dispersed into restaurants and bars. A cool breeze swept down from the ridgeline. Spring daytime temps in Leavenworth often reached the mid-seventies to low eighties, but nights tended to stay cool, thanks to our alpine air. It was our own version of natural air-conditioning and meant that a slight crack of a bedroom window was all that was needed for a restful night's sleep.

I zipped my sweatshirt as I passed the gazebo and crested the hill toward the highway. Technically Highway 2 runs through the village, but it's a two-lane road with gorgeous hotels on each side and crosswalks for pedestrians every few hundred feet. *Willkommen,* or welcome, pennants fluttered on antique lampposts. Music from rounded turrets and balconies serenaded me.

The walk home took less than five minutes. I still couldn't believe I had taken the plunge on the cottage. I had fallen in love with it the minute I had done a walk-through. It reminded me of something out of the pages of "Hansel and Gretel," with its storybook design, wraparound porch, and view of the miniature golf course from the backside of the house.

Once inside, I made myself a cup of tea and curled up with a good book. Alex was staying at Mac's for the weekend, so I was alone. I must have drifted off at some point, because I woke with a start. My body was drenched in sweat, and I thought I heard pounding.

I must have had another nightmare. They're getting worse.

So was the pounding.

I rubbed my eyes and blinked. Was someone at my door?

I climbed out of bed.

The banging was faster and more frantic.

I wasn't dreaming.

I raced to the front door. My thoughts immediately went to Alex. Had something happened? Was he okay?

I half expected to open the door and see Chief Meyers standing there to tell me something horrible had happened to my son. It was a scenario I'd played out in my head hundreds of times.

But the shock was even stronger when I turned the door handle.

The woman who had run from me twice earlier was standing on my front porch with trembling hands.

"Hello?" I said, looking behind her to see if she was alone.

"Can I come in? I need to come in!" She laced her fingers together again and again, speaking in a breathless tone. "You're in danger. We both are!"

CHAPTER

FOUR

"WHO ARE YOU?" I blocked the door frame with my body.

"I'm who you think I am. I'm Marianne." She looked to her left, then to her right. There was something about her crazed eyes that made me wonder if she should be trusted.

"I don't understand."

"Sloan, please, listen to me. It's not safe out here."

She used my name, which brought me no comfort.

"He could be watching us." She darted her eyes from side to side again, reminding me of a skittish cat. "He's probably watching us. If you'll just let me inside, I'll explain everything."

"How do I know you're not going to hurt me?"

She ran her hands through her silver hair, causing it to frizz out in every direction. "Hurt you? I'm trying to protect you. A woman is dead—my God! An innocent woman! Right down the street in my hotel room, and I know why. It was supposed to be me. He's found us. After all these years, all my work trying to keep you safe, he's finally found us."

She wasn't making sense.

I considered my odds. She didn't appear to have a weapon. That was a good sign. Plus she was at least twenty years older than me. She was about my height, with a similar oval face and olive skin. Wrinkles creased her forehead and feathered at the sides of her dark brown eyes. She was dressed in black from head to toe. Black slacks and a black trench coat, fit for a detective. Her shoulders were slightly stooped. I couldn't tell if it was from age or fear, but I was fairly confident that if it came down to a physical battle, I could take her.

"If someone is dead, we need to call Chief Meyers."

"Fine. Just let me in." Her tone was frantic. She glanced behind us, her voice rising an octave. "Please. Let me in."

I stepped to the side to allow her entry. Then I shut the door behind me.

"Lock it," she insisted.

I followed her direction, wondering if I was making a mistake.

She looked at the living room, letting her eyes linger on the stone fireplace and wall of windows that faced the mini golf course and Blackbird Island. "These windows aren't secure. Is there anywhere we can talk with more privacy?"

"The kitchen, maybe?" I pointed to the attached kitchen.

"Yes. This is good." Marianne went straight to the large window above the sink and pulled down the shade.

"Do you need some water or tea, maybe?" I couldn't shake the feeling that she wasn't stable.

"No. I'm fine." She paced between the deep farm-style sink and butcher-block island that Hans had made for me.

Fine wasn't the word I'd have used to describe her demeanor. Her chest caved in. She rocked slightly as she moved from the sink to the dining nook and then back again. Her fidgety movements, rubbing her hands on her slacks, and swallowing like she was trying to gulp down air, put me on high alert.

"You have to tell me what's going on. Otherwise, I'm calling Chief Meyers right now." I had wisely grabbed my cell phone from my bedside table when I went to answer the door. I held it up as proof.

Marianne waved her arms. "No. Not yet. You're right. We can call the police, but you have to give me five minutes to explain myself first. You have to." She sucked in her cheeks. "If they arrest me, I need to make sure you stay safe."

Arrest her? She definitely wasn't stable. This was a mistake.

"Five minutes." I tapped the clock on my phone. "That's it. Then I'm calling the police."

"Sloan, give me a minute." She clutched the counter. "It's amazing to see you up close after all these years." Tears welled in her eyes. "I wish it wasn't under these circumstances. I've imagined what this reunion would look like since you were a young girl, and I never anticipated this."

I didn't respond.

She sighed. "Okay, I can tell that you don't trust me, and I understand. Sloan, I'm your aunt."

"Aunt?" I heard the word come out of my mouth, but it sounded like it belonged to someone else.

"Yes. Your aunt. You are the beloved only daughter of my younger sister, Claire."

"Claire?" I found myself repeating the last word of Marianne's sentences.

She brushed a tear from her cheek. "Claire was my world.

She adored you. It's hard to describe how much she loved you."

"You're speaking in past tense. Is Claire dead?"

A look of surprise flashed on Marianne's face, but she recovered quickly. "Yes, she died when you were young."

I didn't trust myself to respond. In the same sentence, I had learned my mother's name and that she was dead. A faint ringing echoed in my ears. My legs suddenly felt weak. I, too, clutched the countertop for support.

Marianne returned to pacing. "I took custody of you after Claire's death, and I'm the one to blame, Sloan. I made some terrible mistakes, including bringing you here all those years ago. That fateful trip to Leavenworth turned the tide in the wrong direction."

"I don't understand." I pressed my hands tighter onto the counter. Everything went blurry. Was I about to pass out?

Marianne rubbed her face and scratched the top of her head, sending her long gray hair into wild, frayed strands. "No, you wouldn't, and I know we need to call the police, so let me give you the brief recap so that you can understand the gravity of the situation."

I wondered if I should call Chief Meyers right now, but after forty years of not knowing anything about my past, I couldn't bring myself to do it.

"I got your letters. I've been formulating a plan for the last six months." She stared at a vase of sunflowers resting next to the sink. "I know you've been working with Sally, and I know she means well, but she made a mistake in reopening your files. I'm the one who destroyed them, Sloan. It was my only choice, otherwise he would have gotten them."

"Who?" I found myself struggling with how to respond.

"Forest."

"You mean the man who tried to swindle Otto and Ursula?" My voice sounded quaky, like it didn't belong to me.

"Yes, but it's so much more than that. He's dangerous, Sloan. He's a killer, and he'll kill again." She froze. "Did you hear something?"

"No."

She pressed her finger to her lip. We stood in silence. The faint sound of music from the Maifest tents echoed in the distance, but otherwise it was quiet.

Marianne waited a minute longer. "Sloan, Forest has been in prison for many, many years, but I have some disturbing news. He was released a few months ago. He's coming after you."

"Me? Why?" The ringing sound in my ears was getting worse.

"This is where the story is long and complicated. Forest was arrested when we were here in Leavenworth all those years ago. Don't you remember?" She squinted, studying my reaction.

I shook my head.

"Okay, well, I thought we were going to be okay, but the charges against him didn't stick. That's why I had to do what I did. He has very powerful friends, and he'll stop at nothing to get to you."

"Slow down." I held out my palm. "This makes no sense. First, how old is Forest now? He must be well into his sixties."

Marianne nodded. "He is, but that doesn't make him any less dangerous. He's had a single mission to kill you. That's

44

why I did what I did. That's what I'm trying to tell you." She wouldn't stop moving. "I placed you in the foster care system. I knew it was going to be hard on you. It was the worst thing I've ever had to do in my life, you have to believe me, but it was my only choice. It was the only way to hide you. If I had kept you, he would have found us and killed us both."

She broke down in tears. Her shoulders collapsed.

I gave her a moment to compose herself. "Would you like a tissue?" I moved to the breakfast nook and handed her the box.

"Thank you. I'm sorry to be so emotional. It's just that I've watched you from afar for all these years, and to be here with you now is overwhelming." She dried her eyes with a tissue, then balled it up in her fist. "Like I said, Claire and I were always close. She was my best friend. We never fought. I know that sounds strange for sisters, but we were each other's cheerleaders. I was there with her the day you were born. Her heart broke open in the most beautiful way. I'd never seen her as happy as when she was with you. I felt the same. I got to be the doting aunt, and you were the best baby. You came into this world an old soul."

Her words took my breath away. That was how I always described Alex.

"When she died, I made a promise to myself to raise you as she would have. Leaving you that day was the worst thing I've ever had to do." She started to reach her hand to me, hesitated, then clutched the tissue.

I wanted to comfort her, but it was too much. I wasn't sure what to believe, and I still wasn't convinced that she was in a solid state of mind.

"I don't get the Forest connection. Why is he after me?"

She swallowed hard, as if trying to find the courage to let the words out. "He killed your mother. He murdered Claire, and you were the only witness."

CHAPTER

FIVE

"WHAT?" I RECOILED AT her words. A heaviness invaded my chest, like my breath was being sucked away. I had witnessed my mother's murder?

Marianne moved toward me. She placed her hand on my forearm. Her touch was strangely familiar. "Sloan, you were the sole witness to your mother's murder. You don't remember?"

I shook my head. My early childhood memories were fuzzy at best. "No. Not at all."

"They said that could happen. That's good. Yeah, that's good. It's a protection your brain provides for you. I'm glad of that. It brings me some relief." She stared off behind me as if speaking to someone else.

"And you think Forest is here now? How did he find me?" This was a lot to take in.

"I don't know." She shook her head and massaged her temples. "I thought we were careful. We moved you often. We never let you stay at one home longer than a year." She trailed off. "I feel so awful for that poor woman who was killed because of me."

I had a barrage of questions circling my head, but I needed to focus and to get her to do the same. She was all over the map. "What woman? Who is dead?"

"The housekeeper at the Hotel Vierter Stock, where I'm staying. I don't know how he found me. I told you he has powerful connections. That poor innocent woman didn't deserve to die."

"Wait, Marianne, you're telling me that one of the house-keeping staff is dead?"

"Yes! Don't you understand what I'm saying? You're in grave, grave danger!" Her frenzied tone had returned. "I got back to my room and found her on the floor. That's when I ran here. I thought he might have already gotten to you."

"We have to call Chief Meyers." I picked up my phone.

"I know." She sounded resigned. Then, as I placed the call to the chief, she muttered something under her breath that I couldn't make out.

Chief Meyers asked for Marianne's room number, told me to stay put, and said that she would be in touch as soon as she'd had a chance to assess the situation.

"Are you sure you don't want something to drink?" I asked, walking to the stove to heat up the teakettle.

"As long as it's no trouble, tea might be good." Marianne picked up a framed photo of Alex and me snowshoeing last winter.

"Not at all." I opened a canister of assorted teas and of-fered it to her, then I grabbed two ceramic mugs. "So you

48

think Forest meant to kill you, but killed the housekeeper instead?"

"I don't think it. I *know* it. I was in the village for the festival. I came to make contact with you, but I'm sure I was followed. There was a black SUV that tailed me the entire way from Spokane. When I checked into the hotel, it was parked three spaces away."

I wasn't sure that translated into Marianne being followed. Hundreds of tourists flocked from Spokane and Seattle for the weekend. Highway traffic in both directions would back up for miles on Fridays when people came into town and again on Sundays on their way home.

"I had planned to find you this morning, but both times I bumped into you, I saw someone in the distance watching us." She returned the photo to its spot without saying anything about Alex.

I turned on the gas stove and placed the teakettle over the open flames. The simple act of doing something normal helped bring my heart rate down. "And you think it's Forest?"

"Yes. I can only imagine that your head must be spinning. This is a lot to dump on you."

That was an understatement. In the last ten minutes, I'd learned that my mother had been murdered, and I'd been the only witness, and now her killer was potentially stalking me.

"It doesn't add up," I said to Marianne. "Isn't there a statute of limitations on murder, and aren't we well past it by now?"

"No. There's no limitation on homicide in the state of Washington." She spoke with authority.

That was news to me. So much for Mac's police procedural shows versus real world knowledge.

Before I could ask Marianne more questions, a knock sounded on the front door.

Marianne grabbed my arm. "Wait, don't answer it. It could be him."

"Or it could be Chief Meyers." I turned the burner to low as steam began to pour from the top of the kettle and went to the front.

"At least ask who's there," Marianne cautioned, the wild look returning to her eyes.

I used the peephole and saw Chief Meyers standing on the porch. "It's okay. It's her." I unlocked the door to let the chief in.

"Evening, or is it morning?" the chief said. She was dressed in her standard khaki uniform with a brown tie and a gold star badge pinned to her chest. A walkie-talkie, flashlight, and holster were strapped to her belt. Chief Meyers was in her mid-fifties. Some people might have found her style abrupt, but I appreciated her direct approach. She had grown up in the village, which gave her a distinct advantage when it came to connections with locals and understanding the cyclical swings of our small town ballooning with tourists during festivals and holidays.

"I have no idea. Come in." I showed her to the kitchen and introduced her to Marianne. She asked Marianne about a dozen questions before Marianne cut her off.

Marianne had poured herself a mug of tea. She clutched it with both hands. "Okay, look, I understand you have to follow procedure, but I need to know if you found the body."

The chief frowned. "We did."

"Any sign of a struggle? Evidence? You're probably sweeping for prints now, right?"

"I thought I was the one who was supposed to ask questions." The chief caught my eye.

"Sorry. Habit," Marianne replied.

What did she mean by that? She was used to questioning people. Had Marianne been involved in law enforcement? Was she still? But then, why would she have mentioned being concerned that she might be arrested?

"Can you walk me through what happened tonight?" The chief pulled out a barstool and sat down. She took out a notebook and a pencil.

"Tea?" I pointed to the kettle. Tiny clouds of white steam puffed from the top of the vintage blue teakettle Ursula had given me as a housewarming gift.

"Thank you." Chief Meyers gave me a nod.

I poured her a cup of the boiling water and handed her the container of tea bags.

She opted for a packet of peppermint and plunged it into her mug. "For starters, I'm going to need your personal information."

Marianne hesitated. She stared at me for a moment before addressing Chief Meyers. "I'm Marianne DuPont, Sloan's aunt."

Meyers's personality tended toward stoicism. But even she couldn't hide her surprise. She coughed twice, then moved her eyes from Marianne to me, while her body remained rigid. "Your aunt?"

I shrugged.

"It's complicated," Marianne replied, still pacing, with the mug glued between her hands.

"Complicated is my middle name. I'm investigating a

murder in town, so why don't you go ahead and try me." She tapped her notebook with the tip of her pencil.

Marianne twisted the string on her tea bag around her pinky. "Yeah, I guess you'll have to be in the loop."

The chief caught my eye. I mouthed, "Don't ask me."

Marianne proceeded to give Chief Meyers the same story she'd told me. The chief took notes, stopping her every so often for clarification.

"Can you give me a description of Forest?"

"I can do better than that. I can give you his entire police record. As long as the files are still there. I had the files in my hotel room, but the problem is that I'm sure he had other people watching us. Following us. He's notorious for getting other people to do his dirty work. If the housekeeper is dead, it's probably because he—or one of his henchmen—broke in to steal the files."

"Okay." Meyers sounded even more unsure than I felt. "Yet you mentioned that he was coming after Sloan." She checked her notes to make sure she was repeating Marianne's statement verbatim.

"Yes." Marianne sounded irritated. "You don't understand how dangerous he is and how much power he has. I know that I was followed. Whoever he's hired as his henchmen, they were probably tasked to follow me and watch for me to make contact with Sloan. I would bet money on the fact that Forest told his guys to wait for him. He would want to end things with Sloan himself. He's extremely dangerous."

"Then why attempt to kill you?" Chief Meyers asked.

"They didn't need me any longer. I brought them to Sloan." She sloshed tea on the counter as she spoke. "That's what Forest has been waiting for. I'm telling you, it's his singular goal. This is my fault."

The chief appeared skeptical. "What about Sara Wilder? How well did you know her?"

"Who? Is that the housekeeper's name?" Marianne set her teacup on the counter.

Meyers nodded.

"Not at all. I'd never seen her until I set foot into my room tonight."

"You didn't have any interaction with her? No towels brought to your room? No passing her in the hallways?"

"No. Never," Marianne insisted. "I've trained myself to keep vigilant watch. I study faces. I can tell you every detail you want to know about the front desk clerk who checked me in, the owner, who happened to be in the lobby when I arrived, or the groundskeeper, who was tending to the flower boxes outside, but I never saw the housekeeper."

"Did you interact with anyone who can verify your whereabouts tonight?" Chief Meyers plunged her tea bag in her cup and studied Marianne.

"Wait, I know what's happening," Marianne wailed. "You think I did it. Why would I kill a housekeeper? I understand you have to do your job, but you have no idea what you're up against here."

"I don't believe those words came out of my mouth." The chief sipped her fragrant mint tea.

"You're asking me for an alibi, though. I know what you're hinting at. I know how this works." Marianne stood taller. Her persona shifted. "The answer to your question is probably no. I tried to stay under the radar. I'm telling you that Sloan and the rest of your town are in danger. Forest will stop at nothing to make sure that she's dead. Sara, that's the housekeeper's name? She should be the only proof you need to place Sloan under protective custody immediately. What about the room, did you find any files?"

Chief Meyers didn't respond.

Marianne sighed. Her pinky had turned purple from knotting the tea bag around it. "Arrest me. Do whatever you have to do, but you have to promise me you'll watch over Sloan and her family. Forest won't hesitate to kill anyone who gets in his way."

The chief pursed her lips. "For the moment, I'd like to continue this conversation at the station." She flipped her notebook shut and stood.

Marianne backed away.

"I'm not arresting you. I simply want to have a more detailed discussion at the station."

"It's not that. I'm not leaving Sloan until you can guarantee that she'll be safe."

The chief caught my eye. "I'll put in a call to one of my officers to camp outside her door tonight if that will make you feel more comfortable."

"I don't think that's necessary." I started to say more, but Marianne cut me off.

"No. That's good." Marianne dumped her tea in the sink. "Sloan, don't take this lightly. I can't stress how much danger you're in."

Chief Meyers motioned to the door. "Shall we?"

"When's the officer coming?" Marianne wasn't budging. "I'll go with you as soon as I see a uniform on Sloan's front porch."

Chief Meyers sighed, but made the call.

Marianne moved closer to me. She pressed something soft into my hand. "This is for you. A token from your first baby blanket that I've carried in my pocket since the day I had to leave you." Her words were rushed. "Sloan, don't trust anyone, and promise me you'll stay inside."

"It's the middle of the night. Where would I go?" I stared at the swatch of plush fabric with fluffy faded bunnies and pastel hearts.

"I don't know, but you're not safe. I'll try to be in touch as soon as they let me go, but in the meantime, lock every door and window. Close the shades and don't talk to anyone. Don't call anyone—he could be listening. Don't pick up the phone until I come find you again. Not even to call your family. They're in danger, too. If Forest and his guys find Alex or the Krauses first, they'll end up like Sara."

Her words sent a chill up my spine. Alex could be in danger?

CHAPTER

SIX

AS PROMISED, MARIANNE LEFT willingly with Chief Meyers once a police officer pulled into my driveway. I glanced at the clock. It was nearly three in the morning. There was no chance I was going to be able to sleep, so I cleaned up the tea and curled up on the living room couch with a book. Reading was impossible. I couldn't concentrate. I read the same paragraph over and over, and found myself running my fingers over the plush remains of my baby blanket. It didn't trigger any new memories, but it did make me feel a sense of connection to Marianne. If she was telling the truth and had carried a swatch of fabric with her for all these years, it must have meant something.

But then again, I had to question whether Marianne was sane.

I couldn't be sure one way or the other. Her story matched up with pieces of what Ursula had told me. She certainly seemed scared, but was that because there was a real threat, or was she in need of mental health support? She knew a lot about me. She knew Alex's name. She knew about the Krauses. She knew about my past. How could she know that much if she was lying?

My thoughts turned to Alex. What if he was in danger? How could I protect him and the Krause family?

Had I really witnessed my mother's murder? I tried to force any memory I could conjure from my early childhood to the forefront of my brain. Nothing was complete. Everything was like a flash, a shooting star darting across the sky. I remembered smells—apple orchards and Play-Doh. I remembered swirled chocolate-dipped soft-serve cones, and a bunny. Or was it a cat? I remembered a song about friendship—silver and gold. Sleeping in a tent with the sound of ocean waves crashing nearby.

I didn't remember the name Claire. Or Marianne. Or Du-Pont. I didn't remember my mother dying or seeing it occur.

One thing I did know from my therapy sessions with Sally was that our brains protected us from trauma. If there was any truth to what Marianne had told me, it could be that the cells in my brain had blocked out that memory as a survival strategy.

I wanted to talk to Sally. She was the only person who might be able to make sense of this. Marianne couldn't be right about Forest listening in to my phone calls. She had to be completely paranoid.

I spent the next three hours trying to get comfortable on the couch. Finally sometime before the sun had risen, I gave up, tucked the old piece of fabric in my pocket, and made a pot of coffee. Maybe a strong dose of caffeine would bring me some clarity. I poured a cup for myself and looked through the cupboard for something to bake. I had a handful

57

of bananas that were spotting with brown. I decided to make a batch of banana bread spiked with beer. I creamed butter and sugar together as I mashed the bananas and tried to make sense of Marianne's claims. After adding eggs, a trio of spices, flour, and baking soda, I swapped the milk in the recipe for a cup of beer. It was a technique that Ursula had taught me many years ago. Beer is such a versatile ingredient to bake with and can be substituted for practically any liquid. The end result offers breads and pastries an elevated flavor and a zing of frothiness.

Once the banana beer bread had baked to golden perfection and cooled for a few minutes, I sliced a thick piece and poured another cup of coffee for the officer assigned to my porch, and brought them outside to him.

A pinkish light illuminated the top of the mountains as the stars made their retreat. The early morning air was cool and crisp, tinged with the floral scents of spring, and filled with birdsong.

"Thanks for staying on watch. Can I offer you a coffee and banana bread?" I handed him the cup and plate. "I'm Sloan, by the way. I know I've seen you around the village, but I don't think we've been formally introduced."

He took both. "I'm John. I'm fairly new. Came from Spokane a couple months ago." He didn't look that much older than Alex. His head was shaved in a buzz cut, and he wore a khaki uniform. I noticed that he kept one hand on his holster after he set the banana bread on the porch railing. "It's no problem on night duty. It's been quiet so far. I heard from the chief about twenty minutes ago. She should be by in the next hour."

"Great. Can I get you anything else?"

"This is perfect. Thank you." He gave me a nod, keeping his hand ready to pull out his weapon with a second's notice.

I returned inside to get dressed. On a typical morning I would have taken a long walk through Blackbird Island and gotten an early start on breakfast for the guests at Nitro, but this wasn't a typical morning.

While I waited for the chief to arrive, I went through my closet to find a dress for Kat, and one for me. I had no intention of wearing my dirndl to Nitro, but I could change before the parade. For Kat I decided on a pretty pale green dress with pink and white trim and a matching ruffled apron. It was youthful and flirty without being revealing. I opted for a classic red and white dress for myself with a black apron that Ursula had sewn with yellow, orange, and red flowers. It should be fitting for the parade, and it would appease April.

I studied my face in the mirror. My eyes looked sunken and red from lack of sleep. I splashed cold water on my face and massaged my cheeks with moisturizer, hoping to restore some of my natural color. I braided my long dark hair into two braids and twisted them together on the crown of my head. It wasn't my normal look, but I knew that everyone in the village would embrace traditional Bavarian fashion for the parade. I folded the dresses in a bag along with a change of shoes and a pair of knee-high socks. Then I tugged on a pair of jeans and a thin, pale tangerine Nitro hoodie with our logo in gray. The color brought out some of my naturally tanned skin tone and made me feel like my face had a bit more life.

A knock sounded on the door as I finished getting dressed. "Sloan, it's Meyers."

I went to open it.

Chief Meyers looked like she'd been up all night, too. Her eyes were squinty, and her uniform wrinkled.

"How are you? Do you need coffee?"

"I never turn down coffee."

We went into the kitchen. Had it only been a few hours ago that we were in this same spot?

"Well, what do you think?" I asked, pouring her a cup of coffee and slicing her a piece of the banana bread without asking.

"That's a good question. One that I'm not sure I can answer yet." She gulped down the coffee, which was still scalding hot. Then she took a bite of the bread and let her eyes roll back in her head. "My God, Sloan, I don't know how you do it, but your baking is out of this world. This is so good." She took another big bite.

I wanted to shift the conversation back to the topic at hand. "Do you think she's telling the truth?" I cradled my coffee in my hands, waiting for it to cool a little.

"We're looking into it." She paused to polish off the rest of the bread and then used her fingers to get the remaining crumbs. "You don't know anything about her, correct?"

"Last night was the first night I ever met her. She showed up pounding on my front door." Saying it aloud made it sound even more bizarre then it felt.

"She could be your aunt. She looks like you. Same bone structure. Same skin tone. You've had no connection with her prior to last night?"

"No." I went on to explain what I had recently learned from Ursula about my past.

"That could line up." She jotted down a note. "I'll talk to the Krauses."

"What if she's right, though? What if we're in danger?" I felt a tightness return to my chest.

"Sloan, Leavenworth is about the safest place you could possibly be." She made eye contact with me. Her gaze was direct and firm. "Maifest crowds or not, it's hard to hide here for long. We've got you covered. I'm not concerned about that."

"Do you think she's overreacting?"

"I didn't say that." She chose her words carefully. "I believe that *she* believes you're in danger."

"Did you find the files she was talking about?"

"No. There was nothing in her room other than her luggage." She paused for a minute before continuing. "I can tell you this much. We learned from the hotel owner that there have been some break-ins at the hotel. Petty theft. Nothing major. Cash, cell phones—that sort of thing. The owner thinks the thefts have been internal, an employee. And they have been occurring for over a month. Much longer than Marianne claims to have been in town." She stopped again and took a long drink of coffee. I got the sense she was stalling in an attempt to figure out what to say next. "We're going to be following up on the thefts. While Marianne couldn't provide proof about Forest, she was able to direct us to a contact in Seattle. We've been in touch with our colleagues in Spokane and Seattle."

That didn't sound like Chief Meyers was completely dismissing Marianne's claims.

"What about Sara, the woman who died?" I finally took a sip of the coffee. It barely had any taste.

"That's an open investigation. It's too early to rule anything out."

"But you think she was murdered?"

"She was murdered. There's no doubt about that. Blunt force trauma to the head. The question is whether this has any connection to Marianne's theory or if this is a separate case."

"What should I do?"

"My advice?" She took another drink of her coffee. "Go about your normal business. I'm assigning you a tail, who'll keep watch. John's on that duty for now. He told me you brought him coffee this morning. That was nice of you. He's young and eager, so I don't think there's much to worry about with him watching you, other than him pulling the trigger on a poor unsuspecting deer that might pass through your front yard."

I tried to smile.

"Seattle is considering sending a team, so depending on how that shakes out, you might end up with someone new. I'll keep you posted."

"A team?" A wave of fear sent my stomach gurgling.

Chief Meyers sounded calm, but I noticed there was a grimness to her tone. "It's Maifest weekend. We already have everyone on deck, plus extra hands on duty from Wenatchee and Spokane. I think an abundance of caution is a good move at the moment."

"Okay." I nodded, trying to ignore the tingly sensation running up my spine.

"I've released Marianne for the time being. I'm sure she's going to make contact with you soon. That's good. That's what we want. You're going to be my best source for getting information out of her. I suspect that, like me, you have some concerns about her mental state. At this point, I'm leaning toward believing her, but not without plenty of eyes on her, too. Regardless, I don't think you're in any danger with her. She could have your best interests at heart, but the question is going to be whether that's warranted or not."

"I guess, but then why call in extra help?"

Her answer didn't pacify me. "Like I said, extra precaution. Our motto is better safe than sorry." She finished her coffee. "As long as you're comfortable, let Marianne stick near you. See what else you can learn. You're wise and discerning. I think you'll be able to get a sense of her stability, and in the meantime, until extra help from Seattle arrives, I'm going to have John or another member of our team on you. They will give you a perimeter of privacy, but they'll stick close by you. I'm going to be putting every effort into learning what I can about Marianne and Forest while leading the investigation into Sara's murder."

"Okay." I didn't know what else to say.

"Before I go, a word of caution. Keep your phone on you, okay? And stay alert."

"Okay."

The chief left.

I wasn't sure if our conversation had made me feel better or worse. Sitting at home dwelling on it wasn't going to improve the situation, so I gathered my things and decided to head to Nitro. John had finished his coffee. He handed me the empty mug. "Thanks again for that, and it sounds like we're going to be seeing a lot of each other for a while. The chief has assigned me to be your shadow until a replacement arrives. I'll try to stay out of your way, but if you need anything, you just wave or holler, got it?"

"Yeah. It's weird, but it will be a relief to know that you're close by."

"At all times. I won't be more than a few feet away. My training at the academy is finally going to come to use. I've never been assigned to tail someone before. I'm excited about it. I'll try to stay as discreet as I can." His face looked even more boyish as he spoke.

Excited wasn't the word I would have used, but I didn't blame him. I was sure this was the most action he'd seen in the entire time he'd been in Leavenworth. I brought his coffee cup inside, and then locked the door on my way out.

It was strange to know that he was following me as I walked to Nitro. I was going to have to explain my new friend to Garrett and the rest of the crew at the pub. I wasn't sure how to do that without alerting them. Probably my best bet was to keep as close to the truth as possible. I would tell them that it was connected to Sara's murder and I was helping Chief Meyers investigate.

In addition to feeling unsettled with my shadow, it was surreal to see my fellow villagers putting the finishing touches on their shop windows and storefronts in anticipation of the parade, none the wiser that a woman had been murdered.

I didn't get far. Marianne stood at the corner of Fourth and Front, right next to the ten-foot-high carved-wood nutcracker statue. She hadn't changed since I'd seen her last. Her black trench coat was cinched tight around her waist, and her gray hair was tussled and frayed.

"Sloan, come quick." She waved her hand toward her face.

"What's going on?" I glanced behind me, wondering if John would try to keep out of sight.

"I want you to come see my hotel room. I think it will help set the scene."

I looked to my watch. "Okay, but we have to make it

quick. I need to get to work. There's a ton to do before the parade."

"This won't take long." She stepped onto the street and was nearly run over by a work crew carting supplies for the parade on two ATVs.

"Careful." I followed after her.

For being in her sixties, Marianne was spry. She moved with agility, darting past shop owners sweeping their walkways and colorful tape marking the parade route. Hotel Vierter Stock sat three blocks down on the far side of the Festhalle. It was ironic that the hotel was named Vierter Stock, which translated to Fourth Floor, given that it was only two stories. Its white stucco siding, chocolate brown timbers, and forest green shutters blended in beautifully with the Leavenworth aesthetic. Lush hanging baskets greeted guests at an arched entranceway. The hotel blended Bavaria and the forest landscape with potted evergreen trees and rock fountains.

"This way." Marianne bypassed the front entrance and unlatched a waist-high iron gate that took us through a sweet garden and patio. A young man in his early twenties wearing a hotel uniform deadheaded geraniums as we walked by.

"Morning, ladies," he said, tipping his baseball cap. "Did you try the breakfast buffet? Best pastries and omelets in town."

Hotel Vierter Stock was known for its delectable made-to-order gourmet breakfasts. Actually, that was true of most hotels and B&Bs in town. Sticking with the German tradition of hospitality, guests were treated to fresh coffee, tea, strudels, the most delicious assortment of pastries, and made-to-order omelets—a hearty start for a day of hiking, rafting, or perusing the shops.

"We're not interested in breakfast." Marianne brushed

him off and moved down a narrow brick pathway toward a bank of rooms opposite the garden.

He flipped his cap on his head and continued his work.

"This was my room," Marianne announced, stopping at the second door. Police caution tape blocked our access. "They moved me upstairs to the second floor." She looked up to the second story.

"Okay."

"Here's what I think happened. It was dark, and the garden and pathway are only lit with a few lights. I think whoever was following me hid right there." She pointed to a vending and ice machine. "They could have easily hidden there and waited for me. Then followed me into my room. Not me, obviously—Sara. If it was dark, she could have been mistaken for me. She was about my age with a similar height and long hair. Don't you think it would have been easy for the killer to get confused?"

"I don't know." I surveyed the area, sensing that we were being watched. Then I remembered, we were. John stood near the center of the courtyard, pretending to be admiring a hummingbird feeder near one of the patio tables with a bright red sun umbrella.

The gardener caught my eye as he turned on a copper sprinkler to water the lawn.

"I told the chief to have her team sweep the vending machine for prints," Marianne said.

A woman in the room next door to Marianne's cracked her window and leaned her head out. "Can you keep it down? It's only seven thirty. Some of us had a late night."

"So sorry," I said, automatically moving away.

Marianne took a different tactic. "Did you hear what happened last night?"

"Huh?" The woman rubbed her eyes.

"A woman was murdered right here! In the room next to you. You didn't hear anything? The police have been here all night."

"What?" The woman scowled. "Hang on." She closed her window. A minute later, she appeared at the door, wearing a plush white bathrobe and slippers.

"Were you here all night?" Marianne asked. She removed a small notebook and pencil from her trench coat. I couldn't believe she was interrogating a guest. That was Chief Meyers's responsibility. Although she did look official in her trench coat and slacks.

The woman peered around us. "Is that caution tape?"

"Yes. There was a murder," Marianne repeated.

"When?" The woman massaged her temples. I guessed her to be in her mid- to late forties. Her short brown bobbed hair was highlighted with streaks of honey, and it looked as if she'd slept in her makeup.

"Where were you last night between the hours of eleven and one?" Marianne moved closer to try and get a look inside the woman's room.

"Uh, I don't remember. I had a bit too much to drink." She rubbed her temples again. "I'm Eleanor, by the way. Eleanor Wolfe of Wolfe Valley Wines. I'm in town for the festival and went to a tasting party with some other vintners last night. I don't remember when I got back to the hotel. It was probably after midnight. I took a sleeping pill and crashed. I don't remember hearing anything until just now."

"Did you see anything unusual?" Marianne pressed on.

Eleanor tried to force her eyes to adjust to the light. "No. I don't think so. Like I said, the tasting party turned into a bit of a blur. You know how it goes with industry people. We like to show each other up. There was a lot of wine flowing."

"Think about it. Retrace your steps," Marianne said, encouraging her. "Where was the tasting party?"

"At the winery in the village—Blumpiwen. We all congregated back there after everyone finished serving at the Sip and Stroll. We each brought bottles to share. Like I said, the details are pretty hazy after tasting a bunch of different wines. I knew that I didn't have to drive, so I wasn't worried about that. I think it was midnight. It could have been much later. I left the winery and walked back here. That's all I remember." She paused, and then gasped. "No, wait, I do remember something. I remember thinking I heard a scream when I came into the courtyard. I forgot all about that. I waited for a minute, right over there." She pointed to a bistro table on the patio.

"And then what did you do?" Marianne asked.

"Nothing. I didn't hear it again. I figured it was probably other people stumbling home after imbibing like me. I went to bed."

"Thank you for your time. That's very helpful," Marianne said.

I agreed. Had Eleanor heard Sara's scream right before she had been killed? If so, she could have been the last person to hear her alive.

CHAPTER

SEVEN

CHIEF MEYERS AND TWO uniformed officers arrived at the hotel. "What do we have going on here, ladies?" she asked Marianne and me.

Eleanor looked from the police officers to us. "Wait, you're not with them? I thought you were detectives."

"No. Craft brewer." I raised my hand. "And concerned citizen."

"I'd like to ask you a few questions in a minute," the chief said to Eleanor. "If you want to get dressed, I'll be back in fifteen or twenty minutes to take your statement."

"My statement? Yes, of course. Whatever you need." Eleanor glanced behind her. I thought I heard the sound of a shower running. "Are you going to want to talk to me here in my room?"

"Wherever you're comfortable," Meyers responded.

Eleanor shot another look behind her and shook her head.

"Uh, maybe the breakfast room in fifteen minutes? I could use some coffee."

"Fine." She turned to Marianne. "Can we talk in the dining room?"

They left together as the officers entered the room where Sara had been murdered.

"What just happened? I'm confused." Eleanor stared at me. She brushed smudged mascara from underneath her eyes, giving her the appearance of a football linebacker.

"Marianne was staying in the room. She found the body."

"Oh, how horrible." She placed her hand over her heart. "I wish I remembered more."

"Think on it. You might be surprised at what comes up." I glanced at my watch. "I should go. Brewing calls."

There was a soft thud in her room. She snapped her head around, and shook it twice. Then turned back to me. "Sorry. That startled me. Just my book falling off the bed."

The thud had sounded louder than a book, and was it just my imagination, or did Eleanor seem jumpy? It made me wonder if someone else was in the room with her.

She tugged the door closer to her body. "So, you're a brewer?"

"Guilty as charged." I pointed to my hoodie with the Nitro logo.

"That's so great. We're kindred spirits. There aren't that many women in head roles in the wine or beer industry. I'd love to chat and swap stories if you have time while I'm in town."

"Sure, come by the pub. Nitro."

"I'll do that, but first I need coffee and a bottle of Advil." She rubbed her head and retreated to her room.

On my way out, I passed the gardener again. He was having a hushed conversation with a young woman who appeared to be a member of the housekeeping staff, based on her uniform—a green German frock and a ruffled white apron with an actual feather duster tucked into the front pocket.

When I approached, they broke apart.

"Don't mind me, I'm on my way out."

The housekeeper scurried away without a word.

"She's just freaked out by everything that went down last night," he said to me. "I saw you talking to that woman and the police. Are you involved in the investigation?"

"Me? No. I work at Nitro."

"Oh, yeah, I've seen you around before. I'm Bozeman. Me and some of the guys have come by for pints. You guys make great beer."

"Thanks." I should have returned to the pub, but I couldn't pass up the opportunity to see if he knew anything. And Chief Meyers had asked me to stay alert. "Were you here when it happened?"

"No. I work the day shift. Vienna, who just ran off, was here. She took the night shift for Sara."

"So Sara wasn't on duty when she was killed?"

He shook his head. "I don't think so. She was in charge of housekeeping. On busy weekends like this, she would sometimes help transition a room or two if needed, but she managed the staff, supplies, guest requests, that sort of thing. She was a legend around here. She worked here for over two decades. In fact, she was planning to retire in the fall. Too bad."

His words were sympathetic, but his body language was rigid and controlled.

"Did you know her well?"

"Sara? Everyone who worked here knew her, even if you tried not to."

"How so?"

"She was a stickler for the rules. She wasn't even in charge of the grounds, but she'd always keep an eye on what I was doing out here, and she never hesitated to go to Jay, the owner, if she thought someone was slacking." He dug dirt from beneath his nails as he spoke.

I was surprised to find him so forthcoming.

"Did that happen a lot?"

"Nah. She and Vienna got into it a few times because Vienna is constantly on her phone. They got in a big fight yesterday. Sara told her that if she caught Vienna on her phone one more time when she should have been cleaning a room, Vienna was going to get axed. That's why she's so skittish. She thinks the police are going to arrest her."

"For having a fight with her boss?" I asked.

"Because that's a motive for murder, right?" Bozeman yanked off his Hotel Vierter Stock baseball cap and scratched his head. "I don't think she did it, but I get why she's freaking. She's been out of cash for a while. Times are tough up here. Things were slow this winter and early spring, so getting a job here was a big deal, and losing it is a pretty solid reason for offing her boss. That's what we were talking about. I told her to go to the police."

"That's good advice." I didn't mention the fact that regardless of whether Vienna wanted to talk to the police or not, she didn't have a choice.

"My money is on that other woman you were talking to. The one in the trench coat who thinks she's CIA or something. She's been sneaking around and acting shady. I caught her lurking in the supply shed yesterday and trying to sneak into the employee lounge."

"When was this?"

He shrugged. "I don't know. I went to fill a wheelbarrow with bark after lunch yesterday, and I caught her in there. She claimed to be looking for lightbulbs for her room. Vienna saw her in the employee lounge last night."

This was also news. I made a mental note. Marianne could have been paranoid about being followed, or she could have been up to something else.

Bozeman changed the conversation. "Anyway, you guys got anything new on tap? Maybe I'll have to stop by later, avoid the crowds at the Festhalle, you know?"

"I do know. It's going to be a mob scene today. Come by anytime. We'll be pouring our new spring line all weekend." I glanced at the smartwatch Alex had insisted I buy for myself. I had to admit that I enjoyed tracking my steps, especially since living in the village and walking everywhere. On brew days I usually logged well over twenty thousand steps. There was something rewarding and slightly obsessive about knowing how physically taxing brewing could be. "I should get going," I said to Bozeman, leaving him with a half wave.

After I was a block away, I thought of a dozen other questions I could have asked him.

It's not your battle, Sloan, I reminded myself as I returned to Front Street and headed to Nitro. I loved walking through the village at this hour. Sunlight kissed the baroque rooftops, two red-tailed hawks drifted in the cloudless blue sky framed by a fortress of craggy alps, and the early hum of excitement hung in the air as shop owners prepped their storefronts for the parade. The rounded glass windows at the Nutcracker Shoppe displayed delightful spring nutcracker bunnies, a nutcracker with a pineapple crown, a rainbow ballet soldier, and a farmer bearing a basket of his garden's bounty. Das Bonbon enticed potential customers with a droolworthy assortment of marzipans formed to resemble cherries, pears, and wild blackberries. The toy store had wisely catered to its youngest audience. I paused, remembering when Alex would beg us to visit the shop to spend his allowance on giant wand bubbles and a wooden xylophone.

When I arrived at Nitro, the pub's front door had been propped open with our chalkboard sign that read COME ON GET HOPPY NOW!

The bistro tables had been set up with mason jar vases filled with bunches of spring wildflowers. Kat was awake and stringing green and white bunting cut in the shape of hop cones from the top of the door frame to the fence.

"Wow, you're up and at it early," I said with a grin.

Kat twisted a thumbtack into the bunting. "Big day. I'm so excited for the parade."

"On that note, I brought you a gift." I held up the bag.

She climbed down from a step stool and tied off the bunting. "Can I see?"

I handed her the bag. "The top dress is for you."

Kat pulled out the girly dress and held it over her shorts and T-shirt. "This is amazing, Sloan. Thank you so much! It's so pretty, and it will cover my backside, which I greatly appreciate."

"It will look lovely on you." I tucked the bag over my arm. "Have you started breakfast? Should I get going on that?"

"That would be good. I made coffee, and water for tea is already heated, but our flowers got delivered so I started decorating."

"Keep at it. I'll make breakfast, and we can regroup in an hour or so. Is Garrett already awake, too?"

"Yep." Kat fluffed the ruffles on the dress. "He's in the brewery."

"Have fun with the decorating." I left her with a wave. Inside, the tasting room was still dark. A huge box of wild-flowers sat at the bar, along with two floral crowns and a package of pastel colored mints in the shape of tulips.

"Morning," I called to Garrett, who was checking the gravity of our Pucker Up IPA.

"Hey, Sloan." He pushed back his chemistry goggles.

"How's the gravity looking?"

He studied the sample. "Right where it's supposed to be."

"That's what we like to hear." I pointed to the kitchen. "I'm getting started on breakfast. Need anything?"

He siphoned a taster from the clarifying tank. "Want to try it?" Garrett offered me a sample.

Before I could respond, Kat raced into the brewery. "Sorry to interrupt, but there's a police officer across the street. He's just staring at the pub. It's kind of creeping me out. Is there something going on out there?"

"Oh, that would be because of me." I told them about the murder at Hotel Vierter Stock, leaving out the details of my relationship with Marianne.

"That's terrible." Kat's cheeks lost their flush of color from running inside to find us. "That poor woman. Who would do something so awful? And in the middle of a festival weekend." She shuddered at the thought.

Garrett wasn't as easily contented. "Does Chief Meyers have any suspects?"

"Not yet, at least as far as I know." That was true. I didn't know that Marianne was a suspect, although I guessed that the chief had her on a short list.

"Such sad news, with the festival this weekend, too," Kat added. "I wonder if it was a guest. I know there was a group that got pretty out of hand last night."

"Could be," I replied. "Chief Meyers is on it. As you both know, she doesn't miss much. It's just an extra precaution to have one of her team members nearby."

Garrett looked like he wanted to say more, but thankfully he didn't.

"Team meeting in an hour?" I asked. "I'll bring muffins." With that, I went to the kitchen to start breakfast before Garrett had a chance to dig deeper into why the chief would feel compelled to place an officer on watch. I whipped up a batch of lemon blueberry muffins, with a splash of our Lemon Kiss IPA and juicy fat blueberries that I had found at the market earlier. Then I scrambled eggs, hash browns, sausage, and peppers together. Within a half hour, I had a platter of muffins, fresh fruit, and the scrambled eggs delivered to the communal breakfast table upstairs. After I finished the dishes, I plated the extra I had set aside for our team and took it to the front. The twins had arrived.

"How was the rest of the night?" I asked them, handing everyone plates.

"Easy. We drained the kegs, but that's a good thing,

right?" Jack unwrapped a muffin from its paper liner. "We missed you, Kat. You disappeared."

"Oh, I ran into some friends, and we ended up at the Festhalle."

"There was one group that was wild, though," Casey added. "We had to cut them off. That's the first time I've ever had to do that."

"It won't be your last," Garrett said.

I cradled my coffee. "Kat said something similar. Were they tourists?"

"No. I know one of the guys. He was a couple years older than us in school." Jack devoured the muffin in two bites. It reminded me of Alex. Where did teenage boys, or young adults in Jack and Casey's case, put their food? I swear I would stock up on groceries only to have them vanish in an hour when Alex was home.

"Yeah, his name is Bozeman, but in high school they used to call him Boozeman." Casey laughed. "I guess some things don't change."

"I just met him," I replied. "He works as a groundskeeper at Hotel Vierter Stock, right?"

"Yeah, he's part of the group I saw last night at the Festhalle," Kat said, stabbing her egg scramble. "He got into a huge fight with a couple of women. I don't know what happened. I heard the screaming on my way back here."

"When was this?" My curiosity was on high alert.

"Late. Maybe midnight. Twelve thirty."

"We cut him off at ten when the Sip and Stroll ended," Jack said. "He and his friends must have gone to the Festhalle or one of the bars."

"I'm surprised anyone else would serve him. They were

all pretty drunk." Casey chimed in. "This is really good, by the way." He pointed to his nearly empty plate.

Garrett shifted gears to our plan for the day. I had trouble concentrating. I couldn't stop thinking about Bozeman. Who were the women he was arguing with, and if he was drunk, could that have led him to do something rash like kill Sara?

CHAPTER

EIGHT

THE REST OF THE morning was a blur of activity as we prepared for the busiest day Nitro would experience since Ice-Fest. Having Jack and Casey had been invaluable. They were steady workers and brought new energy to our small crew. Since everyone in town would participate in the parade, our plan was to open Nitro after the Maipole dance, the last event of the annual promenade along Front Street. Jack helped Garrett transfer new kegs to the front. Casey restocked pint glasses and made sure we had a supply of recycled plastic glasses in case we needed them. I had a feeling the odds were good that could happen. We would constantly rotate empty pint glasses from the front to the kitchen, where we would run them through our industrial dishwasher. That process didn't take long. The issue was cooling the glasses. There's nothing worse than serving a cold pint in a scalding hot glass. It ruins the beer. Disposable plastic glasses aren't ideal either, but they will do in a pinch.

There were some brewers who had recently embraced the trend of serving their beers at room temperature, but Garrett and I were old-school. We preferred to serve Nitro's offerings at a cool yet drinkable forty-six to fifty degrees. Temperature is one of the finer points of craft beer that tends to get overlooked. Drinking a beer at the preferred temperature allows our customers to really taste the subtleties in every pint. Too warm, and a beer ends up flat. Whereas if a beer is served too cold, between thirty-eight to forty degrees, it reduces the carbonation and the beer loses its aroma. In fact, we had been on a mission at Nitro to ban the term "ice-cold beer" from our clients' vocabulary. No beer should be served ice-cold—ever.

When I gave tours of the brewery, guests were often shocked at how much technique goes into pouring a perfect pint, from the temperature of the glass to the style. I loved getting to share my craft beer knowledge and showcase our brewing process. It never failed to amaze me how many people were shocked by the amount of time and effort that went into each pint. Part of our tour was designed to educate visitors about our use of local ingredients, partnerships with organic farms, and handcrafted brewing methods.

I would tell our tour participants that they could definitely drink a beer straight from the bottle or can, but as a brewer, I always recommended pouring a beer into a glass. First and foremost, drinking a craft beer from a pint glass ensures that the drinker will be able to experience the beer's aroma. Drinking a beer from the bottle cuts off that sensory experience. A beer's aroma can completely alter how we perceive flavor. The same goes for being able to see a beer. A pint glass can showcase a beer's color and clarity. Not to mention those tiny effervescent bubbles that erupt from the bottom, swimming and popping up to the foamy surface.

The twins would be responsible for keeping the bar stocked and managing food orders. Kat, Garrett, and I would work the bar. We had extended our outdoor seating into the back alley. Kat had set up extra tables and decorated them with more bunting, twinkle lights, and flowers. We anticipated a continual rush throughout the afternoon and evening.

After reviewing assignments, we split up to change. I slipped on my German dress, tightened my braids, and finished the look with a pair of knee-high white socks and black patent leather shoes. I added a light blush to my cheeks and a soft, creamy shadow to my eyes. Then I applied some shimmery lip gloss. With my olive skin, I didn't need a lot of makeup, but this was a special occasion. I stood back to appraise myself. *Not bad, Sloan.* The dress was romantic and flirty, and the makeup masked my lack of sleep

I returned to the tasting room, where Kat danced in wearing the dress I'd given her. Her skin glowed. She had twisted her bouncy curls into a messy bun. "Sloan, I'm in love with this dress. Thank you again."

"It looks great on you. You can keep it."

"What? No, I couldn't." She smoothed the front of the Bavarian frock.

"Kat, listen, after you've lived in Leavenworth for a few years, you'll have a closet full of German dresses. It's a prerequisite to becoming a full-fledged citizen. Take this as a gift, please. My closet is not in need of any more dirndls."

"If you're sure?"

"Yes, it's meant for you."

"Yay!" She did another twirl.

Garrett stepped into the front, and both Kat and I gasped. I had never seen him in anything other than shorts, jeans, and T-shirts. Since Nitro didn't subscribe to the Bavarian vibe inside, he had never donned a costume. I had to admit that he looked like a natural in his black lederhosen, crisp white shirt, suspenders, and knee-high socks.

"I never thought I would see the day that Garrett Strong would be wearing lederhosen," I teased, ignoring the fluttering feeling in my stomach.

"Only for the parade. And, I'm going to do my damndest to avoid April Ablin like the plague. She can't see me in this. I'll never hear the end of it."

That was true.

"By the way, I got you two a gift for the occasion." His eyes drifted to me. For a second, we held each other's gaze. I caught a fleeting look of longing before he squared his shoulders and smiled at me and then Kat. "You both look lovely, by the way."

"Thanks." Kat looked to me. "A gift, really?"

I shrugged.

Garrett picked up the two floral headbands resting on the bar. "When I ordered flowers for the pub, the florist asked if I wanted to add in any hair accessories for my female staff, and I thought why not? You don't have to wear them if they're cheesy. She mentioned that a lot of locals wear them for the parade. I guess they're kind of a tradition for Maifest."

"It's beautiful." Kat swooned and donned her flower crown.

The crowns had been weaved together with fragrant green bay leaves, eucalyptus, sprigs of rosemary, and lavender, and entwined with pale white orchids, spray roses, and magnolias. It was a sweet gesture from Garrett. I was acutely aware that we were far from being alone at the moment, but that didn't stop my heart from racing or the way my body wanted to pull toward him. Ever since things had blown up with Mac, I'd been careful not to let my heart open to anyone new, but there was no denying that my growing attraction to Garrett was threatening that.

"Too weird, Sloan?" he asked.

"Not at all. I'm with Kat. They're gorgeous. Thank you." With that, I placed mine on my head, drinking in the dainty scent of the blooms.

"No one can accuse Nitro of not being in the Maifest spirit," Garrett said. "They look great on both of you, but let's make a promise right now, that the minute the parade is done, we change back into our T-shirts for the afternoon rush."

"You won't get a complaint from me," I replied.

Kat shook her head. "I don't know. I'm kind of vibing on this look. I might have to wear it for the entire day. After all, Maifest is only once a year."

Ah, to be in my twenties again. I was glad that at least one of us embraced the Bavarian spirit. Actually, there was no part of me that longed to return to my youth. I enjoyed the wisdom and confidence that came with age. Some of the decisions I'd made in my early twenties, like marrying Mac, had come to haunt me.

Jack and Casey had finished setting up the back area and changed into lederhosen, too.

"Whoa, you guys look awesome," Kat said, reaching for her phone. "Let's take a group selfie before we go."

I watched Jack push Casey out of the way so he could

stand next to Kat in the photo. "Say prost!" Kat snapped shots of us standing in front of the taps.

We headed outside to find Front Street packed with families noshing on pastries and sipping German chocolate mochas. Kids raced through Front Street Park, chasing balls and bubbles. A trio of accordion players piped out upbeat tunes in the gazebo, and the street vendor tents were already bustling with activity. People were selling flower wands, crowns, earrings made from rose petals, and Bavarian-style leis. The longest line was at the caramel corn tent, where the sweet smell of huckleberry and green apple caramel corn drifted my way. The *Bier* wagon, decked out with kegs and flowers, stood at the ready to lead the procession. Bernese mountain dogs with yellow daisy collars trotted like regal ambassadors, stopping to be petted by their adoring fans.

Spring celebrations like Maifest dated back thousands of years. Originally a pagan holiday signaling the return of spring and fertility, the joyful merrymaking had evolved over the years. Villages in Germany had marked the occasion with parades and dancing around the Maipole, which was believed to bring good luck and great wealth to the village and its inhabitants. The arrival of spring and the reawakening of the earth after winter's cold darkness was most certainly cause for dancing in the streets in my opinion. The budding apple and pear trees agreed with me, putting on a fragrant blossoming show for our weekend guests.

"April said we're supposed to congregate between the library and pool," Kat told us as we blended in with the crowd moving west along Front Street toward the highway.

I assumed that we were being followed by John, my

personal protection team, but I didn't turn around to check. At the gathering site I spotted so many familiar faces that I was immediately whisked into conversation after conversation. Catching up with friends was a welcome distraction from the last few hours.

Ursula and Otto came up to me as I moved to take my place in the parade line.

"Sloan, over here!" Ursula called. Her silky gray hair was wrapped in two braids around the crown of her head. She and Otto wore matching outfits like last night, only this time in bright spring greens and pinks.

"How was the dance? You two looked pretty great up there last night," I commented, greeting them with a hug. It was a relief to know that I didn't have to worry about their past. Part of me wanted to tell Ursula about Marianne. After all, she had known Marianne. She might be able to lend insight into whether she had thought Marianne was stable those many years ago, but I resisted the urge. I had made a promise to Marianne, and if there was any chance that she was telling the truth about Forest, I didn't want to put the Krauses in harm's way.

"We stayed out later zan we have in years." Otto's light blue eyes twinkled. "Once Ursula is on ze dance floor, she will not leave."

"I'm glad you enjoyed yourselves. The crowd loved you."

"Stop, Sloan, you will make us blush." Ursula waved me off.

"Mom!" a voice called from nearby.

We turned to see Alex and Mac approaching. My heart thudded in my chest. I tried to remain calm, but shot a look in both directions. Villagers crowded around us. If Forest or one of his henchmen were watching me, there would be no way for me to know. I stood on my tiptoes and was relieved to see John only a few feet away. He looked like he belonged. A number of police officers stood waiting to lead the procession and make sure that the streets were cleared for us.

Whew. I let out a sigh.

Play it cool, Sloan.

"Don't you look dapper," I said, planting a kiss on his cheek.

"Mom." Alex wiped my kiss away. "You can't kiss me in public. I'll lose my street cred."

"Street cred?" Mac laughed. He wrapped a burly arm around Alex's shoulder. "You're going to have to teach your old man your tricks."

They were nearly the same height. In fact, on closer inspection, I couldn't be sure that Alex hadn't inched over the top of Mac's head. They looked like father and son, with their rosy cheeks and bright eyes. Mac's build was stockier, whereas Alex had a long and lean soccer player's frame. His cheeks had begun to fill out, and his voice had deepened. It was surreal to watch him transform in front of my eyes.

"April got to you guys, too?" I teased.

They both wore Der Keller's traditional *Trachten* shirts, suspenders, and shorts.

"I'm in charge of handing out coasters." Alex reached into his pockets to show me a stack of coasters with the Der Keller family crest, two lions waving German flags.

"That's a great job for you."

We walked together to join the parade procession.

"You would have been so impressed with this kid of ours," Mac said, ruffling Alex's hair. "He must have run five miles going back and forth between the patio and kitchen last night."

"That should make your soccer coach happy," I said. "How was it? Are you going to turn in your resignation this morning?"

"No way. It was awesome. There were a couple of jerks in the mix, but for the most part, everyone was chill and happy, and my shift went by so fast because we were busy the entire night."

"Just wait for today," Mac cautioned. "You think last night was busy? Tonight is going to be triple the crowd."

"Bring it on." Alex flexed.

We made it to the back of the line, where we were ushered to our different spots. I had been slotted to be part of the flag-waving group. About twenty of us were handed small German flags. I noticed Bozeman—or Boozeman, as the twins referred to him—talking to Vienna the housekeeper. They were both assigned to my group. I hung back and watched them for a minute. Vienna appeared to be pleading with Bozeman.

The sound of the alpenhorns at the front of the line signaled that the parade was about to start. We slowly shuffled forward. A man wearing the Hotel Vierter Stock uniform squeezed in next to Vienna and Bozeman, who continued to argue.

I recognized the man. He was Jay Hunter, the owner of the hotel. I didn't know Jay well. He had moved to Leavenworth from the East Coast three or four years ago when he bought the hotel. I'd bumped into him at a few chamber meetings and seen him at the pub a handful of times, but our conversations had never been more than casual. I'd been fine with that. Jay was handsome in a slick way that had put me on edge from the moment I met him. I remembered at our first meeting moving away from him when he had smiled with unnaturally white teeth that made me conjure up images of Little Red Riding Hood into the Big Bad Wolf.

Vienna tried to scoot away from him. I saw why. As the horns bellowed again, Jay reached beneath her skirt and grabbed her ass.

CHAPTER
NINE

I PUT MY HAND to my chest. The thought made my skin crawl.

She swatted his hand away and moved to the other side of Bozeman.

I considered myself a pretty good judge of character. Vienna's reaction and her rigid body posture told me she didn't welcome Jay's advances. It appeared that I needed to add sexual harassment to the list of issues at the Hotel Vierter Stock.

We proceeded toward Front Street to the happy applause of the crowds. Tourists pushed together on the sidewalks for a firsthand view of the polka bands, giant puppets, colorful floats adorned with lush spring flowers, and clopping Clydesdales. A group of women in pretty dresses with red, black, and yellow aprons tossed fuchsia pink and canary yellow carnations to bystanders. Children perched on their parents' shoulders noshing on pretzels the size of their heads. The brilliant blue sky above and sturdy mountains surrounding the village served as the perfect backdrop for the whirl of color, thumping of music, and cheerful laughter. I waved my German flag high in the air and kept an eye on Vienna. She made a concerted effort to stay as far away from Jay as possible. I didn't blame her.

I made a mental note to mention the interaction to Chief Meyers. If she was already investigating a murder at the hotel, she could probably do a bit of digging into employee/management relations or report what I'd witnessed to HR.

We sauntered along Front Street, waving to happy visitors. They snapped photos and steadied their cell phones to capture our Festzug on video. Kids in tiny German costumes danced on the street and tossed candy to parade watchers. A line of six alpenhorn musicians led the procession. The melodic sound of the delicately carved wooden instruments brought a grin to my face. They were followed by a traditional horse-drawn carriage guided by two long-maned mares with floral saddles. April sat with the mayor and sprinkled her adoring fans (as I'm sure she imagined the spectators were) with rose petals.

It was hard to argue that there was any place more magical than Leavenworth at the moment. Our version of Bavaria was on full display, with authentic costumes and the pulsing beat of shiny tubas, as the band high-stepped down the street. The budding trees and gazebo draped with silky ribbons and dainty twinkly lights caught the sun, creating sparkling patterns that reminded me of falling snowflakes. The smells of roasting nuts and aromatic flowers brought a smile to my face. Everyone clapped and swayed along when the high school band broke into the "Beer Barrel Polka." German maidens spun in circles carrying a miniature version of the Maipole. I wondered how they weren't dizzy by the end of the route. I caught Garrett's eye in the crowd. He grinned and waved, as he dutifully followed the *Bier* wagon that carried the all-important wooden keg, which had been decked out with dozens of red and white blooms. He had been assigned to the poop scoop crew, who wore matching felt hats and darted after the horses with their wheelbarrows and shovels.

The parade didn't take long. Within twenty minutes, we had made it to the Festhalle. I hadn't spotted Marianne or anyone looking nefarious in the crowd, but I had felt the eager gaze of my young police detail burning the back of my head. I wondered if anyone else had noticed that John marched by my side or a few paces behind for the duration of the parade, rather than up front with the other police officers. I tried to ignore the thought that I was being watched and focus instead on the jubilation.

It was hard not to feel upbeat and festive in the midst of so much joy and happiness.

This is why you love Leavenworth, Sloan, I thought, stopping at the corner near Der Keller to watch the remainder of the parade. Our village might have its fair share of quirks and challenges, but we came together for events like this in a way I had never experienced in my youth or young adulthood. The entire village embraced the return of spring and our collective desire to share that with our guests.

I was about to return to Nitro when I spotted Vienna coming toward me. She was making a beeline for Der Keller, but there was already a line queuing halfway down the block. She stopped at the corner and sighed.

"It's already packed," I commented. "You basically have to pitch a tent on the sidewalk the night before parades if you want a seat inside."

She frowned and nodded. "Bummer, I was just hoping to sneak in for a slice of pizza and pint before the parade finished. Guess I missed my chance."

"I think some crafty paradegoers got smart and used their spot in line to view the parade." Der Keller's patio tables were packed with tourists enjoying strudel and giant beer steins. From their rosy cheeks and the way different groups crammed together around the long picnic tables, I suspected they'd been there for a while. "I work around the corner at Nitro. I can pretty much guarantee that we won't be packed yet, but that might change soon. If you want to follow me, I can hook you up. We don't have pizza, but we have ample beer and some delicious lunch specials."

"Oh yeah, one of my friends was talking about Nitro. I haven't checked it out yet. I live in Wenatchee, so usually I head straight from the shuttle to work and then back again." Vienna nibbled on the tip of her pinky. Her fingernails were painted like a rainbow and dotted with little stars. "Good thinking. As long as you have food. I forgot a lunch, and I'm working a twelve-hour shift today."

"We do," I replied. I felt someone watching us, and when I turned, I realized it was John, who stood casually leaning against one of the hop vine trellises that Hans had built. "I'm Sloan, by the way. I saw you at the hotel."

"Vienna." She reached out her manicured hand. While her nails were painted and buffed, her skin was rough, chapped, and calloused. "Yeah, I work there, although I don't know for how long. You're not hiring for a housekeep by chance, are you?"

"Not at the moment, but you never know." We walked together. John faded into the horde filing into shops. "Why? Are you thinking of leaving Hotel Vierter Stock?"

"I'm not thinking of leaving. I think I'm getting fired."
She chomped harder on her pinky.

Her words echoed what Bozeman had told me earlier. I was stunned that she would admit it to me. Maybe she had a different side to the story. "Oh no. Why do you think you're getting fired?"

"Did you hear about Sara, the woman who died?"

"I did. I'm so sorry."

"Yeah. It's crazy. It's still hard to believe." She kicked a plastic cup that someone had left on the sidewalk.

I stopped to toss it in one of the keg barrel trash cans. Crews would work around the clock for the duration of the festival, making sure that the trash cans didn't overflow and that our cobblestone sidewalks remained clean.

"Had you worked with Sara a long time?" I asked.

"Not that long. I've only been on staff for about a year, but she was my boss the entire time, so I guess I knew her pretty well. She was tough. She had high standards for us, and she hated cell phones." She fiddled with her platinum blond braid, wrapping it around her finger and then letting it go again.

"Really?"

"She freaked out anytime I happened to be on my phone. I kept telling her it wasn't a big deal. She didn't understand my generation. It's not like I talk on the phone. I would shoot a text to a friend or check in on my TikTok. It didn't stop me from doing my job."

I didn't respond, especially since I was in Sara's camp on the issue of phones at work. If it was slow in the pub, I never minded that Kat would use that time to take pictures for our social media and website, but Garrett wasn't paying her or any of us to scroll on our phones for hours. There were always endless projects to be done when working for a small, family-owned business. Work ethic had been essential to my success. It was one of the things I tried most to impart to Alex. His life hadn't been filled with the same challenges that I had experienced in my youth. While I would never have wished him the instability that I'd had, my years in foster care also made me resilient. I wanted that for him.

"So it sounds like you and Sara didn't have a great working relationship?"

"That's what the police kept asking me earlier. I don't know what the big deal is. She was my boss, and she was, like, forty years older than me. It's not like we went out for beers after work or hung at the spa together, but isn't that the way it's supposed to be?"

"Definitely," I agreed. "I think it's important to have some boundaries between management and staff."

"Yeah. Exactly." Her phone buzzed. She reached into her pocket and responded to a text as we continued along the sidewalk.

I was impressed that she could text and walk simultaneously.

"Sorry, I had to text my mom real quick." She stuffed her phone back into her skirt pocket. "See, that's what I told Sara. I'm fast. What's the big deal about taking a few seconds to shoot off a text? I never take long lunch breaks or anything. I'm a hard worker. I need this job."

I wasn't sure how to respond, but Vienna seemed open, so I decided the best route was taking the straightforward approach. "Did that cause problems between you and Sara? Is that why you're worried about getting fired?"

"No. Sara threatened to fire me a bunch of times. I knew she would never do it."

"Why?"

"Because I'm the best cleaner she had. I'm the most reliable. I've never skipped a shift or showed up late. You can't say that about some of the other staff members. Sara warned me to put my phone away all the time, but she wasn't going to fire me. It was an empty threat to make a point. That's all."

"Then why are you worried about getting fired?"

She bit her lip. "Uh, because of my other boss. He won't keep his hands off of me."

Jay.

"Vienna, what do you mean?" I stopped. Although I already knew how she was going to answer.

"The hotel owner is a serious creep. He is always trying to grope me. I told Sara about it, and she had my back. That's another reason I know she wasn't going to fire me. She told me to stay away from Jay and that she was going to help me file a formal complaint."

This was major news. I wondered how it might tie into Sara's murder. "Good. No one should have to suffer through workplace harassment." I could hear my tone shifting into concerned mom mode, but it was true. Vienna deserved to go to work without fear of unwanted touching from her boss—or any other staff member, for that matter.

"I know, but now I'm stuck. I don't know what to do. Sara was going to help. She's dead, and I'm alone. Jay has told me on more than one occasion that if I don't sleep with him, he'll fire me." Vienna sounded dejected, as if she was out of options.

"That's illegal, Vienna." I could feel my heart rate increase. How dare Jay take advantage of his power like that? "I'm so sorry that Sara is dead, but her death doesn't mean that you have to suffer through this situation. There are laws in place to protect you. Did you talk to Chief Meyers?"

"She asked me some questions earlier. Someone told her about Sara threatening to fire me, but I didn't say anything about Jay because I was worried that she might tell him and then I'd get fired for sure."

"No, listen, you need to tell her. It's important. Chief Meyers and I have been friends for a long time, and I promise that she'll protect you. Whatever you tell her will be in confidence. You don't have to worry about her confronting Jay, but you do need to tell her what's been happening, not only for your sake but because he could be doing this to other women on staff."

"Yeah, I guess I didn't think about that." She didn't sound very sure.

I wanted to add that Jay's sexual harassment could also be connected to Sara's murder, but I decided it was best to leave that out of the equation for the moment. Vienna had enough to deal with.

We arrived at Nitro. John took up a post near the patio doors. I invited Vienna inside and poured her a pint and got her a to-go box of our cheese and meat plate.

"You'll talk to Chief Meyers, right?" I asked when she paid for her lunch.

"Yeah. I will. Thanks for listening."

"Anytime. My door and my bar are always open." I ran my hand along the wood bar top. "Vienna, Sara was right to help you. I've worked in this industry for many years, and I have had plenty of run-ins with guys like Jay. This isn't your fault. And if you need extra support or someone to talk to, I'm here."

Her eyes misted. "Thanks. It's so embarrassing."

"For him." I met her eyes and reached my hand out to console her. "Really, Vienna. This isn't on you. Workplace harassment is a huge issue. If anyone should be embarrassed, it's Jay. Not you."

She nodded, but she didn't look convinced.

"Sorry, it's the mom in me." I patted her arm and moved away. "This is how men like Jay manipulate the situation, to make *you* feel bad or like it's somehow your fault that he's crossing a major line. It isn't. This is on him."

"Yeah, I guess you're probably right." She took her to-go box. "Thanks again for listening. I need to get back to the hotel."

I watched her leave. Hopefully she would follow through and talk to Chief Meyers. If she didn't, I would. I wasn't about to let Jay get away with harassing his young female staff. Not to mention if Sara had confronted him, that could have given him a motive for killing her.

CHAPTER

TEN

AS EXPECTED, A POST-PARADE surge poured into the pub. Within thirty minutes, there wasn't an empty seat to be had in the tasting room, on the patio, or outside in the temporary section we'd set up in the back. People were in good spirits, which was fortunate because, even with five of us working, there was a constant line at the bar. The twins were earning their keep. I thought of Alex many times when I watched them sprint from the patio to the bar to pick up trays laden with pints, bowls of fresh pea soup, meat and cheese platters, and my Lemon Kiss trifle.

I had to stop multiple times to dab sweat from my forehead and rehydrate with a glass of water. There was no time to think about Marianne or Sara's murder with the steady stream of customers, which was not a bad thing. I checked on John a few times, bringing him pub snacks and Arnold Palmers. He was appreciative but refused to engage in small talk; rather, he kept his eyes forward, constantly scanning the sidewalk.

"How you doing, Sloan?" Garrett asked when I came behind the bar with a new round of orders. He poured a pint of Lemon Kiss and blew the keg. Foam shot everywhere.

I grabbed a towel, cleaned the tap, and helped him connect a new keg.

"Not bad. It hasn't slowed down, though. I thought we might have a lull between lunch and dinner, but it doesn't look like that's going to happen." I wiped beer splatter from my dress. "I haven't even had a chance to change."

"True. True." Garrett tugged on his suspenders. "We didn't follow through on our pact, and I'm dreading the thought of April venturing inside and seeing me still wearing lederhosen. I'll never hear the end of it, and neither will you. Imagine being forced to dress like a nutcracker every day."

"Ah!" I pretended to gag.

Garrett brushed a strand of hair from his face. "There is good news, though. Our till is overflowing, metaphorically speaking," he said, nodding to the iPad mounted on the end of the bar. We used a point-of-purchase system. Rarely did we get cash. The vast majority of our clientele paid with credit cards or their phones.

"I just hope we don't blow another keg." He finished connecting the hose and tested the tap.

"Don't quote me on this, but I think we may get some relief during the dinner hour. That's when the headliners start at the Festhalle. People tend to wander over that way for dinner and music."

"I can't believe I'm saying this, but that would be good." Garrett topped off the frothy pint. "Not that I don't want to sell beer, but I want to have some left for tomorrow. If we keep pouring at this rate, we'll be dry, and our next batch won't be ready for a week. Do I sound like I'm starting to panic?"

I chuckled. "Not at all. You sound like every brewer I know."

One of the biggest challenges for small operations like Nitro was supply versus demand. Our ten-barrel system limited the amount we could brew at any one time. Ten barrels translated into twenty kegs, which might sound like ample beer, but in comparison with a brewery of Der Keller's scale, it was nothing. Der Keller brewed on a behemoth fully automated brewing system, giving them the ability to have close to a dozen unique beers on tap at all times. I would often share stats on brew production with guests during tours of the nanobrewery, and watch jaws drop when I explained that the big guys, the national chain breweries (that produced that watered-down, flavorless beer found at grocery stores) had two-million-barrel setups.

For Nitro, our small-scale brewing meant that for busy weekends like Maifest we had to plan well in advance and hope that we had produced enough.

Garrett got pulled into a conversation. I went to check on the tables on the patio. The late afternoon sun beat down on the colorful umbrellas. Everyone's cheeks were red and rosy, either from the beer, the sun, or both. I drank in the smell of the flower bouquets placed at each table and the hearty scent of grilling meats and veggies wafting from Front Street Park. The entire village was alive and buzzing. A group of retirees in matching green and orange costumes pranced past the patio doing high-kicks and belting out German soccer chants. I could hear the sound of the chainsaw carvers competing near the gazebo. I made a mental note to go check out their finished artwork later.

I picked up used glasses and took orders for refills. As I was about to return inside, someone tapped my arm. I nearly dropped the tray I was balancing.

It was Marianne. She had changed into a long, flowing peasant skirt and a silk tank top with a thin yellow wrap. Her look was completely the opposite from the dark spy-like trench coat she'd worn earlier. "Sloan, how are you? Have you seen anyone?" She craned her neck toward the sidewalk, where a family walked past noshing on chocolate-filled pretzels and drippy ice-cream cones.

"I'm fine, and no, everything's cool. Just the Maifest rush." I looked up to see John keeping a close watch on Marianne. Did he know something I didn't?

She had planted herself in a chair propped next to the short four-foot fence that housed in the patio.

"Can I get you anything?"

"I suppose I could try a beer." She had taken our paper menu and rolled it up into a long tube.

"Do you have a style you prefer?"

"No, bring me your favorite."

That was a sentiment that newcomers often repeated. Picking a favorite beer would be like picking a favorite child—every beer we had on tap was a labor of love—but I didn't have time to give Marianne my normal speech on the topic.

Instead, I took the dishes inside, poured four pints, and returned outside. After dropping off the other orders, I handed Marianne a glass of our hibiscus rose spring ale. It was a light floral beer with low IBUs (International Bittering Units).

For non-beer-drinkers it was a great starting point, without being heavy in hops or malty.

"Here you go. It's a spring favorite."

Marianne stared at the glass. "It's almost a rose color."

"That's what we were going for. We brewed it with rose hips."

"I like it," she said after taking a sip. "It's almost too pretty to drink. You have a talent, Sloan. You get that from your mom. Did you know that Claire used to make wine? She was one of the first women in the area to dive into the craft of wine making. I loved watching her take on the good old boys of the industry. It was just a hobby for her, but she crushed the men. I loved watching them squirm when she showed up with a few cases of her artisan wines at local farmers markets and sold out in minutes. She could have made it a career."

I wanted to scream. Until a few hours ago, I didn't even know her name. To Marianne, I shook my head. "No. I don't know anything about her."

Marianne attempted to smile, but it didn't reach her eyes. "There's so much I want you to know about Claire. She was ahead of her time, like you. She was blending different varietals of grapes long before the Yakima Valley was on the map as the West Coast's premier wine destination, and she was the only woman for miles around. She'd show up at competitions with a few cases of wine in her trunk and absolutely destroy winemakers who had inherited family acreage and had been producing grapes for decades. It was something to watch. She had so much spunk." Marianne trailed off.

Did that mean that she'd lived in Yakima? Did that mean that I had grown up in Yakima before being placed in foster care?

I wanted to ask Marianne so many more questions, but this wasn't the time or place.

"You're busy. I won't keep you. I'll wait out here until you have a break, okay?"

"Feel free."

Was she staying so she could watch me?

Probably.

I wished I could get a better read on her. I wanted to believe her, but she seemed unreliable. If only I could find time to talk to the chief. I wanted to know what, if anything, she'd been able to glean from Marianne.

As expected, the rush finally died down a little after six, as tourists slowly made their way to the Festhalle for the evening's entertainment lineup. That didn't mean that Nitro was deserted, but it did mean that there wasn't a huge line waiting for beers and snacks.

"That was fun," Kat commented, filling bowls with Doritos and mixed nuts. She was still wearing the dress I had given her. "We haven't been that busy since Oktoberfest. The back patio has been a hit. We should definitely set it up for every festival. Maybe we could even squeeze a small band back there. People love the enclosed alleyway vibe, and it's shady."

"Glad it's going well," I commented, glancing around the tasting room. "Do you need a break? There's finally a lull."

"Nope. I'm in my element. It's so fun to get to be this busy."

Garrett overheard our conversation. "Sloan, you should take a break. There's a woman who's been sitting on the patio for the last two hours. Every time I've asked her if she needs a refill, she says she's waiting for you."

He didn't say more, but I could tell from the winkles in his forehead that he had questions about Marianne.

"I'll go check on her." I left before either of them had a chance to respond. But first I went to the small private bathroom attached to the brewery to change out of my Bavarian dress into my shorts and T-shirt. I splashed cold water on my face, staring at my reflection in the mirror in hopes it would provide some clue to my ancestry. Again, I wished I could talk to Sally. Was there really any danger in calling her? I could use her grounding wisdom now.

On a whim, I went into the office and placed a call. Sally didn't answer, so I left her a lengthy voicemail giving her the highlights. I knew she would get back to me soon.

I felt better knowing that Sally was in the loop. With that off my mind, I folded my dress and knee-high socks and went outside. Marianne was in the same spot I'd left her. Her beer was empty, but her eyes were sharp and focused. She scanned every group that passed by on the sidewalk—kids holding giant flower balloons on silky ribbons and college students in fraternity and sorority lettered T-shirts heading to the Underground, a basement bar across the street from Nitro.

A bachelorette party had taken over most of the patio. The bride-to-be wore a sash and plastic crown over a black tank top with gold lettering that read DRUNK IN LOVE. Her bridesmaids wore matching tank tops with the words JUST DRUNK written across the front. Wedding season in Leavenworth brought continual bachelor and bachelorette parties into the village. Brides and their crews tended to opt for wine tasting tours and spa days, whereas the groom and his mates went white-water rafting and golfing. We had created special beer tastings and brewery tours for wedding parties, which was a lucrative business from now through late October. "How did you like the beer?" I asked, pulling a chair next to her.

Marianne held up her empty glass. "The beer was wonderful. Like I mentioned, I don't consider myself a beer fan, but I think you've converted me. It was a pleasure to drink, and it brought up so many memories of your mom. She would be so proud of you." Her voice broke.

I sat down, not sure how to reply without breaking down myself.

"Sloan, I'm sorry." She sighed and bowed her head. "I never intended to involve you like this. I was planning to reach out to you. Honestly, I was, but then I learned that Forest was closing in, and I panicked. I didn't know what else to do. After so many, many years of trying to protect you and keep you safe, I couldn't let him get to you first. I know this is a terrible time. I see how busy you are. I see how happy you are. I can't believe what a life you've made for yourself here, and now because of me, that's in danger." There was a softness about her that was different from last night, and not just because of her bohemian outfit, which looked especially out of place against the sea of colorful dirndls and barmaid dresses.

"Marianne, are you sure this threat is real?" I rubbed my forearm. "Is there any chance that you may be blowing things out of proportion?"

"I can see in your face that's what you think of me. You think I'm crazy, don't you?" She gave her head a soft shake. She was much quieter and less animated than she had been earlier.

"I wouldn't use those exact words, no."

"You don't need to. It's obvious. That's why this is so hard. I wouldn't believe me either. I would look at me and think, 'She's some nut job.'" She ran her index finger along her bottom lip. "That's why I'm saying this isn't how I intended our first meeting to go. I had planned to have documentation for you. I know he took it. It was in my hotel room. I was so careful. You have to believe me. Everything was in the files. If you had seen them, you would be terrified, too. It's my word against an unknown threat, but, Sloan, I promise I have your best interest at heart. I always have. I always will. I don't know how I'm going to do it, but somehow I'm going to earn your trust."

"What did Chief Meyers say?" I wished I could believe her. I wanted to believe her. I wanted to sit outside with her for hours and hear every story she had to tell me about Claire and my early childhood, but I couldn't let myself go there.

"Nothing. They're checking the room for fingerprints and any other evidence the killer might have left behind. They won't find anything. I already told her. Forest is a professional. He's not going to leave a single strand of hair behind or let any of the people he hires to do his dirty work do the same. I guarantee the room will be spotless. It's probably cleaner than when I checked in. That should be her red flag."

"Chief Meyers is a professional. She'll do her due diligence."

"It won't matter. She's a small-town cop, and it's too late anyway. He's here. I can feel it." She looked around us as if expecting to see Forest jump out from behind a group on their way to the Festhalle.

"I spoke with Vienna, one of the young housekeepers, earlier, and it sounds like there are some other issues at the hotel." I kept my tone measured and steady. "Do you think there's a chance that Sara's death has nothing to do with Forest? I think there's a strong possibility that she could have had issues at work that led to her murder."

Marianne clenched her jaw. "I understand why you want to think that. I would, too. It's easier to live in denial versus fear, but I can't stress enough that Forest is *dangerous*."

"I don't doubt that. I can tell that you're scared, and I'm taking your warning to heart. Chief Meyers has me being watched around the clock right now. What I'm talking about, though, are the odds that Sara's death has any connection to Forest. It seems much more likely that the two are unrelated."

The bachelorette party cheered as Jack delivered a round of drinks to their table.

"You're not going to believe me, are you, Sloan?" She sounded broken, as if I had wounded her.

"Marianne, you said it yourself. You can't expect that after over forty years I'm going to implicitly trust everything you say. I'm following your instructions. I'm limiting my contact with my family. I'm keeping both eyes open. It's not as if I have plans to take any major risks. I'm not going to jump up on the gazebo stage and announce that I'm here, but if Forest really wants to find me and he's as dangerous and connected as you say he is, what can I do?"

"Leave." Marianne pursed her lips together so tightly that they formed a single narrow line. "You can leave the village now. It's not too late to enter witness protection. I can take you to Seattle tonight. The next train leaves in an hour. I already bought us two tickets."

"What?"

"I've thought through every option, Sloan, and the only choice you have is to run."

CHAPTER

ELEVEN

"WHAT?" I STARED AT her as if she was speaking a foreign language. "Run? You want me to run? Leave behind Alex? The Krauses? Garrett, Nitro, everything? No way. Not a chance."

"If you stay, you're putting all of them—everyone you know and love—at risk." She placed her hands on the table, formed a steeple with her fingers, and held my gaze.

"I'll take that chance. I spent my entire childhood moving. Do you know what it's like to never have a sense of permanence? I'm not doing that again, and I'm not abandoning Alex."

"We could take him with us," she suggested.

"And force him to leave his father, grandparents, uncle, friends, everything he knows and loves? Absolutely not. I won't do that to him." I shook my head so hard it hurt.

She folded her hands in her lap. "I was worried this would be how you would react."

"I can't imagine anyone else reacting differently."

"No." She sighed. "You're right. It's probably in my head. Maybe I've let my paranoia get out of hand. I think I'll go back to the hotel and try to rest."

I was surprised by her 180-degree shift, but I didn't disagree. "That's a good idea."

She stood. "If you change your mind in the next hour, come find me. The tickets are booked. We simply need to get ourselves to the train station."

"I'm not changing my mind." I shook my head with force again.

For a minute I thought she was going to try and convince me again. Her facial features sagged as she stood up. "Thank you again for the beer. It was lovely." With that, she turned and walked away.

I stayed at the table. I needed a second to collect my thoughts before I went back inside. The more time I spent with Marianne, the more I was beginning to wonder if I was in any serious danger. Her personality had completely shifted. Within the same breath, she had gone from insisting that we run away to dropping the whole idea. How stable could she be? Was Forest even real? I needed to face the fact that I knew little to nothing about her. For all I knew, could she be trying to kill me. Then again, why? She'd had plenty of opportunities and had yet to harm me. Nothing made sense. If only she had tangible proof. Maybe then the rational side of my brain could believe her outlandish story.

I tried to force the fuzzy memories of my early years to the forefront without luck. The few memories I had prior to my years in the foster care system were like wispy clouds floating across the sky. A woman pushing me in a swing, the scent of jasmine perfume, a hand clutching mine outside Sally's office the day I was placed in care. I had no memory of my mother or of her death.

Could Marianne be making that up, too?

A new thought began to take shape. What if she was actually my birth mother? Maybe the guilt of giving me up had overwhelmed her. The story of Forest and my mother's murder could be a coping mechanism. A way for her to try and rationalize abandoning me. If I thought about it, it made more sense than a crazed killer stalking me decades later.

I was slowly becoming resigned to the possibility that Marianne was not only my mother, but also not in control of her mental capacity.

What did that mean for me? For Alex?

I tried to push the tidal wave of emotions deeper inside. I had to stay focused. There was no one I trusted, aside from Garrett and Chief Meyers in the short term. If I could help Chief Meyers figure out who killed Sara, then I might be able to have a better sense of whether Marianne should be believed.

That's what you need to do, Sloan. I stood and rotated my shoulders. I had one mission—find Sara's killer. Once I accomplished that, I could shift gears and put energy into what to do about Marianne.

The bachelorettes had finished their beers and were moving on for shots at the Underground. I wanted to caution them to pace themselves, but I doubted it would do any good. I returned to the pub, where the crowd had dispersed. The twins cleared tables and bussed dishes. Garrett wiped down the bar with a cleaning mixture.

"Everyone took off, huh?" I noted.

He squeezed a towel into a bucket of cleaning solution.

"You nailed it, Sloan. The question now is whether we stay open for the remainder of the evening or close up shop and go enjoy the fun?"

"In my experience with Maifest, the Festhalle tends to be the gathering spot for the night. It's your call. I'm sure if we stay open we'll get a handful of people in but nothing like this afternoon."

We had discussed the possibility of an earlier closure when making our plans for the weekend, but decided to play it by ear based on the crowds. That was one of the pros of running a smaller operation. We could make decisions like that on the fly. Der Keller on the other hand, couldn't open their large tasting room, restaurant, and patio without ample time to staff up.

"I vote close," Garrett said. "That way we won't need to worry about running out of beer tomorrow. I had quite a few people tell me that they're going to stop in on their way home for growler fills."

"That works for me." I didn't elaborate, but if we closed Nitro early, it would give me a chance to do some more digging into Sara's murder. Maybe if I could prove that Sara's death wasn't connected to me in any way, shape, or form, Marianne would back off. And if that ended up being the case, I could work with Chief Meyers to get her the help she seemed to be in desperate need of.

"Consider it done." Garrett directed the twins to help Kat clean up the outdoor seating. I took on the kitchen, making sure everything was in order and ready for breakfast prep tomorrow.

Normally, I would have hung around and waited for the rest of the crew to head to the Festhalle together, but

I wanted to be alone. "See you over there later?" I said to Garrett on the way out.

"You bet. I'm going to finish tallying today's profits and head out in a while." He pointed to his German costume. "That is, as soon as I change. I'm sure I'll find you over there."

"Sounds good."

Outside, I took a moment, breathing the warm apple-blossom-scented air and considering my options. I could head to Hotel Vierter Stock, or I could join the party in the Festhalle. My decision was made for me when a familiar face appeared on the sidewalk.

"Oh, hello. Sloan, right?" It was Eleanor, the winemaker I had met at the hotel earlier when Marianne had interrogated her.

"Yep, good memory. Nice to see you again." I glanced to Nitro's patio. "Were you coming in for a pint? We're closing up, since the crowd seems to have moved to the Festhalle, but I'd be happy to do a tasting for you."

"Oh, I couldn't trouble you for that. It's not a big deal." She wore a pair of beige slacks and a silky blouse. A large diamond ring glinted on her left hand.

"No, please. I'd love to."

"Are you sure?" She hesitated. "I can gladly come back another time."

"Absolutely. Garrett is cleaning up. It's lovely out here. We can sit on the patio if you like."

"That would be great. To tell you the truth, I could use a reprieve from the noise. The music is fun, but it's so loud. Does that make me sound old?" She twisted her wedding ring.

"No. I feel you on that. It's one of the reasons we like this location. Close enough for tourists to walk and find us, but not so close that the bar rattles from the drums on busy weekends like this."

"Smart." Eleanor pointed to one of the tables. "Should I take a seat?"

"Make yourself welcome. I'll go pour a tasting flight." I returned to the bar.

Garrett raised an eyebrow. "I thought you were taking off, Sloan."

"I was, but we got a last-minute customer wanting a taster flight, and I couldn't turn her down."

"The consummate customer service from Sloan Krause." Garrett gave me a half bow.

I didn't have the heart to tell him that my motives weren't entirely pure. Sure, I never pass up an opportunity to showcase our craft, but more than anything, I wanted to talk to Eleanor alone and see what she might know about Sara's murder.

"This one's on me," I said, as I poured sample beers into our tasting glasses. "That way you don't have to balance the accounts again."

"Just call it on the house, Sloan."

I poured myself a pint of the Lemon Kiss and took everything outside.

Eleanor put down the menu she'd been reading when I set the tasting tray in front of her. "I was reading your descriptions. It's funny how many similarities there are between craft beer and wine. Everything sounds delicious. Where should I start?" She gazed at the tasting tray.

"Like with wine, you should begin with our lightest

ale—the hibiscus rose—and work your way to the hoppier IPAs. Typically we would end with a black IPA or stout, but we don't have either on tap at the moment. Since we're a nanobrewery, we have limited runs for each season. If you had been here in January, you would have found three or four stouts on tap, but right now it's light spring offerings, and we're already in the middle of planning our fall line."

"You're able to be so much more nimble than we are in the wine industry." She picked up the first taster. The ale had a subtle rose tint, the color of ballet slippers. "Aging wine takes longer, as I'm sure you know. We only do a yearly release. Bottling never gets easier. Every year I'm a bundle of nerves. I'm crossing my fingers and toes hoping that the wine is going to be a success, but never quite sure. Do you get that feeling when you brew?"

"Yes, it's a nail-biter every time we brew. Of course, we only have to wait a few weeks to see how a beer has turned out."

Eleanor tasted the ale. I appreciated that she took her time to smell the aroma and let the beer linger on her palate. She was obviously a craft expert herself. "This is wonderful. Refreshing and herbal. Very unique. My husband is an avid beer drinker. He would love this. He's not a wino, which is a constant issue with us. I keep trying to convince him that if he would involve himself in the process of harvesting grapes and making the wine with me, he might appreciate it more, but I can't convince him." She blew out a breath and made a face. "Husbands, what can you do with them?"

"I hear you on that topic, and I'll just say that I agree and leave it at that." I chuckled. "Your husband didn't join you on this trip?" I thought back to our interaction at the hotel. I could have sworn there was someone else in Eleanor's room.

"No." She swished the beer like mouthwash, another telltale sign she was a professional. "He hates crowds and schmoozing. I'm on my own. That's why it's so nice to spend some time with you. It's always hard to travel and not know anyone in town. It can get lonely."

"I'm sure." Her words made me appreciate that my job didn't require much travel. Hop and grain vendors delivered to us. We didn't distribute our beer outside of Leavenworth, and Garrett and I had concurred that when and if we started doing the beer festival circuit, we would hire younger staff to manage those events. In the Pacific Northwest, rarely a weekend went by when there wasn't a beer festival within a hundred-mile range. Sour ale festivals in the spring, fresh hop festivals in the fall, winter ale festivals in the winter, the list went on and on. Beer festivals were a great way to raise a nanobrewery like Nitro's profile and often led to partnerships with distributors, but we weren't ready to take that next step yet.

Eleanor swallowed the sip of beer she had been swishing. I thought about how to naturally steer the conversation to Sara's murder without coming on too strong. She gave me the perfect opportunity.

"I have to admit that I needed something like this. The aroma makes me want to slow my breathing and inhale. Today has not been what I had imagined at all. I thought we—uh, I mean." She shook her entire body, as if trying to reset. "What I meant to say, was that I was hoping for a relaxing day. I had plans for a long sleep in, breakfast in bed, maybe an afternoon nap after the parade, but the police have been in and out of the room next to mine. I can't stop thinking about that poor housekeeper."

"It's horrible," I agreed.

"She was very helpful when I was checking in. We had a long conversation about wine. I can't believe she's dead."

"How did wine come up?"

"She noticed my wine boxes when I was unloading my car. She was very thoughtful and told me that she would get someone to help so I didn't have to lift the heavy boxes and carry them into my room."

"That was kind of her."

"Did you know her?" Eleanor finished the hibiscus rose ale. "I know Leavenworth is small, but I'm not sure how small."

"We're pretty small, but not quite that small. I know most people in town, but Sara, like many hotel and restaurant workers, didn't live in town. She commuted from Wenatchee. I've seen her around, but I didn't know her well."

"Such a shame." Eleanor placed her hand over her heart. "I received a notice from the front desk that there have been some break-ins recently. I can't help but wonder if it's connected. It's a bit unsettling. I hate to say it, but my first thought was housekeeping staff. They have access to the guest rooms. It would be easy enough to steal cash or credit cards and stick them in a uniform pocket. I considered changing hotels, but everything is booked, and management said that they're working with the police and encouraged guests to lock up valuables in our in-room safes and report anything suspicious immediately."

"Really?"

"Not exactly what I expected from a small town like this." She pulled her wedding ring on and off her finger.

"I can assure you that that's not normal. The joke around town is that the only reason anyone ever locks their front door is to keep the bears out," I said. "Leavenworth is very safe."

Did break-ins at Hotel Vierter Stock lend more credibility to Marianne's claims that her files on Forest had been stolen? Maybe Sara had been the culprit. If she had been caught in the act while rifling through a guest's personal belongings, that certainly could have gotten her killed. And then there was Vienna. She also had access to guest rooms. She had admitted that she needed the job. What if, in her desperation for cash, she had turned to theft? If Sara found out, that could be another reason that her job was in jeopardy, more so than getting in trouble for texting, and it gave Vienna a motive for murdering Sara.

"The woman who you were with this morning, she knew the housekeeper, right?" Eleanor asked, shaking me from my thoughts.

"Marianne? I don't think so, why?"

Eleanor picked up the taster of our honey wheat ale. "I can smell the sweetness in this. It almost reminds me of our riesling."

"I can see that," I agreed. "What were you going to say about Marianne?"

"This is lovely, quite impressive." She raised the taster. The straw-colored ale caught the sinking light, making it appear as if it were glowing. "I assumed that she and Sara were connected. I saw them talking privately yesterday before Sara was killed."

This was news.

A sudden coldness hit me at the core. What could that mean? Sara and Marianne had spoken? Marianne had insisted, multiple times, that she had never met the housekeeper. My heart thudded in my chest.

"Do you remember when?" My smile felt stiff as I asked the question.

"It was early afternoon. Not long after I finished checking in and unloading my wine. I don't remember for sure, but I would guess maybe one or two."

"Where were they?" I didn't want to spook Eleanor by asking too many questions.

"In the garden. This is going to sound strange, but I could have sworn that they were arguing about the security cameras. Maybe I heard wrong. Marianne seemed to be upset about the cameras. From Sara's response, I got the impression that Marianne had tried to dismantle them, but again, I could be mistaken. I was leaving my room when they were arguing, so it wasn't as if I was within earshot."

"They were arguing?"

"Yeah." Eleanor polished off the honey wheat ale. "Marianne was furious."

That changed everything. Marianne and Sara had been fighting. Could that mean Marianne had something to do with the housekeeper's death? I wasn't sure, but I knew one thing—she had lied to me.

CHAPTER

TWELVE

ELEANOR DIDN'T STAY LONG. She finished her tasting flight and invited me to stop by the hotel lobby later so she could reciprocate with a wine offering. "I'm having a few other wine friends meet up around nine. Please join us. I'd love to share our wine with you and introduce you to some of my colleagues. The Yakima Valley really is such a community when it comes to vineyards. That's why we're here to build lasting partnerships and raise up the region as a whole."

Her sentiment was similar to what I had experienced in the craft beer world. Patrons were often taken aback when we recommended they visit Der Keller while staying in the village, or talked up one of our guest beer taps. There was a deep sense of connectedness when it came to brewing, one of the many reasons it was the perfect career choice for me. Sure, there were the occasional head brewers who tended toward paranoia and jealousy, but in general as brewers we understood the inordinate amount of work involved in crafting quality ales. Garrett, Hans, Mac, Otto, Ursula, everyone I knew in the industry lived by the creed of raising up one another. We also had a special pact to finish any beer we ordered, even if it was undrinkable.

To Eleanor, I said, "Thanks, I'll see how long I last, but I might take you up on that."

Garrett and I kept a few bottles behind the bar for wine drinkers. We prided ourselves on being able to convert the most insistent beer-averse visitors, but there were still occasions when customers asked for a glass of vino. It might be nice to rotate some regional options into our small collection of artisanal wines.

After bringing in our glasses and checking on the pub one last time, I made my way to the Festhalle. The grounds had been transformed into a floral extravaganza. It looked like a scene from *The Sound of Music*. The dazzling show of colors and alluring aromas made me feel almost light-headed. It was nearly impossible to take it all in. Gorgeous overflowing flower baskets hung from vendor tents. Rows and rows of fresh herbs, potted strawberries, and veggie starts lined tables. There were bundles of wildflowers and an assortment of floral jewelry for sale, including everything from the crowns that Garrett had bought for Kat and me to dainty bracelets, earrings, and bountiful necklaces dripping with ranunculus and wisteria. Intermixed with the floral booths were crafters selling local honey, fudge, mountain jams, fresh produce, and handmade art.

I spent some time wandering between the booths, sampling blackberry preserves and chocolate orange fudge. It was hard not to feel upbeat while mixing in with the happy festival crowds. Kids licked creamy lemon ice pops and devoured bratwurst sausages. The music in the Festhalle pulsed outdoors. My cell phone buzzed. Relief flooded me when I looked at the screen and saw Sally's number.

"Sloan, how are you holding up? I got your message." Her normally steady tone was animated. "I can't believe it. Marianne is really there? In the village?"

I wound my way to a less crowded area of the market farther from the thumping beat of the music. "I know, I can't believe it either." I told her about Marianne's bizarre behavior and my continued confusion.

As always, Sally had an innate ability to calm me. Her even, reassuring style returned as we talked through different possibilities. "Sloan, I'm inclined to believe her," Sally said as we wrapped up our conversation. "It matches my earlier theory that she could have been the person who placed you in care. I was wrong about the Krauses and their involvement, but much of what she's saying adds up—Forest, your mother, you. I've said since the first day you tiptoed into my office that whoever left you did it out of love. Please stay safe and keep me posted."

When we ended the call, I felt better. Just hearing Sally's voice was a reminder that I wasn't alone. I weaved back through the booths toward the Der Keller beer tent at the far end of the market. It stood out from the sea of white awnings with its baby-blue-checkered pattern. Massive strings of spring garlands with bouquets of roses, lilies, and greenery had been strung around the tent.

"Hey, Sloan," Hans called as I walked up to the elaborate temporary bar handcrafted from giant slabs of wood and roped with more aromatic garlands made from hops and assorted greenery. He held a Der Keller pint glass at an angle beneath the silver tap handle and slowly poured a light copper Maibock. The classic German spring pale ale was made with malt imported from Munich and Vienna. It was one of the most popular beers Der Keller brewed with its toasty aroma and fruity hops.

"How did they manage to sign you up for tap duty?" I asked, coming around to the side of the tent so as not to be in the way of waiting guests. The Der Keller tent was more like a small city. As opposed to the six-by-six-foot tent we had erected last night for the Sip and Stroll, the Der Keller tent took up nearly half a block. The inside of the massive canopy had been transformed to resemble the pub and restaurant. Giant balls of twinkle lights hung from the ceiling. There were dozens of tables draped with red-checked plastic tablecloths. Every table had a large vase with red, yellow, and black carnations and miniature German flags. Flower garlands were strung from each side of the tent, and a stage that rivaled that of the Festhalle offered even more entertainment options. Festivalgoers swayed from left to right, balancing steins as they moved to the beat of the band. A handful of people danced in front of the stage as barmaids deftly carried a half dozen heavy steins in each arm. Kids chomped on bratwursts and waited in line to get their faces painted like unicorns and superheroes.

Hans's tanned face broke out into a smile. "You know how it goes with my folks. They look at you with those sweet German blue eyes and say, 'Hans, if it is not too much of a bother do you zink you could take a shift at ze festival?' How can you say no to that?"

"You can't. It's not possible. Otto and Ursula are far too kind to turn down. I feel you. Remember, I tried to decline their generous offer of giving me a percentage of Der Keller, but that ended it before I got two words out."

"It's not worth trying to resist them." Hans poured a golden amber pint and handed it to a waiting customer. "What brings you out of your brewing cave? Are you thirsty?"

"No thanks. I'm saving myself for some wine tasting in a little while." I told him about Eleanor's offer. "I figured I would come take a peek at the flower market. I need to outfit my patio and deck. I have a good start, thanks to the planter boxes you built for me and a few baskets the previous owners left for me. Now that I'm living in the village, my house can't be the only place on the street without abundant hanging baskets and greenery."

"True. Can you imagine the notes April Ablin will tack to your front door if she feels like your front porch isn't bursting with Bavarian blooms?"

"Thanks a lot." I would have punched him in the shoulder, but I didn't want to spill the beer he was pouring.

"Speak of the devil." Hans looked up and nodded.

April pushed her way through the line. "Sloan Krause, there you are! I've been looking everywhere for you!"

Damn.

Even for April, her outfit of choice was a shocker. The plunging neckline on her fuchsia barmaid's dress left nothing to the imagination. Her lacy black bra was on display for everyone to see. As were her legs. I wasn't sure how it was possible, but her dress was shorter than the one she'd given to Kat. It looked like it had taken every effort for her to squeeze herself into the revealing ensemble.

"Why were you looking for me?" I asked, trying not to stare at her bustline. It was hard to avoid, since her pushup bra had lifted her breasts halfway to her chin and she had smothered every inch of skin with a shimmery lotion.

"Like you don't know." She waved her index finger in my face. Her nails had been painted in fuchsia polish, and each had a different flower design in the center. "I gave Kat explicit instructions on Nitro's interior and exterior design, along with costume recommendations. I was just at the tasting room, and none of the materials I sent back with Kat are on display. You know as well as anyone in this village that every resident and business owner needs to embrace Maifest. It is our duty as a *Gemeinschaft*—that means 'community,' by the way—to welcome visitors with the most elaborate German décor they've ever seen."

"Garrett and I have been nothing short of welcoming all weekend, I can assure you of that."

"Ha! With your sterile scientific blah—white walls and black-and-white photographs is not embracing our community spirit. You must remember that the reason visitors come to our version of Bavaria is for *Bavaria*. They can get boring, minimalist warehouses like Nitro in Seattle. It is imperative that we all embrace the German aesthetic. It's what has kept our village growing and thriving for the past thirty years. Need I remind you of darker times when Leavenworth nearly didn't make it? You know how the story goes. If it weren't for our Bavarian forefathers, our town would be in utter ruin. Nitro is single-handedly threatening our future survival."

That was a stretch, to say the least. April wasn't wrong about Leavenworth's past. In the sixties, the town was on its last legs after the railroad was rerouted. Many industries vanished, and townspeople left in droves in search of a better life for their families. Fortunately, a handful of community members rallied together to save the town. Given our proximity to the alps of the North Cascades, the entire town underwent a major renovation. Buildings were redesigned in the German aesthetic, and our famously popular festivals like Maifest were created.

"I highly doubt that," I said to April. "We were packed this afternoon, and everyone loved the experience."

April let out an exasperated sigh. "Sloan, I don't have time to go round and round on this. You didn't even have the decency to stay in your dirndl. I can't deal with this at the moment because right now I have at least a million fires to put out. You can't begin to imagine what it's like to be me during festival weekends."

We could agree on that much.

"I'll stop by Nitro first thing in the morning with some new swag for you to distribute to your guests tomorrow. We may not have been able to wow them with German delights at the pub today, but at least we can salvage their return trip home with some custom stickers, key chains, and souvenir glasses." She gave me a hard stare. "I'll be there at nine sharp, understood?"

"You got it, Captain." I couldn't resist giving her a salute. She stormed off.

Hans chuckled. "I'll never get tired of watching April get under your skin. There aren't many people—if any—who I've ever seen rattle you, Sloan, but April does it every time."

"She doesn't bug you?"

He shrugged. "I take it in stride. She is the textbook definition of schadenfreude. Plus, she's given up on me. After asking me out in less than subtle ways at least a dozen times, I think she's finally realized that it's not going to happen and has set her sights elsewhere."

There was something about his tone and the way he emphasized *elsewhere* that gave me pause.

"Wait, what? You don't mean what I think you mean?"

He nodded. "Oh yeah. She's been at Der Keller every day for the past two weeks. She sits at the bar, nurses a glass of gewürztraminer, and flashes her fake lashes at Mac."

"What?" That was low. Not that I would put it past April, but after helping her out of a jam and using her to purchase my cottage, I would have thought she would have the *decency* not to go after my ex-husband.

"Don't worry about it. Mac is clueless, and even if he wises up to April's overt flirting, he has no interest. Trust me. For starters, she is way too old." Hans winked.

That didn't make me feel any better.

"She rotates through every single guy in town, tourists, too. She'll tire of Mac, just like she did with me, but if you want a good laugh, drop by the pub at lunchtime one day next week, and you can watch her feminine wiles in action."

"No thanks. That is definitely not something I need to see." The thought of it made me want to poke my eyes out. It did explain April's shrinking outfits, though.

I changed the subject. "Hey, is Alex at the restaurant? I might pop in and say hi before my wine tasting."

"He was there earlier. I can tell you that he must have inherited his work ethic from you and not my brother. He was literally running from table to table to try and make sure there was never an empty pint glass. I know I'm a biased uncle, but you've got a pretty cool kid on your hands."

"You won't get an argument from me on that. Do you think he'll be mad if he catches me spying on him?"

"Never." Hans laughed. "What teenager doesn't want their mother lurking around?"

"But I'm a chill mom."

"I'm not sure that chill moms exist in the eyes of teenagers." He raised an eyebrow. "Oh hey, that reminds me. There was a guy at Der Keller asking about you earlier."

I froze. My throat tightened, and my pulse thudded in my neck.

"Who?" I hoped my voice sounded casual.

"I didn't catch his name. He was older. No one I recognized. He said he knew you from community college. He must be one of your old professors?"

"Right. Probably." I clenched my fists. None of my professors had kept in touch. A cold chill ran up my arms, and I didn't think it had to do with the temperature.

"Anyway, he thought you were still working at the brewery. I told him he could find you at Nitro. He'll probably stop by tomorrow. Just to give you a heads-up."

"Thanks." I forced a smile. "Did he say anything else?"

"No. Not anything that stuck out." Hans thought for a moment. "He seemed excited to meet you. He said this was his first time in Leavenworth and he was looking forward to the festivities. I didn't have a chance to speak with him for long. I was dropping off some new tasting paddles and happened to overhear him asking about you at the bar."

"Great. I'll be on the lookout for him tomorrow. Did he say when he was going to come by?"

Hans shook his head. "No, sorry. I guess I should have asked more questions. Like I said, we had a brief conversation, and he just said he would swing by Nitro and say hi."

"Don't sweat it. It sounds like I'll see him tomorrow."

I left the beer tent and made a beeline for Der Keller. A feeling of dread invaded every cell in my body. I could hear my heartbeat reverberating in my head, and sweat began to bead on the base of my neck. Less than an hour ago I had convinced myself that Marianne's claims that I was in danger were unwarranted. Had I made a fatal error?

Could Forest actually exist and, worse, be here in Leavenworth looking for me and my family?

CHAPTER

THIRTEEN

I FELT GRATEFUL FOR my police escort as I left Hans and headed for Der Keller. The knowledge that John was nearby helped soothe some of my fears, but for the first time since Marianne's arrival, I felt truly afraid. What would I do if Forest showed up at Nitro tomorrow? Did I need to warn Garrett and the rest of the staff? My instinct told me that maybe it was time to loop in Mac. Marianne had been so adamant about not saying anything to anyone other than the police, but if there was one thing I knew about Mac, it was that he would do whatever it took to protect Alex. He would never let harm come to our son.

I made up my mind on the spot. I could handle myself, but Alex was a different story. If anything happened to him . . .

Stop, Sloan. You can't think like that.

I exhaled and crossed Front Street toward the restaurant and pub. The patio was wall-to-wall people with a line stretching down the block waiting to get in. I waved to the hostess, who I had hired a few years ago when I was still working at Der Keller.

"I just need to chat with Mac for a second."

She let me through.

Inside, the bar was equally jammed with customers pressing toward the long row of taps. Every seat in the restaurant was full. Upstairs a German polka band serenaded the crowd. The energy was alive and electric. I scanned the space, looking for Mac.

"Oh hey, Sloan," one of the waitstaff said as he passed by me, balancing a huge tray loaded with German potato salad, sausages, and sauerkraut.

"You haven't seen Mac by chance?"

The waiter turned toward the kitchen. "Last time I saw him, he was putting out fires in the back."

"Thanks." I squeezed through the throng to the rear of the restaurant. Der Keller was by far the biggest property in the village. The restaurant and pub, along with the outdoor patios, brewery, and kitchen, encompassed nearly half a block. Across the street was the bottling warehouse—soon to be canning plant, offices, distribution, and dock sales.

I went down a short set of stairs toward the brewery on the lower level. This area was off-limits to guests for obvious reasons. Der Keller's brewing operations made Nitro look like we were brewing in kettles on our kitchen stoves. Its massive shiny brite tanks and grain silo stretched twenty feet in the air. A network of platforms and scaffolding stretched between the copper tanks. Epoxy floors and skylights made the brewery feel even more spacious. Everything was automated with state-of-the-art equipment. The Krause family legacy had humble beginnings. In the first years after immigrating to the United States, Otto and Ursula had taken out a small loan to start Der Keller and follow their passion for brewing German-style ales. Over the decades, they had grown and expanded to become a household name not only in Leavenworth, but throughout the entire Pacific Northwest. They were the ultimate American dream.

"Sloan, what are you doing here?" Mac nearly plowed me over as he stepped out from behind the brite tank.

"Looking for you, actually."

He dabbed his brow with his hand. "Whoa, that doesn't happen very often. I would say I'm excited, but I have to admit I'm kind of scared. What did I do now?"

"Nothing. This time it's all me."

His blue eyes squinted. "Huh? I don't understand."

"Do you have a minute? I need your help."

He reached for my arm. "Sloan, you know I'm here for you, always." His voice developed a husky quality.

"Mac, this is serious."

"I'm being serious." He threw out his hands in frustration.

"Can we go to your office?"

He glanced at the front. "Sure. Let me tell the team that I'm stepping out for a minute. I'll meet you over there. You know the code."

I took the back exit and crossed over to the other building. It shared the same Bavarian architecture as the taproom and restaurant, but the interior lacked charm. Not that it was necessary, since visitors didn't access the building. John dutifully followed behind me, giving me space as I let myself in with the keypad, and followed the stairs up to a narrow hallway with offices on each side until I got to Mac's. It was on the second floor with a large six-pane window that looked out over the village.

"I'll wait out here. Holler if you need me," John said, taking up a post in front of Mac's office door.

I thanked him and went inside. It had been a while since I'd been in his office, and not surprisingly, not much had changed, except it looked like he'd actually purged the usual stacks of unread paperwork that tended to pile everywhere. Photos of the three of us in happier times lined his desk: us at Otto and Ursula's fortieth anniversary celebration and hiking in the Enchantments, along with pictures of Alex in his soccer uniform and skiing gear.

Brewing medals and awards filled the remaining wall space, shiny gold reminders of Der Keller's domination in the regional and international brewing scene. There were trophies from competitions large and small, framed articles from *Brew Bound, BeerAdvocate,* and *DRAFT Magazine.* Features on the Krause family's success had crossed the globe, making headlines and the front pages in newspapers from Germany to Japan.

One of the perks of gaining notoriety in craft beer circles was the celebrity visits Der Keller had had over the years. Mac always took the lead when it came to giving famous visitors a tour of the brewery or stopping to pose for photos with them. He had amassed quite a collection of pictures over the years from dignitaries and politicians to Seattle Sounders and Seahawks players and A-list celebrities passing through on their way to film on location in nearby Canada.

Mac arrived a minute later. He took a seat behind his desk, which was more organized than I'd ever seen it. "Have a seat."

I pulled up a chair.

"What's going on, Sloan? You look spooked." He pushed aside a stack of grain catalogues and leaned his elbows on the desk. "And there's a guy who looks like he's on presidential detail in the hallway. I'm guessing that's because of you?"

"Yeah." I sighed. "Mac, I'm going to tell you something that no one else in town knows except for Chief Meyers. I mean, *no one*. You have to keep this between us, understood?"

"No one knows, not even Hans?" There was a slight edge in his voice.

"Not even Hans. No one."

"Okay. I guess I'm flattered that you're trusting me. That's a big step for us."

"This isn't about us. It's about Alex. He might be in danger."

"What?" Color spread across Mac's cheeks. He'd never been able to disguise his emotions. He wore them on his skin like an ever-changing chameleon.

"That's why I'm telling you and why you cannot mention a word to anyone about what I'm going to say. Got it?" I hoped that my serious tone was getting through to him.

"Got it." He nodded. His cheeks turned even redder, and his jaw tightened. "What kind of danger could Alex be in? He's an awesome kid. He has awesome friends. I don't understand. He's not into drugs, is he? He can't be. I swear I would know if he was, and he's been working his butt off this weekend. Everyone on staff has said it. Not just me."

"No, no it's nothing like that. Before I tell you, please promise me one more time that you won't breathe a word of this to him or anyone. Not your family. Not your mom, your dad, or Hans." A sluggish feeling invaded my body. Maybe I was being ridiculous, but I couldn't not tell him if there was even a tiny risk to Alex.

"Yeah, Sloan, I got it. I won't, but you're really starting to scare me." He sat up and unbuttoned the top button of his checkered shirt.

"I'm scaring myself." I leaned my elbows on the edge of the desk. "Mac, this is kind of a long story, and a lot of it I haven't told you."

"Okay, well, we're here now. Why don't you start from the beginning."

I told him the abbreviated version of my past, including the fact that Ursula and Otto had known Marianne and Forest. I left out any details about their own story. It didn't have anything to do with the current situation, and that was eventually for them to tell or not to tell.

Mac listened intently, without interrupting once as I gave him an overview of my meetings with Sally and her research into my case files. Then I went on to relay the strange turn of events since Marianne had arrived in town.

"Sloan, you should have told me. I could have helped earlier. I can't believe Mama and Papa knew about your past and never said anything. That must have shattered you. And at the same time that I made the worst mistake in my life. Sloan, I'm sorry. I'm sorry for my entire family." He pounded his forehead with three fingers. "It's so unfair to you."

"It's okay. It's not your fault."

"Not my fault? Of course it's my fault. I failed you, and now I'm learning that my parents failed you, too." He took his fingers off his head, scrunched them into a tight fist, and pounded it into his palm.

"Mac, listen, they didn't fail me. They had their reasons. They thought they were doing the right thing."

"What reasons?"

We were getting off topic, and I needed him to focus on Alex.

"Mac, please, we can talk more about what happened in the past another time, but right now I need you to focus on the *now*. Our son might be in danger. Marianne thinks that Forest is here. At first I thought she was crazy, to be honest. She doesn't seem entirely stable, but Chief Meyers thinks there's a possibility that she could be right. I almost blew her off, but I was just over at the Der Keller booth, and Hans mentioned that someone was asking about me earlier. His description of the guy matches Marianne's description of Forest. She warned me that Forest will stop at nothing to get to me, even involving Alex."

"Involving Alex how?" Mac sat up straighter.

"I don't know. I mean, I've run dozens of worst-case scenarios from kidnapping to hurting him and worse."

"My God, Sloan."

"I know. Maybe I'm overreacting."

Mac stood up. He went to the window, looked outside, and then focused his pale blue eyes on me. "Sloan, if there is one thing that you never do, it's overreact. If you're worried, then I'm terrified."

I started to say something, but he held up a finger to stop me.

"No, listen. It's my turn to talk now. I know that I've done wrong by you. I know that my mistakes led to ruining our marriage, but I can't condone that my family has done this to you, too. You don't need to worry about Alex. I won't let anything happen to him, Sloan. I'll die before I let this Forest guy come anywhere near either of you. I'm going to my place now, and I'll pack a bag. Alex and I will stay with you. I'll sleep on the couch and stay on watch around the clock."

"Mac, that's not necessary. I already told you that Chief Meyers assigned police detail. I'm fine. It's Alex that I'm worried about. He's better off at your place. If there's any truth to what Marianne has said about Forest, then he needs to be as far away from me as possible right now."

Mac threw his head back and groaned. "Oh crap, Sloan, I just remembered something. I saw a guy who matches the description Hans gave you earlier. He was hanging around the booth when we were setting it up. I didn't think about it at the time. I figured he wanted to be first in line for a beer, you know how crazy people get. But now I'm not so sure. He was real chatty with a couple of the staff. I thought it was odd at the time, but again I figured maybe he was lonely, traveling by himself, trying to make conversation. He asked a bunch of questions about the family who owned Der Keller. I kept out of it. Our staff know better than to introduce any of us as the owners, unless we step forward ourselves. Here's the scary thing—he left before we tapped the kegs. Sloan, if this is the guy. He's good. He's really good. Slick, subtle."

"Yeah." I rubbed my temples. "It could be that I'm blowing this out of proportion. There are some sketchy things about Marianne, too." I didn't go into detail, but that was the truth. I still wasn't convinced that she was living in reality despite everything that had happened.

Mac picked up a pen and tapped the cap on his forehead. I recognized the nervous tic. "Maybe. I'm with the chief. I don't think we can be too cautious. He told Hans he was going to stop by Nitro tomorrow? I'll be there. I'll be there when it opens, and I'll stay until the last car has left the village tomorrow night."

"No, that's what I'm saying." I was starting to second-guess my decision to loop him in. "I want you to be with Alex. I'll be fine. Garrett will be there. Kat, the twins, and my police escort. Alex is my priority. I need you to be with Alex. Don't let him out of your sight."

"He's at the restaurant right now." Mac glanced out the window again. "Should we go get him?"

"No! He can't know." I reached out to stop him, as if he was about to jump out the window and go rescue our son. "This is just between us, remember? I don't want to freak him out, especially if it turns out to be nothing."

"Sloan, I don't know if that's a good idea. He's a bright kid. He's strong—physically and emotionally. He can handle knowing."

"Mac, you promised. I don't want him to know. I think Der Keller is the safest place for him right now, anyway. It's hardly like Forest would try to snatch him in the middle of so many people. Just make sure you guys go home together and don't let him out of your sight tomorrow."

"Okay. If you're sure." He sounded anything but convinced. However he returned the pen to its holder and stood up.

"I'm sure." I stood, too.

Mac moved toward the door. "I have him on the schedule for a half day tomorrow."

"Good. Don't let him take off with friends when his shift is done."

"I won't. You have my word, Sloan. I will make sure he's safe." His intense, powerful gaze made me want to collapse in his arms. Not in a romantic way, but because he was the only other person on earth who loved Alex as fully, as wholly, as me. Alex was the best of both of us. I knew he was telling the truth. I knew he would do anything and everything in his power to protect our son.

"Thanks." I squared my shoulders and swallowed hard.

I wasn't sure what else to say. A sense of relief came over me. It felt good to share the burden of fear with Mac. Not that I had any interest in renewing our relationship, but Alex was our common ground. I didn't doubt for a second that he would ensure his safety. Now I needed to focus on mine.

CHAPTER

FOURTEEN

I LEFT MAC BEFORE he could continue to try and convince me that I would be safer having him and Alex in the house. It was nearing nine, so I decided to take Eleanor up on her wine tasting offer. I enjoyed learning about other artisan processes, but I was also hoping that I might have a chance to observe staff and guest interactions at the hotel and perhaps see if Marianne was still lurking. The thefts couldn't be a coincidence, and there was the issue of Jay's inappropriate behavior with female staff. There had to be a connection between Sara's murder and the hotel.

As I entered the boutique German manor, I stopped at the lobby to see where Eleanor was hosting the tasting. The clerk directed me to the *Frühstücksraum,* or breakfast room, located just off the lobby.

John stopped short of the breakfast room doors. "I'll wait here in the hallway."

He must be exhausted, I thought. He'd been on duty since

the middle of last night. "Are you going to get a break any-time soon? Can I get you something? Coffee? A snack?"

"Don't worry about me, Mrs. Krause. I'm fine." His boyish face was still beaming with energy. I would have been a walking zombie if I were him. "The chief is sending a replacement soon, but I'm good."

"You deserve a raise." I smiled, reaching for the door handle. "I'll be sure to tell her that."

The sound of laughter greeted me in the elegant breakfast room. Eleanor and six other vintners were seated around a large mahogany table. The room was impressively ornate with dark wood paneling, a large iron chandelier, bucolic prints of the German countryside, and walls of bookcases.

"Sloan, you made it." Eleanor waved me in. "Have a seat. We are just about to get started."

I took the empty spot at the end of the table. Two wine goblets sat at each place setting. I assumed one was for tasting reds and one for whites. Bottles of wine filled the table like pretty chess pieces.

"Everyone, this is Sloan, she's a craft brewer at a new small brewery here in town, Nitro," Eleanor introduced me. "I was lucky enough to be able to sample their line earlier today and was very impressed. If you have a chance to stop by before the weekend is done, I highly recommend you do."

She made brief introductions. I noticed that the gentleman sitting next to me seemed to cling to her every word. His eyes didn't leave her as she reached for a bottle of pale apricot chardonnay.

"Do you know Eleanor well?" I asked him.

"Me? No. No. We just met. What gives you that impression?" He clutched his wine goblet in one hand and dragged his gaze away from Eleanor. I guessed him to be similar in age to Eleanor and me—mid- to late forties. He had a ruggedly handsome look. A dark, scruffy yet groomed beard, deep brown eyes, and dark, graying hair. He was dressed impeccably by Maifest standards, in well-cut navy slacks, a crisp white button-down shirt, and a skinny navy tie.

"Nothing. Just making conversation."

He extended his hand, which was slightly damp. "I'm Russ. I own a vineyard in Wenatchee. Hawks. You may have heard of it."

"Hawks, of course. We serve your wines at Der Keller."

"I thought Eleanor said you work at Nitro?"

"True. I do, but I was with Der Keller for years and am still a partial owner."

"Lucrative. You'll have a brewing monopoly here in Leavenworth soon." His eyes drifted back to Eleanor as she rounded the table, filling glasses and describing tasting notes for the first wine.

"That's the master plan. Total brewery domination." I winked. "How do you like traveling for events like this? Eleanor mentioned that it can get tiring to be on the road so much. That's one of the reasons I'm glad to be working at a nanobrewery. Everything we do is hyper-local, which means I don't have to leave Leavenworth very often."

"I don't mind it. There's a certain thrill to travel. Never knowing who you'll meet. Who you'll bump into. Seeing gorgeous places along the way. But I get why some people don't like it. That's not true for Der Keller, though, is it?" Russ asked, holding out his glass for Eleanor to pour him a taste of buttery chardonnay. "I see the Der Keller tents at nearly every beer festival throughout the west."

"Yes. We have an entire team dedicated to outreach." I waited for Eleanor to fill my glass.

She placed her hand on Russ's shoulder and let it linger for a moment. "Play nice with our brewer, Russ."

He reached for her hand and then quickly sat up.

The gesture of affection wasn't lost on me, but Russ changed the subject as Eleanor moved on to pour for the rest of the table.

"Did you hear about the murder?" he asked, dipping his nose halfway into his glass.

"Yes, it's such a tragedy."

"I'm sure. A small town like Leavenworth. I would guess news of a murder is rocking everyone's world."

I wouldn't have phrased it exactly like that, but he wasn't wrong.

"The crazy thing is that I think I saw the maid right before she was killed. She was scurrying around. It made me wonder if she was up to no good."

"Really? Does that mean you're staying here, too?"

His face turned as white as his wine. "No. I'm staying on the other side of town. I was here for the tasting last night."

That was interesting, because unless my memory served me wrong, Eleanor had said that last night's tasting was across the street at Blumpiwen.

"I stopped in the lobby for a drink of water. You know how it is after a tasting, especially with a bunch of wine snobs. My mouth was parched. I saw the maid and the owner of the hotel going at it."

"Going at it?" I repeated.

"They were having a heated argument. I grabbed a glass of water and got out of there before they saw me, but I told

Eleanor that I wouldn't be surprised if he did it. He was out of control. Hurling insults and his fists."

"Wait, are you saying that Jay, the owner of the hotel, hit Sara?" Jay was sounding worse by the minute. Sexual harassment and physical violence.

"No, he didn't hit her, but he punched the wall. I bet his knuckles are nice and sore today."

Eleanor interrupted our conversation by dinging on the side of her glass. "I'd love for everyone to take an initial taste of this 2017 chardonnay. We weren't sure how the year was going to do. If you recall, there were large wildfires in Canada and eastern Washington that year, but I'm happy to report that the grapes did really well, and we ended up with this touch of earthiness that beautifully balanced the chardonnay." She went on to explain how some of the cooler terrain of the Yakima Valley was home to over half of Washington's chardonnays and rieslings.

I sipped the delicate wine and kept one eye on Russ. I wasn't sure that I trusted him. Something was obviously going on between the two of them, and he'd let it slip that he and Eleanor were more than new acquaintances. Could he have been in her room? It would explain his lie about staying at the hotel. The question was whether they had any connection to Sara's death. What if Sara spotted them? Eleanor was married. If they were having an affair and she accidentally discovered them, could that have given them a reason to react? Maybe it had been a moment of panic. Or maybe Sara, if she was the person responsible for the thefts, had threatened to blackmail them. It was a stretch, but I couldn't rule out the possibility.

"Have you mentioned any of this to the police?" I whispered as we finished the first wine.

"Mentioned what?" Russ knocked back the few sips left in his glass.

"The fight you witnessed. That could be important information in their investigation."

"No, I don't want to get in the middle of it. It's not my problem." He held his empty glass out to signal Eleanor he was ready for the next.

Eleanor directed us to the next bottle. As we tasted five more estate-grown wines, including a spring pinot noir, a fruit-forward syrah, and a bold cabernet, I couldn't get Russ to say much more. Every question I asked that related to Sara's murder was met with silence. Obviously, I had hit a wall.

By the time our tasting flight was complete, my head was slightly dizzy and my cheeks were warm. Eleanor's wines were delicious. There was no debating that. I would definitely recommend buying a few bottles for Nitro. I made a mental note to talk to Garrett about that in the morning.

I excused myself when a couple of the winemakers brought out more bottles to sample.

"Thanks so much for inviting me," I said to Eleanor. "It's been enlightening, and we're definitely going to get some of your wine for the pub."

"Great. You have my information. Email, call, or text, and I'll set you up. Or if it's easier, I can drop by tomorrow on my way out of town. I have a few cases left."

"Sure. I look forward to that and to introducing you to Garrett."

I left the breakfast room to find John standing at attention as promised. He followed me to the lobby. I wanted to see if Russ had been exaggerating about Jay. Sure enough, there was an indent in the Sheetrock near a stuffed grizzly bear statue. I wouldn't have called it a hole, but if Jay had punched the wall hard enough to leave an indent, he must have been extremely angry.

"Can I help you?" A voice behind me made me jump.

I turned to see Jay standing three feet away. "Sorry, I didn't hear you come up behind me." I caught John's eye. He stood near the lobby doors with his hands on his holster.

"Sloan, right? We've met at chamber events, I think. You're not one I would forget." His tone was suggestive, as was his wicked grin. "Were you looking for something?"

"Right." I could feel his eyes staring at the damaged wall. "I was going to take a picture of the bear for my son. He's a high schooler here in town, and I'm constantly nagging him to be on the lookout for bears when he and his friends are hiking. I thought it would be funny to send him a warning text that the bears have infiltrated the village. You don't mind, do you?"

Jay's shoulders relaxed. "Sure, go for it. You know, we had been talking about doing a social media bear hunt. Like the nutcracker hunt."

I wasn't thrilled with the idea of being close to him. "Good idea. The nutcracker hunt has been very popular amongst tourists and going on for at least ten years." I was trying to shift attention, but there was truth to my words. The nutcracker scavenger hunt sent kids and sleuths of all ages throughout the village with a handful of clues on a journey to track down hidden nutcrackers tucked into unexpected nooks and crannies. Successful adventurers could return to the chamber of commerce for fun prizes.

"So I hear. I've owned the hotel for three years, and I still feel like a newcomer. Does that ever end?"

I became acutely aware of Jay's lewd stare that continually drifted below my sight line to my chest. Thank goodness I had changed out of my more revealing dress into a T-shirt. It was no wonder that Vienna was spooked by him. I stood taller. "How so?" I was surprised to hear that feedback. The village had always embraced newcomers. Maybe rumors about Jay's behavior had already spread.

"You know, everyone has an idea or an opinion on how things should be done." He rolled his eyes and snuck in another gawk at my chest. I didn't know whether he was a killer, but he definitely did not give me good vibes, and I was a grown, adult woman with a teenage son. I could only imagine how uncomfortable his younger staff, like Vienna, must feel, especially when her livelihood depended on a paycheck signed by him. "Apparently we're not cutting it when it comes to being in line with the German aesthetic in the rest of the village."

"Oh, I know exactly what you're talking about. I take it you've had some chats with April Ablin?" I inched away from him.

"Yeah." He pointed to the bear. "She wanted me to put lederhosen on the bear for the weekend. I refused. I'm not going for that vibe here. I want a high-end German hunting lodge."

"Don't listen to anything she says. She doesn't speak for the village."

"It seems like it. I understood when I bought the hotel that there might be resistance at first from an outsider coming in, but I thought by now people would be over it."

"Is it more than April?"

He moved closer. I could smell stale coffee on his breath. "Yeah, it's my staff, too. They're constantly complaining."

"About what?" I moved away again.

"Everything. The previous owners had different protocols for everything. I thought the village was going to have a chill vibe, but it's the opposite. People are so uptight."

"How so?" I wondered if he would bring up Sara.

"Look, you're about my age, right? I think there's a certain sense of having to be politically correct about everything these days. One of my staff members freaked out that I put my hand on the girls' shoulders. What's the big deal?"

Unwanted touching was a pretty big deal to me and could easily put him in legal trouble, but I let him talk.

"They were claiming that they were going to file a lawsuit against me. Yeah, right. What judge is going to take that case?"

Had he read my mind? "Your staff is threatening to sue?"

"Not anymore. I think that it all blew over, but like I said, I wasn't expecting everyone to be so rigid and intent on following the rules. I thought this was a mountain town with a bunch of ski bums and river rats."

"We have a lot of that, too." I wasn't sure how to respond.

Fortunately, Jay got called over to the front desk. I took that as a sign that it was time to make my exit.

I had learned a couple of important things tonight. The first was that I suspected Eleanor and Russ were having an affair. I wasn't sure how or if it related to Sara's death. One hypothesis was that she had walked in on them and they freaked out. Maybe it was a crime of passion—literally.

But, then again, Jay seemed like a much more likely suspect. He had blatantly admitted to sexually harassing his female staff. What did he mean by not being worried about a lawsuit any longer? Had it blown over as he stated, or could it be that he killed Sara to put an end to future legal action?

CHAPTER

FIFTEEN

I LEFT THE LOBBY and stepped outside. Darkness had settled over the craggy mountain peaks. The garden was illuminated with tiny golden string lights. John waited for me next to a bubbling fountain. I glanced to the room where Sara had been killed. Yellow caution tape still stretched across the door. Marianne was nowhere in sight, which I hoped was a sign that she was getting some much-needed rest.

That's what you need, too, Sloan. A restful night's sleep might make everything clearer tomorrow.

A brisk breeze made me wish I had brought a sweatshirt. I rubbed my arms, and as I wound through the grassy area, I heard voices and stopped. Vienna and Bozeman were huddled next to a lilac bush.

"Please, Bozeman," Vienna begged. Her long hair shimmered under the golden lights. She had changed out of her housekeeping uniform into a pair of skinny jeans, flip-flops, and a thin sweater that hit her at the knees.

"We've already gone over this, Vienna. You need to stay out of it." Bozeman's tone was harsh.

"But I could help. You should let me. The staff is talking, and rumors are starting to spread." She tried to grab his arm.

"No!" He yanked it away. "You need to drop it and get out of here. I'm tired. I need to go find my dudes and grab some beers. We've been working twelve-hour days, and I'm not sticking around to fight with you when I'm off the clock."

"But if you would just listen to me. I have an idea that might help," Vienna pleaded.

He threw his hands in the air. "Nope. I'm outta here. See you tomorrow." In a slick move, he jumped like a hurdler over the low fence and took off.

Vienna stared after him. For a minute I thought she was going to follow him, but instead she hung her head and turned in my direction. I walked straight toward her. "Good evening."

"Oh, hi. I didn't know we weren't alone." She sucked in a breath.

"Sorry. I didn't mean to eavesdrop. I was just on my way home."

She looked even younger under the glow of starlight. Tears welled in her eyes.

I stepped closer. "Are you okay?"

"Bozeman can be such an ass. He won't let me help him." She pulled her hands into the sleeves of her sweater.

"Why does he need help?"

"It's just work stuff. It's not a big deal." She clammed up. "I should go. It's late, and I have to be back here bright and early tomorrow. You'd think having everyone depart would make my job easier, but it's actually worse. We're going to have to turn over every room. It's going to be a long day."

"I can walk out with you."

"No, that's okay. I have a couple things to get out of my locker." Vienna started to move toward the lobby, but froze. She was looking at something behind us. "On second thought, yeah, yeah, let's get out of here. I can deal with my locker tomorrow."

Vienna hurried to the gate. I followed her, taking a quick look over my shoulder to see what had made her change her mind. It wasn't what. It was who. Jay lurked near the lobby doors. Was that why he'd been hanging around? To try and catch Vienna alone?

I shuddered at the thought.

"Did you have a chance to speak with Chief Meyers about what we talked about earlier?" I asked.

"Not yet. We were slammed. I've been running from room to room restocking toiletries and making beds. I'll try to find her tomorrow, if there's time." She didn't sound very likely to follow through.

"Wasn't Chief Meyers at the hotel most of the day?" I had thought that she and her team had been on-site investigating Sara's death.

"Yeah." Vienna stopped at the corner and pointed down the street. "I'm heading that way to the shuttle stop."

"Okay. I'll check in with you tomorrow, but I really want to encourage you to share your experience with Chief Meyers. You can't let Jay get away with this. She'll know what to do, and she'll be extremely discreet and have your best interests at heart."

"Thanks, I'll see if I can find her tomorrow." Vienna left to catch the shuttle. I had a feeling she was blowing me off, but maybe she was late for the bus.

Leavenworth ran a shuttle service to different stops through the village, the outskirts of town, and to Wenatchee and Lake Wenatchee, shuttling tourists and hotel and restaurant staff back and forth on busy festival weekends. The chamber encouraged workers to use the shuttle service in order to reduce the number of cars on the highway and coming into town. In fact, at a recent chamber meeting, a group of business owners had proposed banning vehicles from Front Street. Their point was that only allowing pedestrian access would provide more flow during festival weekends and allow restaurant owners to take advantage of more outdoor seating. Garrett and I had thrown our support behind the idea.

I turned in the opposite direction and walked through the village to get home. The air had grown chilly under a canopy of stars. The hazy streaks of the Milky Way cast a pale glow above. An opaque moon rose over the jagged ridgeline of Mount Stuart.

By the time I made it home, I'd begun to regret declining Mac's offer. It would have been nice to have company, but I pushed those thoughts away and crawled into bed. What I needed was a good night's sleep. Hopefully by morning things would start to make sense. I intended to take my own advice that I had just offered to Vienna and call Chief Meyers first thing. In the blur of evening activities, I realized I had yet to inform her that Forest may or may not be in town and there was a possibility he could be making an appearance at Nitro tomorrow.

When I unlocked the house and left John at his post, I noticed a plain envelope had been slipped beneath the door. There was no name on the envelope, but I assumed it must be for me. I opened it to find a grainy Polaroid inside. The photo was of Marianne when she was much younger. In it, she was standing in front of a brick schoolhouse with her arm wrapped around another woman, who had to be Claire. The sisters could have been twins. Claire was slightly taller and wore glasses, but otherwise, they shared the same olive skin, defined cheekbones, dark hair, and smiling eyes. They looked carefree, as if they were ready to take on the world.

A wave of nostalgia washed over me. It was nice to see them in their bell-bottom jeans and flowery blouses posing for the picture, each with one hand on her hip and a goofy grin.

Why had Marianne left me the photo?

She was impossible to get a read on. Every time I came to the conclusion that she was delusional, she did something like this. There had to be some truth to her story. The scrap of my old baby blanket, this picture, were they clues? Or was it her way of trying to connect?

My sleep was less than restful. I did manage to drift off a couple of times but was woken with night terrors. After the second nightmare, I gave up. My T-shirt was drenched in sweat, and my skin was clammy. It was nearly six, so I decided to take a long hot shower and get an early start to what I imagined might be a strange day.

The shower helped revive my energy, as did a steaming cup of coffee. I pulled on a pair of shorts, a T-shirt, and a lightweight sweater and left for Nitro. No one was stationed on my front porch, but a different squad car was parked in the driveway. I gave the officer a wave as I approached the vehicle. The words SEATTLE POLICE were painted in blue on the side of the white squad car.

He opened the door and stepped out of the car. "Morning, Mrs. Krause, I'm Officer Downs, and I've been assigned to your protective duty. My approach might be different than what you've experienced so far. I'm going to be within a few feet of you at all times." Officer Downs reminded me of Sasquatch. He was easily well over six feet with a burly body and bushy beard. I had felt safe under the watchful eye of John, but there was nothing to worry about with Downs on duty. He looked like he could snap anyone attempting to harm me in half with one move.

"Hi, thanks for being here—I'm relieved to hear it, actually. I'm heading in to work at Nitro. Do you know when Chief Meyers starts her day?"

"She's working around the clock with the murder investigation and the arrival of our team. Why? Did you need something?"

"No. I'll call her." I thanked him and walked into the sleepy village. Nothing would open for a few hours. Sundays tended to be leisurely, with visitors sleeping off a night of fun. Fortunately the coffee kiosk near the gazebo opened early. I stopped to pick up lattes for Garrett, Kat, and myself, taking in the early morning splendor of the village while I waited for the barista to make our drinks. Vendor tents had been closed tight. The faint smell of roasted nuts lingered in the air. Blue jays hopped on spindly feet, collecting any remnants left behind last night. A cleaning crew rumbled along the street, picking up garbage and giving the stunning flower displays a healthy watering.

Nitro was equally quiet when I unlocked the front door and showed Officer Downs inside. He did a sweep of the first floor before taking up a post in the front while I got to work in an empty kitchen. It was one of my favorite times in the brewery. I enjoyed puttering around in the kitchen or tinkering with our brews while everyone else snoozed up-stairs. Since we wouldn't serve our overnight guests break-fast for a couple of hours, I had time to bake something special, but before I got started, I placed a call to the chief. I got her voicemail and left a message detailing what Hans had told me last night and that there was a chance Forest could make an appearance at the pub.

I felt relieved knowing that she was looped in, so I focused my attention on my morning bake—beer bread cinnamon rolls. We tried to infuse our pub fare, including our break-fasts, with our product. It was a way to allow our guests to fully immerse themselves in the craft beer experience and showcase our beer. Much like my banana bread, the beer would add a hint of zest to the cinnamon rolls and help ac-tivate the yeast.

For the rolls, I started with yeast and sugar. Once the yeast had activated, I added flour and a cup of our Pucker Up IPA. I allowed the dough to rise before forming it into a large rectangle; generously slathering it with butter, cinnamon, and sugar; and rolling it into a log shape. I sliced the dough into hearty rolls and set them in the oven to bake.

Garrett wandered into the kitchen as the scent of the spicy rolls began to waft from the oven. "Hey, Sloan. What are you doing up this early?" He rubbed sleep from his eyes. I won-dered if I had woken him, since he was in a pair of sweats, slippers, and a heather gray T-shirt that read MY BLOOD TYPE IS IPA. "And why does everything you bake have to smell so good?"

I chuckled and offered him a latte. "You might need to zap this in the microwave. Consider it a peace offering."

He clutched the coffee. "If you bring me a latte, I'll pretty much forgive you for anything."

"Sorry, I didn't sleep well last night. It's going to be a busy day anyway, so I figured I would get to work now."

"Are you going to tell me what's really going on, Sloan? Or are we going to keep pretending that everything's fine?" Garrett eyes were etched with concern.

"Is it that obvious?"

"No, but you've trusted me with your story, Sloan, and I can tell there's more going on. I hope you know that you've got a listening ear if you need it." He took off the plastic lid and added a half spoonful of sugar to his coffee. "Plus there's a guy in uniform in the bar who nearly had me in a headlock when I came downstairs, so yeah, I think something is up."

"Sorry about that." I winced. "I wouldn't want to be on the receiving end of an Officer Downs headlock."

Garrett pretended to massage his scalp. "Tell me about it."

He was right. My breakup with Mac had taught me that closing myself off to the people who cared about me wasn't what I needed. This past year had brought an unbelievable amount of change. Some of it hard. Some of it rewarding. The most important lesson that continued to resonate was that I had created a community of friends around me. Friends like Garrett. If Forest was really here and really coming after me, I needed his support now more than ever.

CHAPTER

SIXTEEN

EVERY DETAIL POURED OUT of me as we sipped our lattes and waited for the beer cinnamon rolls to bake. When I finished, I expected Garrett to lecture me on not saying something sooner, but instead he leaned against the kitchen counter.

"Wow, Sloan, thank you for trusting me. I can't imagine what you must be going through, but I want you to know that I'll support you however I can, and if Forest shows up here, he's going to meet my mash tun paddle and an entire Leavenworth armada."

"That might be difficult, given that we're landlocked," I joked.

"It's a figure of speech. You know what I mean. He's not welcome here, and the minute he steps onto my property, I'll have him arrested."

The timer dinged. I went to check on the rolls.

"What does Chief Meyers think?" Garrett asked.

"I haven't talked to her yet. I left her a message earlier. She obviously knows everything Marianne told her, but I am worried that the news from Hans might prove her right."

"We can't be too careful." Garrett surveyed the kitchen like he was trying to assess our weapons cache.

The industrial kitchen was stocked with plenty of bread and cheese knives, but I doubted they would provide much protection if Forest was really as dangerous and savvy as Marianne had described him.

"There's a chance this is a figment of Marianne's imagination," I said. "Don't forget that. I'm still not convinced that she hasn't inflated the danger, or she could be connected to Sara's murder."

"Sure, but then who was the guy asking about you? You said yourself that you didn't keep in touch with any of your professors from school. It's a pretty odd coincidence, don't you think?"

"Yeah, that's the thing I keep coming back to in my head." I slid on a silicone pot holder and removed the pan of golden cinnamon rolls.

Garrett ran his fingers through his hair. "Sloan, we need a better plan. I think you should go find Chief Meyers now. The more I think about it, we can't minimize this. I'd rather err on the side of being overly cautious than take a chance. If Forest is the reason you were placed in protective care, then I'm inclined to believe Marianne's dire warnings. Maybe we need to lock everything down."

"Don't do anything rash," I cautioned. "That's what Officer Downs is here for. Up until now, the police have been keeping an eye on me from a distance. I think the official term they used is a personal perimeter, but not any longer.

He's going to be inside at the bar today. You saw him. He's not going to let anything happen to me."

"Rash?" Garrett sloshed some of his coffee as he spoke. "Sloan, if the man who murdered your mother is in town, he's here for one reason—you. We can't be too careful. I'm not willing to take a chance on this. We have to do something right now. I'm glad that Officer Downs is going to stick by you, but it's not enough."

"What do you want me to do?" I moved to the sink to wash my hands. I had found a hop-infused soap at the farmer's market a few weeks ago, and anytime I scrubbed up in the kitchen, the calming scent of hops helped to center me.

"I want you to go to the police station. Wait there until the chief arrives. She needs to know everything. Don't wait for her to come to you. Take Officer Downs." He set his paper cup on the counter. "While you do that, I'm going to make sure every door and window in this building is locked tight. There are so many windows and extra doors here, it's ridiculous." When Garrett inherited the historic building, which was originally a brothel in the late 1800s, then a diner and guesthouse during his Aunt Tess's reign, he spent countless hours reworking the space to make it functional as a brewery and tasting room, including closing off numerous unnecessary exits in the back.

I understood his concern. As far as I was concerned, Nitro was likely one of the safest places I could be. "But what about breakfast? What about our guests?" I motioned to the pan of cinnamon rolls.

"What about them? Kat can serve them and throw together some fruit or eggs. Breakfast is the least of our worries right now. We'll take care of everything." Garrett set his jaw and held his chin high. "Sloan, you have to focus on you."

"You're reacting the same way Mac did."

"Good. This is one time I'm happy to be in alignment with Mac. You're sure he's got Alex?"

"Positive. They're both working at Der Keller this morning and then I told him to keep Alex occupied this afternoon. Not to let him out of his sight."

"You didn't tell Alex?"

I shook my head. "I haven't told anyone. Except for you and Mac."

Garrett scowled. "Sloan, listen, I understand that you're a very private person and this is your life, but you're making a huge mistake. This isn't the time to shrink into yourself. This is the time to rally the troops. Do you know how many people in this village love you? You've been there for everyone else; now it's time for people to show up for you. Otto, Ursula, Hans, Kat, even April, you name it. Everyone needs to know. Everyone needs to be part of protecting you."

"But . . ." For the first time in my adult life, I couldn't come up with a retort.

"No, I'm not going to argue with you on this one." Garrett moved toward me and nudged me to the door. "I'm right, and we both know it. If you don't want to call in the armada, I will. I don't care if you quit. I don't care if you don't talk to me for the rest of my life. Well, that's not true—this place would crumble without you. But you get my point. We need help. We need you surrounded by everyone who loves you."

"Okay."

"Okay?" He sounded shocked. He gave his head a quick

shake. "Okay, then. I'll start making some calls. You go find the chief. Bring her back here, and we'll formulate a plan."

I started to walk away. Then I stopped. "Thanks, Garrett. I think I needed to hear that."

"You did." He met my gaze as we stood in the doorway together. I could smell his minty toothpaste and musky soap. Our foreheads bent toward each other. "You don't need to thank me or anyone else who shows up. You know why, Sloan Krause? Because you've saved everyone in this village. I'm not exaggerating when I say Nitro would be nothing without you. I would be completely lost. Remember how I hadn't even thought of serving anything other than a bowl of nuts or chips when we opened? You came up with the idea of pub fare. You made this place look amazing. I know you've worked countless hours on your own time on recipes, buying groceries for your incredible farm breakfasts for our guests and never turning in receipts. You've made Nitro so much more than a brewery. You've created a welcoming space where everyone feels at home." He placed his hands on my shoulders and leaned in close. His voice was filled with passion as he continued. "Sloan, you've changed me. I'm not just a geeky brewing dude anymore. I'm part of this community, thanks to you. This nanobrewery experiment has wildly exceeded my expectations because of *you*. I can't tell you how much you mean to me as a business partner and friend."

For a minute that felt like an eternity, I thought he might lean in close enough to kiss me.

He released my shoulders. "Sorry. I'm being dramatic because I need you to know how we all feel about you, okay? You've taken care of everyone in the village, now it's your turn to let me and everyone who loves you repay the debt we owe you."

Salty tears spilled down my cheeks. "Okay."

Garrett brushed my tears away with the tip of his finger.

He had seen me emotional before, but something shifted between us with his impassioned speech. I could feel my body pulling into his with the force of a magnet. I couldn't tear myself away. I wanted to collapse in his arms and pretend that this had been a bad dream. Garrett cradled my chin. "We're going to keep you safe, Sloan."

I gulped.

His forehead tilted toward mine. Our lips were inches apart.

Was this happening? Now?

"Mrs. Krause, is everything okay?" Officer Downs's voice broke the moment.

Garrett smiled and shook his head—in disappointment? I couldn't be sure.

"I'm fine," I called to Officer Downs.

"Be safe, Sloan," Garrett said softly. "I'm going to start fortifying this place while you're gone."

I brushed residual tears from my face and sniffed twice before telling Officer Downs my plan. He followed me to the police station, which was actually more like a welcome center, with its wooden POLIZEI sign and pink and purple flower baskets. Chief Meyers and her small staff maintained a presence in the village. They were typically tasked with keeping the peace during busy festival weekends, giving directions, and offering to take photos for tourists. Crime was rare in Leavenworth. A fact that none of us took for granted. Part of life in the village meant looking out for our friends and neighbors. Our small size and remote location meant that it was nearly impossible to stay disconnected. Lately, I had come to appreciate the idea that my fellow business owners knew what I was up to on a daily basis. Garrett was right. It was time to ask for help.

"Is Chief Meyers in yet?" I asked the officer seated at the front desk when I stepped inside. Officer Downs stayed outside on the porch.

"She's on her way. Should be here in five or ten minutes. You can wait." She pointed to two chairs next to the water cooler.

I took a seat and leafed through a map of area wineries. Eleanor's vineyard was listed as one of the map's passport participants, as was Hawks, Russ's vineyard. The concept of a wine passport had come to fruition a few years ago when the local wineries had banded together to promote regional tourism. Visitors picked up tasting maps here in Leavenworth and received a stamp for each vineyard they visited. Once they had stamped their entire passports, they returned them to the chamber of commerce to be added to a monthly drawing for hotel stays and restaurant gift certificates.

The idea had taken flight. From spring through early fall, when the mountain roads were passable, wine lovers spent the weekend traveling from vineyard to vineyard, sipping regional varieties, picnicking on lush lawns, and wandering through rows and rows of organic grapevines.

I thought about last night's tasting. The chemistry between Russ and Eleanor had to have been evident to everyone in the room. The way Russ had followed her every move and their brief physical exchanges—a touch on the shoulder, Eleanor constantly taking on and off her wedding ring—made me confident that they were an item. What was puzzling was whether their affair had anything to do with Sara's death. The same was true for Bozeman and Vienna. I wondered if they had really been arguing about something work related. Vienna had sounded upset.

And what about Marianne? She had vanished after her abrupt change of heart.

"Sloan, what are you doing here?" Chief Meyers interrupted my thoughts.

I returned the map to its spot on a stand of brochures and stood up. "I was hoping for a minute of your time."

"Of course." She pointed to the back of the room where her desk was located. The office wasn't exactly private.

"Do you think we could take a walk?"

Her brows arched together for the briefest of moments. She quickly recovered. "Let me put my things down, and I'll be right with you."

I waited for her on the porch, where Officer Downs tried to look inconspicuous. He scanned the village with a subtle stoic shift of his head. Not an inch of his solid body moved as he surveyed our surroundings. A minute later, the chief returned outside.

"Morning, Downs. You have us covered?"

His only response was a quick nod.

"How are you, Sloan?" she asked, matching my stride as we walked to the gazebo. She had a file folder tucked under one arm. Although Front Street Park was quiet at the moment, the signs of the festivities remained, tent canopies and spring banners flickering from lampposts. The gazebo was decked out with garlands of miniature roses, topiaries with golden twinkle lights, and hanging baskets dripping with eucalyptus and begonias.

"Not great, to be honest."

"Let's talk about it."

I appreciated her approach. She had never been overly effusive, and yet I knew that she cared by the way she intently listened and took careful note of everything I said.

"It's the situation with Marianne and Forest," I began. "At first, I guess I blew it off a bit."

"Hmmm. I disagree. I've never known you to blow anything off," she responded, motioning to the cedar bench in the center of the gazebo that was flanked with fragrant spring blooms. "Should we sit?"

"Sure." I followed her. "Maybe that's the wrong choice of words, but Marianne seems so unstable that I didn't fully believe her. Now I'm wondering if that was a mistake." I launched into everything that had happened in the last forty-eight hours, most importantly, what Hans had told me last night.

After I finished, she didn't speak right away.

"I'm glad you came to me. I have to agree with your assessment, and I have some news from the state authorities that I think you're going to want to see." She handed me the folder.

I opened it. Inside was a mug shot of a man identified as Forest. His photo sent a shiver down my spine. There was something sinister behind his light eyes. The words beneath his picture read ARMED AND DANGEROUS.

CHAPTER
SEVENTEEN

"I DON'T UNDERSTAND," I said to Chief Meyers, clutching the folder. "What does this mean?"

"It means the authorities agree with Marianne. I still haven't been able to find any trace of the files she claims were stolen from her room, but his police record is clear. He was released from prison, but broke his parole last week. He has an APB out on him and is considered armed and dangerous."

"Do you think that Marianne's telling the truth about Sara's murder? Could she have been killed by Forest?"

"That I don't know. It's an open investigation. I can't comment at the moment. I will say that there's no firm evidence as of yet that the two are connected." She pointed to the paperwork in my hands. "This, however, is tangible proof that you and your family are in danger, Sloan. A danger that I don't take lightly. I've called in reinforcements from Spokane and Seattle. People with a higher rank and clearance than me. My entire staff has been alerted. That's why I assigned you Downs and gave him strict orders to keep you in his sight at all times. We're sending press releases to the media with Forest's picture, asking for the public's help in locating him. Flyers will be distributed throughout the village. In the next few hours, his face will be in every shop window. You won't be able to walk five feet without seeing his mug shot. I'm increasing your protection and the protection around Nitro. Officers will be stationed at Der Keller. I know that you're a private person by nature, Sloan, and I'm afraid that there's no silencing this situation. I'm going to have to inform the Krause family. As for the rest of the village, I'll try to keep things as tight-lipped as possible, but I can't make any promises. You know better than anyone that gossip spreads faster than wildfire around here."

"It's okay. I'm fine with that." I nodded. Across the street, shop doors and shutters had begun to open. The smell of breakfast sausage and bacon sizzling on griddles wafted toward us. Soon breakfast crowds would gather. Tourists would fill shopping bags with trinkets and reminders of their getaway weekend before returning home.

If she was surprised, she didn't show it. She crossed one leg over the other and leaned back against the bench.

"Things could ramp up around here. It's not often that villagers see a squad of police officers on patrol. In good conscience, I have to warn you that we're going to have eyes on you, but even so, that doesn't put you completely out of harm's way. Forest could have been holing up here in the village, plotting his attack for the last few days. I'm hoping that we're out in front of this situation, but I have to warn you that we might be playing catch-up."

"I know. I get it." I returned the folder to her.

"Listen, there's lots to be done. Sloan, I know that you

have a sense of the danger, but I want to warn you that there's much more to this file that's classified. I asked for permission to share some of the details with you, but my request was denied. Let me say this much. Forest is a trained assassin. He hasn't just killed before. He's killed again and again. I wish there was more that I could say. I probably shouldn't have even told you that much." She stood. "Please stay on high alert." For a moment, I thought she might hug me. Instead she gave me a pained smile. "Be careful, Sloan."

"I will."

Chief Meyers had ordered three additional officers, who had arrived at the brewery. "I want every entrance covered," directed Officer Downs. "No one leaves their post, understood? I'll be in touch within the hour."

I barely managed more than a wave to my fellow villagers and shop owners as Officer Downs escorted me into Nitro. I felt comforted by his lumbering steps, but I couldn't focus.

I wasn't sure how to feel. My hands were clammy, my forehead tingly, and a strange sensation came over my entire body, as if I were watching events unfold from above.

"Well, what's the report?" Garrett asked. He had moved furniture in the tasting room and used empty kegs to barricade the brewery. Typically a small chain with an EMPLOYEES ONLY sign blocked off the space. He had taken it a step further by creating a wall of kegs. "I see that the chief has called in extra bodies. That must be a sign that she's taking things seriously. Good."

"Yeah. There's going to be even more." I told him about police officers arriving from Seattle and Spokane and the chief's plan to plaster Forest's picture throughout the village.

"Good. Let's get this guy." His voice cracked with anger.

"I've made sure no one can get into the back and locked every window and door upstairs and downstairs."

Meyers's words of warning kept echoing in my head. They were similar to what Marianne had told me. How many people had Forest killed? And why was his file secret?

"Any other day, I'd tell you to get out of here and go home, but I don't think that's a good idea," Garrett said. He had changed out of sweats into a pair of khaki shorts, Keen sandals, and a Nitro T-shirt.

"No, you're right. I think this is the safest spot for me, and I need to do something—anything. I'm going to start freaking out if I just sit around waiting for Forest to come find me." The sweat pooling on my back was proof that I was already freaking out. I wondered if Garrett could tell.

"Fair point." He strummed his fingers on the bar. "What do you think? You want to work the taps or hide out in the back?"

"Work the taps. No question." I stared at the barrier of kegs. "How are we going to get into the kitchen with those stacked like that?"

Garrett pressed his lips together and sucked in one cheek. "Good point. I didn't think of that. I'll make a narrow pathway. I was hoping that you would let us stow you away back there, but I had a feeling you would say you wanted to work the bar. I don't know why I asked." He swept his hands across the row of tap handles. "My lady, the bar, she is all yours."

I chuckled. It didn't lighten the mood.

"Kat is finishing breakfast cleanup. I gave her a rundown of the situation. The twins should be here in an hour. I'll fill them in, so you don't have to, okay? We have everything covered. Casey and Jack can prep lunch. They can work the patio. There's nothing you need to do, got it?"

Garrett had taken charge of the situation. Maybe he was picking up on the fact that I was teetering on the edge of a full-blown panic attack. Normally I prided myself on being a strong, independent woman, but I appreciated not having to do anything other than pour pints at the moment.

"I suspect we'll be busy right from opening, given how many people talked about coming back for growlers yesterday," Garrett continued. "Although depending on how much they enjoyed last night, maybe they'll forget about us."

"People never forget about beer."

Garrett gave me a slow nod. "Nice. I think that motto should hang next to our Nitro logo. That's deep, Sloan. Real deep."

I knew that he was trying to keep my spirits up and my mind off Forest. What I wanted to tell him was that was an impossible task, but I didn't want to hurt his feelings "I'll take over inventory and bar prep."

"Cool. I'll fix my beer keg fortress, then go check the fermenters and see if Kat needs any help." He gave me a brief parting glance and nodded to Officer Downs, who was studying the Nitro menu like it was the most compelling novel he'd ever read. I knew he was trying to be discreet, but I also knew he had heard every word of our conversation.

I was glad for the routine of the bar. Methodically checking off each task on our opening prep sheet felt like a massive accomplishment. At some point I vaguely remembered greeting the twins and chatting with Kat when she brought me bags of Doritos and mixed nuts for the bar, but if I was being honest with myself, nothing felt real. It was as if I was moving through molasses. Each movement took considerable effort. Every time I filled a bowl with pretzels or stacked pint glasses, I had to remind my brain to connect with my body. My waking-dream-like state didn't bode well for managing a busy morning of growler fills. I knew that if I hid out in the back, I would collapse into myself, and I wasn't going to let that happen.

"Who's ready to unleash the beast?" Garrett asked a while later. Time wasn't functioning like normal, at least not in my mind. It felt like we had just made our plan a few minutes ago, and it was already time to open the doors.

Garrett waited by the front door. The clock was about to turn to eleven. "Is everyone ready for one last mad dash?"

"Let's do this." Kat clapped.

I nodded.

Before Garrett officially opened the pub, he checked in one last time with me and Officer Downs. "You're both a go?"

"I'll be right here for the duration of the day," confirmed Officer Downs, taking position between the end of the bar and the entrance to the brewery. "If anyone sees anything out of the norm, you flag me down immediately, understood?"

Kat, Casey, and Jack agreed.

Officer Downs had a photo of Forest on his phone. He passed it around for everyone to study. "Take a close look. You see this guy so much as step a toe inside, and I want you to make noise. You scream, you holler, you do whatever it takes to get my attention."

Our team diligently studied the photo. Everyone was solemn and unified.

"Mrs. Krause, are you good?" Officer Downs gave me the final word.

I nodded. "I'm good."

Garrett opened the doors, and as expected, a line had already formed.

I tried to quench the sense of dread flooding my body. *Focus, Sloan.*

It was nearly impossible not to profile every person who made their way to the bar to place their orders. I found myself constantly checking over my shoulder as I filled growlers and poured pints. Along with a few of our regulars, hospital staff coming off of the night shift, and locals in search of a lunchtime pint, there was a steady crowd of tourists who had indeed returned to fill growlers. Twice older gentlemen matching Forest's description came into the bar. Officer Downs sprang into action both times, placing his hand on his holster and readying himself to tackle them. The first man ended up being a grandfather in search of our root beer for his grandkids. The second was a retired English professor who had promised his wife he wouldn't leave Leavenworth without a growler of our Pucker Up IPA.

Both false alarms hammered home reminders that Forest could be out there in the village, waiting for his opportunity to strike.

Garrett stayed at the bar the entire time. I had a feeling he had also received orders from Chief Meyers not to let me out of his sight. If new glasses were needed or an order for lunch was placed, he directed the twins and Kat to take care of it, never allowing his eyes off of me.

"How you doing, Sloan? Hanging in?" He checked in when we were about two hours into service and the rush had begun to slow. That was typical for Sunday crowds. People wanted to get on the road by early afternoon to beat the traffic and be home before dark.

"I'm good." That was the truth. Being busy had helped take the edge off.

"Nothing out of the ordinary, right?" Garrett scanned the pub. There were a handful of locals enjoying lunch at our high-top bar tables and outside on the patio.

"Nope." Maybe this had been blown out of proportion. Or maybe the heavy show of police had scared Forest away.

I was surprised that I hadn't seen Marianne. I had expected that she might have been waiting outside when we opened the doors.

"You want to take a lunch break?" Garrett asked.

"I'm fine. I can do a sweep of the patio." I started to move. He grabbed my wrist.

"Sorry. I can't let you do that. Chief's orders—you are to stay behind the bar or in the back." He made eye contact with Officer Downs, who gave him a nod of approval.

"So basically I'm under house arrest?"

Garrett tried to smile. His eyes were narrow with concern. "Yeah. You are, Sloan."

"Okay."

Before he could say more, April rushed in through the open patio doors. "Sloan, Sloan! Oh thank God, you're okay."

She knocked over a barstool. It thudded on the concrete floor. April took no notice. She left it on the ground and ran up to the bar.

Officer Downs blocked her path.

She slammed into his sturdy frame and ricocheted backward, nearly falling over. "Hey, I need to get through!"

Officer Downs stood his ground.

"Sloan! Tell him who I am!" she demanded, propping her hands on her hips.

If Officer Downs tackled her and dragged her out of Nitro, would it be such a bad thing? "She's harmless," I said to Downs. That wasn't entirely true. April was responsible for nearly every piece of gossip that worked its way through the village. Part of me thought that being handcuffed by Officer Downs might serve as a lesson.

He let her pass.

"Sloan, oh goodness. Sloan!" She raced to the bar and grabbed my hand. "I've been beside myself with worry. I can't believe you're here and upright."

I yanked it away. "April, what are you doing?"

"Checking on you." She thrust both hands over her chest. "I was so worried when I heard the news, but you're here, so it must be okay." Yet again, she wore another German getup. Today's was a springtime barmaid's dress with pale yellow daisies and matching daisy earrings. I wondered how much she must spend on her wardrobe. It had to be a small fortune. I didn't think I'd ever seen April in the same outfit. Her closet could probably supply a small textile museum with Bavarian skirts, dresses, and accessories.

Leave it to April to overreact.

"I saw the police and the flyers of course. I figured our fine men and women in blue would apprehend the suspect, but I had no idea they'd do it so fast."

There goes any glimmer of hope about privacy, I thought. What did she mean, apprehend the suspect? What was she talking about?

"April, I'm not sure what you mean. Unless it just happened, I don't think there's been an arrest."

She stuck her neck forward and furrowed her brow. "No arrest? Then what are you doing here? I would have thought you'd be out there with them."

"With the police? No. They want me here so they can contain the situation."

April leaned her arms on the bar. "Oh, Sloan, I don't know how you're doing it. How can you be so calm? That's so very brave of you. If my kid was missing, I don't think I'd be able to follow orders. I think I would be out running around the village, screaming at the top of my lungs, doing anything I could to try and find him."

"What?" A cold sense of dread pulsed through me. "April, what are you saying?"

"I'm talking about Alex!" She stared at me with eyes so wide I thought they might burst through their sockets. "My God, Sloan. You don't know, do you?"

"Know what?" I clutched the counter and braced myself for her answer.

"Alex. He's missing."

CHAPTER

EIGHTEEN

THERE HAD TO BE some of kind of a mistake. Missing? Alex wasn't missing. He was with Mac at Der Keller, where Chief Meyers had posted another team of police officers. No way Forest could have gotten to him.

"April, what are you talking about? Alex is at Der Keller. Mac is making sure of that. I might not be Mac's biggest fan these days, but he knows the seriousness of the situation, and he wouldn't let Alex of his sight." My legs felt weak. I needed to sit down.

"Look, Sloan. I don't know what happened, but they're looking for Alex right now." She glanced toward the street.

"Who? Who is *they*?"

"Chief Meyers. The entire police squad. They're search-ing the village, Blackbird Island. They've shut down the highway in both directions. No one is getting in or out of town."

Officer Downs's cell phone rang. He answered the call,

remaining silent as he listened to news or orders from the other end of the line.

I thought I might collapse.

"Garrett, come help!" April yelled.

I felt myself sinking. My knees buckled. My stomach swirled. Was I going to throw up?

Not Alex.

Not Alex.

How?

How could Mac do this? He had stood in front of me and sworn that he would keep our son safe.

"Sloan, Sloan, can you sit up?" Garrett knelt next to me. "Kat, grab her a glass of water!"

I pushed him away. "I don't need water. I need to get out of here. Alex is missing."

He motioned for me to stay on the ground. "Stay there. Don't move."

Officer Downs had ended the call. I looked up into his dark eyes. His nod of remorse confirmed my worst fears.

I tried to stand, but my legs felt loose and floppy, like they were being controlled by a puppeteer.

"Sloan, it's okay." Garrett placed his hand on my knee. "We're going to help. We're going to find him. We're closing right now. Everyone here is going to help. We're going to find him, Sloan," he repeated pressing his hand on my skin. "But you need to keep breathing and drink some water. You're not going to be any good to Alex or yourself if you pass out, okay?"

I took the water Kat offered me. My throat cinched closed as I tried to gulp down a sip. I coughed. "Forget it." I set the water down and pushed to my feet, not caring that the room spun sideways and ignoring the pounding in my chest. Rage took over. "Let's go!"

Officer Downs shouted orders to the team of officers posted inside. He led our small crew outside, where it looked like a movie set for an action film. Dozens of police officers raced in every direction—toward Blackbird Island, fanning out near the hospital and guarding the entrance to Front Street. Every road had been barricaded with orange and white cones. A helicopter's blades whirled above us. Sirens wailed in the distance. Blue, red, and white lights flashed like fireworks.

This was real. It wasn't a lucid dream, it was a waking nightmare.

"Sloan, stay right here." April shoved me onto a patio chair. She addressed Garrett. "Get her to wait here for a minute. I'll go find Chief Meyers." April raced off.

Garrett waited for directions from Officer Downs, who was on the phone again.

How had Forest gotten to Alex?

It didn't make sense. It was the middle of the day. Had he taken Alex from Der Keller? But how? Wouldn't Alex have put up a fight?

The throbbing cry of sirens made it hard to think.

This couldn't be happening.

Not Alex!

Not Alex. Please, no, I begged the universe or whoever else was listening.

I felt myself starting to collapse again. I sagged into the chair, letting my arms hang loose like a rag doll. My vision went blurry.

I felt two firm hands wrap around my shoulders, pulling me upright. "Sloan, hang on. I've got you."

I looked behind me to find Hans supporting me. He kept one hand on my shoulder and pulled up a chair next to me.

"Hans, it's Alex." I broke down. An ocean of tears spilled from my eyes. I collapsed into him, enveloped by the scent of cedar and the comfort of his solid arms.

He let out a long sigh, then closed his golden-brown eyes. "I know."

Hans held me tight. He didn't say anything. He simply stroked my head.

I had no idea how long we stayed like that. Hans unbuckled his tool belt and set it on the table at some point. Officer Downs recruited Kat and the twins to join him and a search team heading to the high school. Activity whirled around us. Friends and neighbors scoured the village. Tents that had been used for yesterday's merriment had been repurposed as temporary checkpoints. The sweet smells of spring evaporated. Gone was any remnant of charm. Our little Bavaria had turned into a stage for the biggest manhunt I'd ever seen.

Hans continued to caress my arms, repeating, "We'll find him, Sloan. We'll find him."

It wasn't until April returned with Chief Meyers that I was able to pull myself together.

My entire body quaked. My legs felt like Jell-O. Hans kept a firm grip on my waist and helped me stand. "Do you have news?"

"Not yet but, Sloan, we've got this. We're following a number of leads, and I'm confident that we are going to find him safe and sound." Chief Meyers met my eyes. Her stare held a resolve that I couldn't conjure up in myself.

"How? He was supposed to be at Der Keller with Mac."

"He was. We have a witness who saw him exiting the back toward the warehouse with an older gentleman." She flipped through her notebook. "Signs indicate that he appeared to leave willingly, but we suspect that wasn't the case."

"What does that mean?" I looked to Hans.

The chief held up a finger to an officer who had approached us. "Give me a minute here. I'll be right with you."

The officer nodded and held back.

"Sloan, we suspect that Forest threatened him in some way. Perhaps he had a concealed weapon of some kind. Or perhaps he used verbal threats. He could have told Alex that harm would come to you, Mac, or the Krauses, something that would have made Alex leave with him."

"Where are they now?"

"They were last seen heading toward Blackbird Island. We have every man, woman, and child in the village involved in the search, along with police teams from Spokane and Seattle." She motioned to the blur of frenetic action around us. "We're going to find him, but we need to move quickly. There's an important window of time right now, and I don't want to delay. We're going to bring him back safe and sound," she repeated.

Was she saying it for me, or did she actually believe it? I wished I shared even a sliver of her confidence. Every worst-case scenario barraged my head. What would stop Forest from torturing Alex, or worse? What must be going through Alex's mind right now?

Hans cleared his throat. "What can we do, Chief?"

"You can stay here and wait for Alex or one of us to call."

"That's not going to happen," Hans replied, shaking his head.

He took the words out of my mouth.

"We've got cell phones. Alex knows how to reach us." He picked up his tool belt and secured it around his waist. "We can't just sit here. No way. Give us an area to search. Right, Sloan?"

"Yeah," I managed to mutter.

The chief's confidence evaporated ever so slightly. She tucked her notebook into her breast pocket and waved the officer waiting nearby closer. She whispered something in his ear, which I couldn't hear. Then she returned her attention to us, addressing Hans. "Okay, take the warehouse. I sent in a team there a while ago, but you two know it well. You hear or see anything, and I mean anything, even the slightest peep—you call the team positioned there for help and then you call me directly on my cell and you wait. Understood?"

We both nodded.

Her pupils had dilated, and her jaw was like stone. "Alex's safety could depend on it."

"Understood," Hans said. His tone was somber.

The chief returned her attention to the waiting officer.

Garrett caught my eye, then he looked to Hans. "You've got her, right? It sounds like they need me to hang around in case they need to access anything inside."

"She's safe with me." Hans clapped him on the back. "Let's go, sis." He looped his arm through mine with such a firm grip I thought I might lose feeling in my wrist. He kept me upright as we passed the hospital. I tried to block out visions of ambulances and Alex arriving on a gurney.

"What happened? How did Mac let this happen?" It took every effort to put one foot in front of the other. My body seemed to move outside of me.

"You know that I don't often defend my brother, but this one isn't on him, Sloan. He's distraught. My folks are with him now. They've cleared out the brewery. They've got police protection with them. He might be in even worse shape than you. He didn't let this happen, Sloan. It was a fluke. Forest must have already been in the building. I'm with Chief Meyers—he must have threatened Alex to get him to leave."

"My God, this is all my fault." I felt dizziness start to take hold. My fingertips were numb and tingly. A strange buzzing filled my ears.

"No, it's no one's fault," Hans replied, clutching my arm tighter. "Like the chief said, we're going to find Alex. The best thing you can do right now is focus on that. Let's think. Alex is a smart kid. If Forest got him outside, what would Alex do? Can you think about anyplace he might have tried to get away to or maybe even tried to lead Forest to?"

Hans's methodical approach made me feel more rational.

I had to focus. Panicking wasn't going to save my son.

Where would Alex go? The soccer fields? The park? He knew Blackbird Island well, but I couldn't imagine him heading there. He wouldn't have gone to the cottage or Mac's condo. The warehouse was a possibility, but there weren't many places to hide amongst the bottling racks and pallets of beer. There was the farmhouse, which had sat empty for the past few months while Mac and I were deciding whether to sell it or convert it into a Der Keller guesthouse like what Garrett and I had done with Nitro, but that was on the outskirts of town. I didn't think Alex would take that kind of a risk if he had any control over his captor. Wouldn't he try to be around more people, not less?

"I guess it depends on the threat," I said to Hans. "Did

Forest take him by gun or knifepoint? Does Forest have a car? If he was threatening to kill me or Mac, maybe Alex panicked. Could they have gone to the farmhouse? Your parents' house?" I stumbled over a pebble in the sidewalk.

Hans caught me. "Maybe." He stopped in front of the Gingerbread Cottage. The sugary and spicy scent of baking cookies, which usually reminded me of Ursula's kitchen, sent a wave of nausea swirling in my stomach. If anything happened to Alex, I would never be able to live with myself.

"Maybe he could have gone to my folks' house," Hans repeated. "But, like I said, Alex is one of the smartest kids I know. I can't imagine him leaving the village, not of his own accord anyway. I feel like they must be close."

"Me, too." Call it a mother's intuition, but I sensed Alex would go somewhere nearby, if he had any say in the matter. "What's Forest's endgame? Do you think he's using Alex to get to me?"

"It seems like it."

"Right. So, if that's the case, he wouldn't want to go far either. I think they're here in the village, Hans." I massaged my temples.

Think, Sloan. Think.

Hans looked equally perplexed.

"Should we go to the warehouse?" he asked. A troop of volunteers ran past us shouting Alex's name.

"We can, but my gut says they're not there. Not if the police really did a full sweep of the building. You know it as well as I do. Where would they hide? One of the offices? The kitchenette? The police must have checked those, right?"

"I agree. Mac was there for that. He wouldn't have left a

stone unturned." Hans sighed. "Should we go to Der Keller and check in with him and my folks?"

"Sure." We'd started to move in that direction when a thought hit me. I stopped and grabbed Hans. "Wait, I think I know where he might be."

"Where?"

"Your shop!"

CHAPTER

NINETEEN

"SLOAN, YES! WHY DIDN'T I think of that?" Hans had already spun around in the opposite direction. His workshop, which was not only his craft space but his showroom and living area, was located down below my cottage, just a couple of blocks away from the miniature golf course.

I couldn't count how many hours Alex had spent in the dust-covered shop over the years. Hans had taught him how to whittle pieces of wood into a fantastical creatures and eventually moved on to bigger projects like how to use band and circular saws, and how to build handcrafted kayaks. The shop was in the village, a space Alex was intimately familiar with, and best of all, it was filled with potential weapons Alex could use against his captor. It was the perfect spot. Hans was right; Alex was a smart kid. If he had gone anywhere, it had to be the workshop.

Hans reached into one of the many pockets on his cargo shorts and pulled out his cell phone. "I'm going to call the chief. I wonder if anyone thought to send a search team or police officers there?"

"Probably not." I felt breathless as Hans broke out into a slow jog while placing the call. The pace wasn't too fast for me, but nevertheless, I couldn't catch my breath.

"We're on our way to my workshop now, Chief," Hans yelled into the phone. "Got it. We won't make a move until you get there."

He hung up. "She's on her way, too, and sending the closest team. Let's go."

"Wait." I froze. "We should call your family. If we're right about this, they should be there, too."

He gave me a nod of approval and placed a call to Mac before we both sprinted five blocks to the wood shop. Volunteer crews were searching the golf course, hollering Alex's name and pacing out steps in a gridlike pattern. I could hear more police activity on Blackbird Island to our left, and made out a police boat zipping along the Wenatchee River's rushing waters, heavy with spring runoff.

Once we were half a block away, I slowed my pace.

Hans stopped abruptly. "Are you okay?"

I knelt down and clutched my knees.

"Sorry, was that too fast?" His breathing was heavy.

"No, I mean yes," I said, sucking in air. "I'm scared now that we're close," I admitted.

Hans squeezed my hand so hard that my fingertips turned ghostly white. I didn't care. I needed the reinforcement.

We continued onward in silence, stopping only when we were directly in front of his house. The exterior of Hans's live/work space was designed to resemble a German mountain cabin. He had refurbished the shop log by log. When he purchased the run-down old pottery studio, he had literally transformed every bit of the one-story structure, from the shingled roof to the attached garden. My favorite feature was the huge pergola he'd built next to a rock garden with large Japanese maples, water fountains, and a wall of herbs potted in handmade cedar boxes. In the summer months he used the garden as a showroom, and in the winter we often gathered round the large brick fire pit for snowy bonfires with hot mulled wine and s'mores.

"Does anything look off?" I whispered, catching a faint hint of warm sawdust.

Hans shook his head. He scanned the arched front door and the side gate that led to the back gardens and workshop. Clients used the gate entrance so that they didn't have to traipse through his living room when picking up a custom order for Adirondack chairs or fireplace mantels carved from madrone wood.

"No. Both the door and gate are latched," he answered, keeping his voice low as well. "The chief gave me strict instructions not to enter until she and her team arrive."

I knew that was the wise move, but every cell in my body told me to get inside. For all I knew, Forest could have a gun to my son's head.

"Sloan, don't move." Hans grabbed my waist. "Listen, did you hear that?"

I froze.

The only sounds I heard were the nearby shouts of villagers out searching for Alex and the wail of sirens.

"No, what?" My mouth felt gummy. I tried to swallow, but it didn't help.

"Wait, listen." Hans placed a finger over his lips.

I strained as I hard as I could to pick up any background noise.

"There! Did you hear it?" Hans asked. His light brown eyes held a spark of hope.

"Was that someone saying 'help'?" I asked, not sure if I was actually hearing something or just hoping that it was true.

Hans perked up. "It sounded like it, didn't it? And it's coming from the yard." He carefully stepped closer to the gate and leaned in.

"Sloan! Hans!" Mac rounded the corner, whisper-yelling. His face was redder than any amber ale I'd ever brewed.

"Quiet," Hans whispered.

Mac's cheeks burned, and sweat poured from his brow. His Der Keller shirt was soaked through, like he'd swum across the Wenatchee River. He bent over and put his hands on his knees to try and catch his breath when he made it to us. "I ran faster than I have since high school football practice," he wheezed. "What's the word? Is there any sign of him?"

"We don't know," Hans replied. "We think we heard something in the side yard."

The three of us remained quiet. Hans cupped his ear to the fence. Mac closed his eyes.

I pressed both hands behind my ears, hoping to amplify any sound. At first there was nothing—only the distant shouts of teams searching the village and mountain crows cawing in answer. I was about to move my hands when again I heard the faintest muffled sound coming from the back.

"That's him! That's Alex!" Mac made two fists, as if he was readying himself to fight. "What are we waiting for? Let's go!" Mac took a step forward.

Hans blocked him. "Hold up. The chief told us to wait. She should be here any second."

"And that could be one second too long. If that's my son in there—your nephew—crying for help, we're going in! I don't care what Meyers or anyone else says." Mac pushed his brother out of the way.

I couldn't believe it, but I was with Mac. There was no time to dally. If Alex was in danger, we had to get in there now.

Hans frowned, but followed after him. "You're right, but we don't have any weapons. What are we going to do if this guy has Alex at gunpoint or something?"

Mac's eyes were black with fury. "Take him down."

I half expected him to kick the gate open, but he flipped the latch and raced through the yard. "Alex, we're coming!"

Hans and I ran behind him.

My pulse thudded so hard in my neck I thought I might burst a blood vessel. *Please let him be okay. Please let him be okay,* I begged internally.

I couldn't face the thought of anything happening to Alex.

As much as I wanted to know if he was okay, I felt my feet slowing. What if he wasn't?

I gripped the fence and dragged myself forward.

At that moment, sirens erupted. Chief Meyers sped onto the street, her squad car jumping the curb and landing on Hans's front lawn. She raced toward me with her gun pulled. Within seconds, three more squad cars had the block surrounded.

"That way, Sloan?" She nodded to the back.

"Yeah." I leaned into the fence as a swirl of blue-uniformed officers thudded past me. I heard the chief shouting orders and Mac's and Hans's voices, but everything sounded far away and blurry.

"We got him!" Chief Meyers's voice rang loud and clear.

Alex. My heart thudded.

"He's okay!"

Thank God. I placed my hand on my stomach and walked with intention to see my son.

What I found in Hans's garden made my knees buckle. Chief Meyers was untying Alex's hands, which were bound to the workbench. He was blindfolded and gagged with rags that Hans used for staining wood. The chief undid the blindfold and freed him from the gag.

Alex coughed. His eyes were wide with fear.

Mac embraced him in a giant hug. Hans placed his arm on Alex's broadening shoulders.

I held back for a moment, trying to get my bearings, too overcome with the weight of relief and the adrenaline of fear. I remembered an old trick that Sally had taught me when I was younger and struggled with anxiety over being moved again and again in foster care. "Sloan, pick five things to focus on. Name them," she would say, trying to give me manageable tools to deal with my big emotions.

I did that now. *Edison-style garden lights,* I said to myself. *Potted tarragon. A three-tiered fountain. Rocking chairs. A hammock.*

My kid. Okay.

Sally's trick worked. I raced over. Mac stepped to the side. I hugged Alex tight, running my fingers through his wavy hair like I used to do when he was young and stroking his eyebrows.

"Alex, I'm so sorry. I can't believe he got to you. It's my fault." I kissed the top of his head.

Alex was shaky. "I'm okay, Mom."

"Let's give him some space," Chief Meyers said, directing an officer to bring over a chair. "Hans, I'm sure you must have a juice or soda inside. Something with sugar would be good."

"You got it." Hans clapped Alex on the shoulder again and then went inside to get him a drink.

"Have a seat, son." The chief pointed to the chair.

Alex looked stunned. "Yeah, okay."

"Before I ask you any other questions, I need to know: Have you been harmed? I don't see any apparent injuries." She surveyed him from head to toe.

"No. I'm fine." His voice sounded off.

I could tell he wasn't fine. I wanted to let him sit on my lap and to rock him the way I had when he was little.

"This might be difficult, but anything you can tell us about what happened is going to be extremely important in apprehending and arresting Forest."

"Who's Forest?" Alex sounded confused.

Was he in worse shape than he appeared? Could Forest have hit him? Maybe he had a concussion.

I suspected the chief was thinking the same thing. She walked around the other side of the chair and examined the back of his head for bumps and bruises.

"The man who kidnapped you," she said to Alex. "His name is Forest."

"He didn't kidnap me." Alex shook his head.

Chief Meyers returned to face Alex. "It's okay. I know you've been through an ordeal. That sends our body into fight or flight and can make things seem off—almost like you're outside of yourself. It's normal in stressful situations like this to feel fuzzy. Dizzy."

"I'm not fuzzy," Alex insisted.

Hans came outside with a root beer. He offered it to Alex, who took a tentative sip.

"Look, I don't know who this Forest guy is, but that's not who did this."

"Would it be helpful to show you a sketch? I have photos of Forest that might help trigger your memory." Chief Meyers motioned to one of the officers to bring Forest's mug shot over.

Alex took a brief look at the photo and handed it back to her. "I don't need my memory jogged, because it wasn't a man who took me. It was a woman—she said her name was Marianne."

CHAPTER

TWENTY

I GASPED. "MARIANNE! MARIANNE did this to you?"

Alex drank more root beer. "Yeah. She came to Der Keller. I noticed her hanging around most of the morning. She sat at the bar drinking the same cup of coffee. She kept saying no to refills when I would check in on her. I kind of had a strange feeling about her—like she was watching me. When I finally went to pick up her empty, she asked me if I was your son. I told her that I was, and she started to cry. She said she's my great-aunt. I couldn't believe it. She knew everything about you, Mom. She even looks like you." His voice cracked. "She asked if I could walk her here. She said she was meeting you and Uncle Hans."

Marianne had convinced Alex to leave with her? Why? It didn't make sense.

"I feel so stupid." Alex hung his head.

"No, it's not your fault." I looked to Chief Meyers. What did it mean? Why would Marianne have kidnapped Alex?

Had she intended to try and take me, too? Was that her plan since I had refused to run?

"What happened when you arrived here?" Chief Meyers asked, trying to keep Alex focused. "It's important to try and remember as many details as you can. Take your time and think about it."

"Uncle Hans and Mom weren't here, so I let us in through the gate." He paused to drink more root beer, which I took as a good sign. "I figured they would be here soon, and we could wait for a few minutes. Der Keller was pretty slow, so I didn't think Dad or the staff would mind if I was gone for a while. Dad was acting weird all morning. He kept checking on me, like I was in trouble or something, but I didn't want to leave her here on her own. I guess I should have trusted myself— once we got here, I felt kind of funny. I don't know how to describe it exactly, but something about her felt wrong."

"Mmm-hmm." Chief Meyers took notes without looking at her notepad. She encouraged Alex to continue, nodding and maintaining eye contact with him the entire time. "Do you remember what time this was or how long you were here before she tied you up?"

"It happened so fast." Alex clutched the glass. "I think it was around noon when we came over here, but I'm not sure. It could have been earlier. I wasn't paying attention to the clock. I just know that the lunch crowds were starting to arrive. I think we were here for maybe ten or fifteen minutes. She was asking a bunch of questions about Mom, and then all of sudden, she picked up Uncle Hans's power drill and grabbed me. Then she tied me up. I probably could have resisted or fought back more, but I was so shocked. It came out of nowhere."

"Alex, did she say anything? Did she tell you why she did this?" I interjected.

"She kept apologizing. She said it was for my own good. It was the only way to get your attention. I don't understand, Mom." The confusion in his eyes pierced my heart.

I rubbed his arm. "I don't either."

Otto and Ursula showed up as the chief continued to press Alex for details on timing and where Marianne might have gone next.

"Ziz is terrible. Why Alex?" Ursula's eyes were bloodshot, and her cheeks stained with tears. She clutched a lacy hand-kerchief in one hand. "We have been beside ourselves. When Mac told us what had happened, we cannot believe it."

"Same for me." I squeezed her hand.

She wouldn't release her grasp. "He is okay. Ziz is all zat matters now."

"Zat and catching ziz horrible woman," Otto added. His normally kind smile had morphed into a stoic frown. He stood with his arms folded across his chest, looking to Chief Meyers for support. "You must arrest ziz woman. What kind of a monster would do ziz to a child?"

"Opa, I'm not a kid. I'm sixteen." Alex rolled his shoulders to prove his point.

Otto patted his head. "*Ja.* I know. You are a young man, but you will always be my *Enkel,* and ziz is terrible. We must find ziz woman and take her to jail immediately."

I didn't blame Otto for sounding furious. My fear was starting to shift into anger, especially since Alex was okay—at least physically speaking. I wondered what kind of emotional toll this experience would have on him.

The chief called me and the entire Krause family over for

a private conversation next to a set of rocking chairs near the fire pit while two paramedics who had arrived on the scene assessed Alex.

"I don't want you to worry. It's standard procedure to call EMS," she explained. "He's in good shape. I'm not worried about him. I do need to call off the search for Alex or, actually, refocus our volunteers and police force."

"You mean to look for Marianne," Mac said. Some of the redness had dissipated from his cheeks, but the way he stood with his feet wide apart and his hands stuffed in his pockets told me he was seething, too.

"Exactly. She can't have gotten far. We already shut down the highway. There's no way in or out of the village until I say there is." She tapped the badge on her chest.

I ran my fingers over a bunch of rosemary Hans had planted between the rocking chairs. The herbal fragrance did little to calm my nerves. "I don't get it. Why take Alex? For show? To worry me? It doesn't make sense."

"I don't know, Sloan. I wish I had answers. I don't at this point, but I'm confident that once we find Marianne and I can interrogate her, many things will come to light, including a motive."

"Was Forest fake, then?" Hans asked. He rocked the chair back and forth with the tip of his ankle-high work boots. "Didn't you say that Alex was seen leaving Der Keller with someone matching his description?"

"He's not fake. Which has stumped me, to be honest." Chief Meyers sounded genuinely perplexed. "I have a hefty list of police records to prove otherwise, and what I learned about his criminal record from my colleagues in Seattle would send terror through your veins. At this stage, I'm staying open to multiple theories, including that Marianne was indeed trying to protect Alex—to protect your entire family. As to the description, I do have some thoughts on that."

"Marianne leaked it," Mac interrupted her.

She gave him a one-finger salute. "Yep. Not a bad play if you think about it. Kidnap, tie up the kid, and then return to Der Keller as a witness who just so happened to see Alex leaving with a suspect matching Forest's description."

"Do you think that's possible?" I asked.

"Not only possible. I think it's probable." She paused and flipped through her notebook. "Yep. Here it is. An unidentified woman placed a call to our office to report the kidnapping at twelve forty-five this afternoon."

Her cell phone buzzed. She removed it from her khaki shorts and glanced at the screen. "I need to take this. Why don't you all, including Alex, head home. We're going to need to do a sweep of your house, Hans. Check for prints. That sort of thing. It might take a while."

"That's okay. Do whatever you need. It's unlocked," Hans replied.

"I'd suggest you stay together in one place. I'll be in touch as soon as I can." She left to reassign her troops.

"We can go to my condo," Mac offered. He tugged on his wet shirt. "I could probably stand to change. At least you might want me to."

"Or you can come to my place," I offered, pointing to the grassy hill above us. "It's only a few blocks away."

"*Ja.* I zink zat would be nice for Alex," Ursula said. "Mac, you can go home and change and zen come meet us at Sloan's, *ja?*"

"It is so nice ziz afternoon we can sit on your deck and

196

be together. Ziz will be good for all of us, *ja*?" Otto caught my eye.

"That's decided," Hans said. He and Mac helped Alex stand up. Not that he needed help, but I appreciated seeing him wrapped in their strong arms.

We made our way past what seemed to be a wall of police officers. I couldn't take my eyes off of Alex.

He's okay.

He's okay. I repeated those two words over and over again on the short walk to my cottage, trying to block out the noise around us, and using Sally's trick again to center myself in the moment. I took notice of the police vehicles and officers patrolling the area, goats roaming on the hillside, the trickling sound of the waterwheel on the golf course, the smell of blooming jasmine and wisteria, and the trot of the horse-drawn *Bier* wagon resuming tours through the village. When we made it to the cottage, I reminded myself to keep breathing while I let everyone inside.

"I'm going to run to the condo and change," Mac announced. "Need anything?"

"I don't think so. Does anything sound good for lunch, Alex?"

His cheeks were an unusual shade of gray, and his hands continued to tremble. "I don't know. I don't think I'm hungry, Mom."

"How about if we go sit on the deck and soak up some sun?" Hans opened the slider and gave me a knowing look.

"*Ja, ja.* Zis is a good idea," Ursula said with a warm smile. "We will put together a late lunch and bring it outside in a while."

Otto joined Hans and Alex on the deck.

"Text me if you need anything. I'll be back in few," Mac said.

"What if we make *Frikadellen*?" Ursula asked, moving into the kitchen with me. "It used to be his favorite when he was little. Do you have beef and pork?"

"I do." Fortunately I had stocked up on groceries before the weekend, knowing that the stores would be packed with tourists.

"Good. Let's get it started, and I can make some of my German potato salad to go with ze *Frikadellen*."

She rolled up her sleeves and got to work mixing ground beef and pork with spices, breadcrumbs, egg yolks, and chopped onion. *Frikadellen* was like a combination of meatloaf and American burgers. Instead of molding the mixture into a loaf pan, she would create patties, which she would flatten, pan fry, and serve on *Brötchen,* German rolls. It was the perfect picnic food and would go nicely with a tangy potato salad.

"Want me to peel the potatoes?" I asked. Having a task, something tangible to concentrate on, was probably a good idea.

"*Ja,* zat would be good." Ursula kept her gaze focused on the counter. "I wish you would have told me about zis, Sloan. I understand why you did not. I know zat we must regain your trust, but it breaks my heart to know zat you have been hurting and scared and alone."

"Thanks." I scrubbed the potatoes in cold water. "In hindsight, I wish the same. I should have come to you. Marianne was so convincing. I believed her. I believed that she had my best interests at heart even when my rational brain told me not to. Why didn't I trust that? I feel so stupid. I feel like she conned me."

"Maybe. Or maybe she did have a reason." Ursula's voice was calm and soothing. "If she is ze same woman I met many years ago, zen I must believe she does have your best interests at heart. Ze woman I remember loved you dearly. Zat cannot have changed."

"Unless she's crazy."

"Well, we know zat Forest is real, *ja*? We know zat he tried to steal Der Keller from Otto and me back many years ago now, and we know zat he has been in jail and zat ze police have reason to believe he could be dangerous. Zis is something. Zis makes me believe Marianne may have had a reason to take Alex. I do not know what it could be, but I will stay open until we hear from ze police." She rolled the meat mixture into large balls. "Sloan, I hope zat you can believe me when I tell you zat you are not responsible for what happened to Alex. Ziz is not your fault, my dear."

Tears welled in my eyes. I brushed them away with the back of my hand. "Nothing makes sense. I hate feeling like this. I feel so out of control and like the only thing I can do is sit by and watch terrible things happen to everyone I love."

"*Ja,* it is so terrible. I'm sorry for what you have had to see, but zis is why I want you to know zat it is not your fault." She placed the balls on a cutting board and used a spatula to flatten them. "Sloan, my darling daughter, will you look at me, please?"

I met her gaze.

Her eyes were misty, too. "Zis is not your fault, okay? Alex is fine. We are all fine, and we are together. You are part of zis family and families support each other. We will survive zis together, *ja*?"

I swallowed hard. "Yeah, thank you, Ursula. It means a lot to have you here. I was feeling pretty alone this weekend."

"You are never alone. You are a Krause. Once a Krause, always a Krause. We will always be here for you, Sloan. Always. No matter what happens with Marianne and no matter what happens with Mac, you will always be my daughter. My only daughter."

Those words finally pushed me over the edge. More tears flowed. I had cried more in the last few days than in my entire adult life. It felt cathartic and necessary. I didn't attempt to stuff them away, I embraced them. My shoulders heaved. Salt stung my skin.

Ursula wrapped me in a hug. "I know, I know, it is unbearable to imagine our children in danger. He is okay," she whispered gently as she stroked my hair. "We will survive zis together."

Her use of the word *survive* had new meaning now. I was beginning to better understand her choices for fleeing Germany and for making an entirely fresh start here in Leavenworth. She had done it for her boys, out of the deepest desire to give them a better life. Any residual anger I might have been harboring for her not being truthful for so long fell away as we held each other in my kitchen that smelled like onions and sizzling meat. Ursula was my family, and I had never been happier to know that I belonged to her.

CHAPTER

TWENTY-ONE

"OH HEY, SORRY TO interrupt." Mac walked into the kitchen wearing a fresh black V-neck T-shirt and a pair of shorts. Since our separation, he had gone through a physical transformation, losing the pudge of a beer belly and defining his muscles by spending extra time lifting weights at the gym. It was good to see him looking fit and healthy. Yet more confirmation that our split had been the best choice for both of us.

Ursula kissed my cheek and released me from her embrace.

I dabbed my eyes with a dish towel. "Did you see the police out there? Is there any more news?" As I asked the question, I wondered what had happened to Officer Downs. He had taken Garrett and the Nitro team with him to search for Alex at the high school. Thinking about it reminded me that I should probably text Garrett to let him know that everything was okay. He was probably worried sick.

"Nothing yet. They thought they had a sighting, but it

turned out to be a dead end." He leaned over his mom's shoulder. "Are you making what I think you're making?"

Ursula swatted his hand. "For Alex. Zis is Alex's special meal. You will be served last, after Alex has had as much as he wants."

Mac raised his hands in surrender. "Fair enough." He pointed to the mound of potato skins in the sink. "German potato salad, too. Lucky kid." He reached for my hand, his voice thick with emotion. "Lucky us."

I caught his meaning. "Lucky us."

He massaged my thumb and then let my hand go. "What can I do? Put me to work."

Ursula pointed to the fridge. "You can get drinks for everyone. Sloan, I'm guessing you must have some beer, but if not, we will send Mac to Der Keller for some growlers."

"No need. We're all set. Otto taught me well. I never have a fridge without at least two growlers of beer. You never know when company might come, right?" I repeated a phrase I had heard often from Otto over the years. One of the many perks of working in the craft beer industry was that my refrigerator was rarely without enough beer for guests. When Mac and I were together, we had a separate fridge at the farmhouse that we kept stocked with Der Keller's ales and pantry staples for the impromptu dinner parties that Mac was notorious for hosting at the last minute. It used to drive me crazy when he would call with an hour's notice to tell me he was bringing six beer reps home for dinner. Now it seemed more endearing, and it was not lost on me that I'd continued stocking the fridge after our split.

"*Ja*. It is our *Gastfreundschaft*—if we welcome you into our home, it is a great honor and means you are like family and we must have ze beer." Ursula grinned. "Do you have a large fry pan?"

I got her set up on the stove, microwaved the potatoes, and whisked vinegar, sugar, and water together for the brine that would go over the warm potatoes. Ursula's traditional recipe also included hearty chunks of bacon and fresh herbs.

Mac rounded up pint glasses, growlers, and juice for Alex. I started bacon frying next to Ursula's sizzling pan of pork and beef patties. Soon our late lunch/early dinner was ready to serve. We took everything outside and gathered around my picnic table, a housewarming gift from Hans. The view from the deck was breathtaking. I could see glimpses of the lush green grasses of the fairways that twisted past cascading waterfalls and dollhouse-sized Bavarian buildings on the golf course. There was a peekaboo view of the Wenatchee through a clearing of evergreens on Blackbird Island. I'd outfitted the deck with outdoor speakers and bird feeders to accompany the hanging flower baskets the previous owners had left for me. It had become my personal oasis. I turned on some classical music on low as I joined everyone.

Otto stood. "I would like to offer a toast." He held up his pint glass.

Everyone followed suit.

"To my wonderful family. You have no idea how much you mean to us." He glanced at Ursula, who nodded in encouragement. "Zis terrible zing with Alex has reminded me how important family is for all of us, and with zat, I need to tell you ze truth."

"The truth?" Hans shot a confused scowl to Mac and then to me.

Otto sighed. "First let us toast to our wonderful family."

We clinked glasses.

I had a feeling I knew what he was going to say. I hadn't expected it to happen like this, but it was time. Holding Otto and Ursula's secret had been weighing on me. Since we were already deep in the throes of emotions, why not rip off the Band-Aid now?

Otto rested his pint glass on the table. "You see, we have not been honest with you boys." He spoke to Mac and Hans. "When your mother and I came to Washington, we were looking for a new start. A new life."

"Yeah, you've told us that story at least a thousand times," Mac teased.

Otto shook his head. "Not zis part, my son. I hope when you hear what we have to tell you, you can forgive us. Almost losing Alex today has shown me zat we cannot keep zis inside any longer. It is well past time we have told you ze truth."

Ursula clutched his arm for support.

Mac and Hans both sat with their legs crossed. Despite their differences in age and interests, their shared genetic code meant their body language often mirrored one another. Alex stared at me, downing his juice and reaching for the container to fill his glass again.

Otto continued. "You see, zis is not easy for us to share. It is a secret we have been keeping for too long, but ze time, it is now to share it with you."

A hushed silence fell over the table.

Otto inhaled through his nostrils before he continued. "Our family, it is not what you zink it is. You see, in Germany my family name, it became associated with ze Nazis. Krause is not our family name—it is vom Rath. You see, ziz was a very difficult time in Deutschland. Zere was major strife. It was after ze war, and Germany, it was trying to re-build itself, and zen we had ze Cold War with ze Red Army. Zere were kidnappings and terror attacks. People were afraid. And zey should be. Ze government was searching for many Nazis who escaped punishment after ze war. Villagers were turning in friends and family when names of assumed Nazis were released in ze papers." He stopped, sighed, took a long drink of his beer, then continued. "You see, I am Friedrich vom Rath, and your mother, she is Helga vom Rath."

"I don't understand," Mac interrupted. He had uncrossed his legs and sat up, leaning across the long, smooth wood table, as if trying to get a better look at his father's face.

"My uncle Ernst vom Rath was accused of being a Nazi. He was not. It was a simple mistake. A shared name. It happened many, many times. We tried to explain to our friends and neighbors in ze motherland zat we had nothing to do with ze Nazis, but times were different. People were afraid. We worried about you boys. How would we raise you with ziz worry and fear? So we made a very hard decision to leave everyone and everything in Germany and come here to start a new life as Otto and Ursula Krause." He continued with the story of his past that he and Ursula had already shared with me. He went on to explain, with Ursula's help, their interactions with Forest and Marianne and how Forest had nearly stolen Der Keller from them.

When Forest and Marianne had arrived in Leavenworth, they had claimed that they were sister and brother. I was just a young child, so my memories of the short time I'd spent in the village with Marianne were fuzzy at best. According to what I had learned from my caseworker, Sally, and Otto and Ursula had confirmed, Forest had made them a very lucrative offer to purchase Der Keller. They were new to the country, and this was long before Der Keller was the successful operation it was today. Forest's cash offer was tempting. They had nearly signed the deal, which would have had disastrous consequences. Forest had no intention of giving them a dime. He preyed on immigrants like Otto and Ursula who weren't well-versed in English yet. The contract was fake. Had they signed it, they would have handed their legacy over to him without any compensation. Sally had learned that Forest had a pattern of trying to swindle property and businesses from unsuspecting families like the Krauses.

When Otto finished telling a story I was already familiar with, everyone remained silent. Tears poured from Ursula's bloodshot eyes, but she didn't bother to dab them.

Hans spoke first. "Thank you for telling us. It's a lot to take in. I'm sure I'm going to have a lot of questions for you, but it explains some holes from our past that I always wondered about. For now, what I want to say to you is that ultimately I couldn't care less what happened in the past. I'm a Krause through and through because of you. You have been amazing parents and given us such a great life here. I couldn't ask for anything else." He stood up and hugged his parents.

Mac took a long sip of beer. "I always suspected you two were secret agents or something. Tell me the truth, are you actually spies?"

Ursula choked back her tears. She laughed and winked at her oldest son. "Could be."

Everyone got up and hugged and kissed. It was like a family reunion, only with a family we already knew.

Alex appeared to be the most confused. "I have lots of questions, but all of a sudden I'm starving. Can we eat?"

Ursula clapped. "*Ja, ja*. Let's eat."

We toasted again, and everyone devoured the meal. Maybe it was the stress or the relief, but I found myself taking second helpings of the potato salad and Ursula's *Frikadellen*.

The conversation returned to the Krauses' past. At first I had wondered if this news on top of the afternoon's event would be too much for Alex, but I quickly realized the opposite was true. He peppered Otto and Ursula with questions about their village in Germany, their life before coming to America, and what the transition had been like.

"How did you get used to being called different names?" he asked, taking a huge bite of the roll, stuffed with grilled patties and beautifully charred onions.

"It was easy," Otto replied. "We picked names zat we loved. We decided it would be easier to remember zat way."

"And was it?" Alex asked. Color had returned to his cheeks. His hands were less shaky.

"No. From ze moment we boarded ze plane to come to America, we became Otto and Ursula Krause. We never spoke our family names again. Not even to each other. It would be too hard. Too many memories and too much of a chance zat we might slip. When Sloan came to us, zat was ze first time I had heard my given name in over forty years."

"Wow." Alex took a big gulp of juice. "My Oma and Opa have a secret identity. None of the guys will believe it. Can I tell them that you're secret agents or spies or something?"

Ursula handed him a napkin. "*Ja*. I zink you should."

"Do you think they'll believe you were nearly killed?" Mac asked, his tone still on edge.

Alex glanced toward the green, where two police officers remained on patrol. "Since the village looks like a scene from a war movie right now, I'd say yeah. I think they'll believe it."

"You're going to have a story to tell and will be the most popular kid in town for a while," Hans warned. "Get ready for fame and fortune."

"It's not exactly how I imagined fame and fortune." Alex scowled.

Hans ruffled his hair. "It never is, kid. It never is."

We continued our meal. The conversation was lively and full of stories from the Krauses' childhood in Germany and early years in Leavenworth.

"Do you remember, Ursula, when everyone would tease us about Hershey's chocolate? We would ask zem for chocolate at ze grocery store, and zey would give us Hershey bars. Ursula would say, 'No, no, zis is not chocolate.'"

"I still say zat." She smiled. "Now I am so grateful for imported German chocolates, but back zen, it was hard and very expensive to get zings sent over."

"And zen you had your first *Kaffeeklatsch*. You remember you sent out ze invitations, and no one had any idea what zey were being invited to? Zey assumed it was a formal event, not just an offer to sit around our dining room table, drink coffee, and gossip."

Ursula chuckled. "Now April Ablin hosts a weekly *Kaffeeklatsch* for ze chamber. Zings have changed for sure."

A knock sounded on the door, bringing a new, tense silence over the table.

"I'll get it." I stood up.

Mac was on his feet, too. "I'll go with you."

Chief Meyers stood on the front porch. "I've got some news."

"Do you want to come in?" I offered.

She declined. "No. There's a lot to be done, but I wanted to make sure you heard this from me first. There's video evidence of Marianne being taken at gunpoint by a man matching Forest's description."

"When?" My stomach dropped.

"Earlier this afternoon. It must have been right after she took Alex."

Mac frowned. "Where's the video from?"

"Hotel Vierter Stock. Their cameras caught Marianne being led out of the lobby. She appears to be in distress."

"What does that mean?" I asked. "Isn't the highway shut down? They can't have gone far, right?"

"Well, that's the thing. We're not entirely sure." She hesitated for a moment.

"How can you not be sure?" Mac raised his voice. "Our son was kidnapped."

"I know. I understand. The problem is the timing." Her walkie-talkie crackled. She turned it off. "We have reason to believe that they may have had help getting out of town from someone on the inside. It's still too early to know, but there's a chance that someone on our side let them through the barricades. If that's the case, who knows how far they could have gone. We have alerted the state police as well as our colleagues in Idaho and Oregon."

"So what you're saying is that they got away?" Mac fumed. "There are dozens of officers in the village, and you're telling us that the woman who took our son is gone?"

"No. We don't know that for sure, but it's one possibility." She motioned to two officers I didn't recognize. "I'm putting a new detail on you. They'll be here around the clock until we make headway."

"That's it?" Mac practically spit as he spoke. "A couple officers on Sloan's porch, and we're just supposed to pretend like everything's normal?"

I understood why Mac was upset. I was, too, but fighting with the chief wasn't going to solve anything.

"What should we do?" I asked, taking a different approach. "Is Alex safe here? I mean, was Marianne right—should we get out of town? Go to Seattle? Somewhere farther away?"

"No. I don't think you're in any danger. I think the best move is for you to sit tight. If Marianne or Forest show up anywhere, we'll get them. I'm very confident that they aren't in the village, and we can keep you safest here. We'll keep protection on you and the rest of the family, and everyone in town is on the lookout. I think leaving is a mistake. I've known you both my entire career, you can trust that I have your best interests at heart." She waited for us to respond.

I spoke first. "I do trust that, really."

Mac shuffled his feet. "Yeah, I guess you're right. The village is on high alert."

"Exactly. My recommendation is to resume your normal activities. I think that might be best for Alex, too. Sitting around and waiting for the worst to happen isn't going to do anyone any good. My team isn't going to let a stone go unturned. I give you my personal word on that." She gave us a curt nod. "As I said, I have work to do. I'll be in touch when I can."

I watched her leave. The relief that I'd felt knowing that Alex was okay began to evaporate. If Marianne and Forest were at large, that meant that we were still in danger.

CHAPTER

TWENTY-TWO

"WE MUST STICK TOGETHER," Otto insisted after Mac filled him in on Chief Meyers's report. "Maybe you should come stay with us for a while? Sloan, you, too. Zere is plenty of room at ze house. We can be together. And be safe."

"There's no need for that," Mac replied. "We're being assigned individual protection. Chief Meyers has two police officers posted outside. She's going to send a team to your house and keep watch on Hans's place, too, as well as have extra officers at Der Keller and Nitro. I think we're going to be surrounded. The chief thinks it's best to try and resume our normal activities and let her lead the investigation."

"Easier said than done," Hans said. He stacked empty plates and divided up the remaining beer in the growlers. "It sounds like you're thinking of going back to work this afternoon?"

"I am." Mac took a pair of aviator sunglasses from his pocket and put them on. "At first I thought it was a crazy idea, but now I'm leaning toward thinking Chief Meyers is right. It might do us good to get back on the horse, so to speak."

"You've never been on a horse in your life," Hans teased.

"I don't know, that kind of sounds good to me," Alex chimed in. "It's almost worse to replay things over and over again. I'd rather be busy and get my mind off it." He twisted a strand of hair as he spoke. I recognized the self-soothing technique from when he was younger.

He was definitely my kid.

Mac caught my eye.

I shrugged, signaling that I agreed.

"Okay, then, there's plenty to do at Der Keller, especially with the highway shut down. We're likely to see a Sunday evening rush. I can put you to work." Mac placed his arm around Alex's shoulder. "Of course, be forewarned I'm not letting you out of my sight."

"Yeah. Fine." Alex gathered the dishes that Hans had stacked.

"You're sure?" Hans looked to me.

"Honestly, I was thinking the same thing. I might wander over to Nitro. I left in such a rush. I should go check in with Garrett and Kat. I feel terrible that I took off with you and haven't let them know that Alex is safe."

"Okay." Hans didn't sound convinced, but he helped clear the table.

Otto and Ursula decided to go to the brewery with Mac and Alex.

"I'll stop by the workshop and then head over later," Hans said, loading the dishwasher. "You want me to walk you to Nitro?"

"That's not necessary."

"Let me rephrase that—I'm walking you to Nitro."

"Okay."

"And Alex and I are staying here tonight," Mac insisted.

"Deal." The truth was I wanted to be by Alex's side, and I knew that some level of normalcy right now was probably important to his long-term emotional well-being.

Hans wrapped me in a giant hug. When he released me, he stared into my eyes and spoke with authority. "Sloan, you are not to leave Nitro until Alex and I come get you, deal?"

"Deal." I didn't have the energy to argue. I was convinced from Chief Meyers's dejected mood that Forest and Marianne were long gone. That didn't mean that there wasn't a lingering threat, but I wasn't worried about either of them making a move tonight.

On the walk to Nitro, I broached the subject of Alex's mental health to Hans. "What do you think I should do? Should I get him an emergency counseling appointment tomorrow? Should we take him to Seattle?"

"He seems okay, Sloan."

"But the long-term impact of this kind of trauma could be huge. I don't want him to close himself off."

Hans paused. "Who are we talking about? You or Alex?"

His words struck a chord.

"I guess both of us. I know about trauma, and I don't want that for him."

"None of us do, and you're right, counseling is probably a good idea, but I would follow his lead. I don't think you need an emergency session or to race off to Seattle." He waited to say more until we had passed a group of tourists heading to the golf range with rented clubs and neon balls. "I think we all need to rally around him. I'll check in with him. You do the same. He has a more solid sense of who he is than half the guys I know who are my age. Trust him. He'll tell you what he needs."

"You think so?" I gnawed on the inside of my cheek.

"I'm sure of it." Hans cleared his throat. "But what about you?"

"What about me?" I noticed that some normalcy had returned to the village as we got closer to Nitro. The roadblocks were still in place and there were police officers at nearly every corner, but the frantic search earlier had evolved into what appeared to be more like a militaristic state. Tourists had returned to shops and restaurants, since they weren't going anywhere tonight.

"Don't pretend with me, Sloan. You can't blow this one off. It's too much."

"Nothing feels real yet. Everything is a strange blur. It's been that way since Marianne showed up. I want answers. I want to know who killed Sara. I want to know why Forest killed my mother and if there's any truth to the idea that he's here for me. Now I'm wondering if Marianne made it up. Or if he's really after her and she used me as a shield."

"That's fair." He waited for me to say more.

"I don't know. I'm with Alex. The only thing that makes sense right now is trying to carve out a little slice of normal. I think a couple hours at the pub will be good for me. That and sleep. I don't think I've slept for days."

"I can live with that." Hans stopped at Nitro's patio. "Call me if you need anything, okay? I'll swing by here before I head over to Der Keller."

"Thanks, Hans." I kissed his cheek.

He pressed his hands on my face and leaned down to kiss

my forehead. "You're not alone, Sloan. You are part of this family—forever. The crazy German Krauses—who aren't really the Krauses—you're one of us, like it or not."

"I like it." My voice caught. "I've never been happier to be a Krause."

He took off. I thought about the meaning of names. It hadn't been until I married Mac that I felt like I belonged. One positive thing had come out of this horrific weekend, and that was that the Krauses were my family, no matter what.

Nitro's front door was propped open, but the closed sign hung from the hook and our sidewalk chalkboard menu blocked the entrance. I was surprised that Garrett and Kat hadn't reopened the tasting room given that people were milling around again.

They were both seated at the bar when I came in. "Hey, guys," I said, trying not to startle them.

Kat nearly fell off her stool. She raced over and hugged me. "Sloan, we were so worried. We were looking everywhere for Alex."

"We found him." I felt terrible for not texting. It had crossed my mind when Ursula and I had started making lunch and then I had completely forgotten.

Garrett nodded. "Don't worry. We heard. Chief Meyers let everyone know, and we figured you were probably with your family. That's good news. Really good news."

"What happened?" Kat asked.

"She might not want to talk about it." Garrett voiced what I was already thinking.

"I'll give you the condensed version," I said, and filled them in. As I relayed the strange twist of events, they seemed even more unbelievable.

"Sounds like you could use a pint." Garrett stood and walked behind the bar. "We were contemplating what to do. With the highway shut down, we've had a bunch of tourists stopping by to see if we're open, but it felt wrong to open."

"No, I think we should." I nodded to the sidewalk, where a steady of stream of tourists passed by. "I don't want a pint. I want to work for a while and focus on something else. In fact Chief Meyers said it was the best thing for us to do—to try and resume a normal routine for a little while."

"Are you sure?"

"Positive." I pointed to the door. "Are you both ready? I can flip the sign right now."

"I'm up for it as long as you are, but . . ." Garrett didn't finish his thought. He sounded unsure.

I didn't wait for Kat to respond. I propped open the front doors and turned the sign to OPEN. Within minutes, people streamed into the pub. I spent the next two hours pouring pints and taking guests on impromptu brewery tours.

As I stopped to grab empty glasses at one of the tables on the patio, I noticed Bozeman and three friends were downing pints. They had pushed two bistro tables together. Their stuff was everywhere—baseball hats, sunglasses, keys, and empty pint glasses. Did they intend to move in for the night? They appeared to be camped out with nowhere to go.

"Boozeman, Boozeman," his crew chanted, urging him to chug a pint.

"You know, gentlemen, craft beer is meant to be savored," I said, picking up a couple of empties from their table. "Usually the price point alone is enough to discourage downing a pint."

Bozeman waved me off. "Nah. We're celebrating. This is mug chug night."

"I think you're at the wrong place for that." I wasn't about to encourage him and his friends to engage in a chugging contest.

One of his friends booed.

"It's cool. She's cool." Bozeman defended me.

I wasn't in need of backup. I'd had plenty of experience kicking frat guys out of Nitro. Our policy on drinking for pleasure versus getting drunk was clear and nonnegotiable. Garrett and I had a no-tolerance policy when it came to overserving. Much of that was dictated by state liquor codes. Any violation could lead to losing our license. But it was more than that for both of us. I meant what I had said to Bozeman and his friends. Craft beer was just that—a craft. A labor of love and artistry. Watching someone gulp down weeks' worth of work brought us no pleasure.

"Actually, it's not cool. I'll have to cut you guys off after this round."

Bozeman rolled his eyes. "Fine. No chugging. We're just trying to blow off some steam. It's been an insane weekend."

I couldn't argue on that.

"Didn't your kid go missing or something?" Bozeman asked, his words slurred together slightly as he swayed in his chair. I was definitely cutting him off.

"He did, but he's been found, and he's fine."

"That's good news. Glad to hear it. The hotel was a crazy train today. There are cops swarming the place again." He pinched the skin between his finger and thumb.

"Haven't they been there all weekend with the murder investigation?"

"No one said that it was murder. It could have been an accident, for all we know." He shifted in his chair. "That's what the staff is saying. They think it was an accident."

I considered pushing back. Chief Meyers had been clear from the start that Sara had been murdered, and Bozeman himself had told me during the parade that he thought Jay was involved. But maybe a few beers had loosened him up. I wondered what else he might have seen.

"How's the investigation going?"

"Why would I know?"

"No reason. Since you're in charge of the grounds, I figured you likely see a lot."

That inflated his ego. "True. I do. I see everything. I know everyone's secrets."

His buddies laughed.

I had a different reaction. Could Bozeman have seen something that might give me a clue about Marianne's disappearance? "Did you see what happened this afternoon?"

"I don't know what you mean." He flipped over his empty pint glass and tapped it on the edge of the table.

"That's going to crack." I took it from his hands. "Apparently one of your guests, Marianne—the woman I was with—was in some sort of trouble." Chief Meyers hadn't told me not to share news, but I figured it was best to stay vague.

"What kind of trouble?"

I stacked his glass with the other empties. "I'm not sure. Maybe that's why there are more police on-site now?"

"Oh yeah. That could be." Bozeman looked relieved.

"You didn't see her, though?"

"Not that I remember. There were a ton of people

coming and going. Everyone checked out and then when the police shut down the highway, everyone checked back in." He drank a hearty sip of beer. "You should talk to Vienna. I saw her and that woman together this morning. I figured she was laying into Vienna for not having enough towels or something."

"Vienna and Marianne were arguing today?"

"Yeah. It's nothing new. If you're in the hospitality business, you know that irate customers come with the territory. It's the job. That's what Jay tells us all the time." Bozeman reached for his friend's beer and took a drink. "He's one to talk, though. That dude doesn't have a leg to stand on. He's a creeper."

"What do you mean by that?"

I could tell that Bozeman's friends were tiring of my questions.

"Jay has more run-ins with guests than half the staff. Not to mention how handsy he is with the female staff. I'm surprised someone didn't try to kill him. He had it coming to him more than Sara."

"Speaking of Sara, can you think of any reason she could have been killed?"

One of Bozeman's friends finished his pint and held it up for a refill.

I ignored him and waited for Bozeman to answer.

"You want to know what I think? I think she saw something she wasn't supposed to and that got her killed. As to who? Go talk to my boss." Bozeman proceeded to chug his beer. When he was done, he slapped a twenty-dollar bill on the table and turned to his friends. "Let's go, boys."

Bozeman thought that Jay had killed Sara, and he claimed that Marianne and Vienna had been fighting earlier. I knew that none of the men in my life—Alex, Hans, Mac, and Garrett—would like it, but I had to get over to Hotel Vierter Stock.

CHAPTER

TWENTY-THREE

"HEY, GARRETT, I NEED to go to the Vierter Stock," I announced when I returned to the bar with a tray of empty glasses.

"What? Why?" Garrett set down a towel and waved his hand. "I don't think that's a good idea. Aren't you supposed to stick around?"

"Yes, but there's been a development." I told him about my conversation with Bozeman.

"Sloan, I don't want to sound like an overprotective boss or friend, but think about what you've just been through."

"That's exactly why I need to go. It's still light outside, and Chief Meyers doesn't think that Forest is still in town. Plus she assigned me extra protection." I pointed to the patio. "Look, there are more police in the village right now than during every festival combined."

Garrett shoved his hands into his shorts pockets and shuffled his feet. He stared outside and then back at me again.

"I don't really want to let you out of my sight. I know that sounds corny, and I know that you can take care of yourself, but—" He didn't finish his sentence.

"Exactly. I'm a grown woman, Garrett. I know the risks, and I also know that I will have a sea of police officers surrounding my every step." Actually, I wondered again what had happened to Officer Downs. Maybe Chief Meyers figured I wasn't in any direct danger after the huge scene of searching the village.

He hesitated. "If you're sure?"

"I'm sure. I have to try and figure this out. Marianne's arrival and Sara's death can't be a coincidence. I'm becoming more and more convinced that she could have had a hand in the housekeeper's killing."

"Isn't that even more reason to leave it to the police?" Garrett suggested.

"The police are focused on finding Marianne right now. I won't be long. If I'm not back in an hour, come find me. Okay?"

"Okay." He couldn't stop me.

I made a beeline for the front door and ran smack into Officer Downs. "Speak of the devil. I was just talking about you."

"Talking about me, or trying to shrug your detail?" He cocked his head and gave me a sideways glance. There was no chance I could make it past his burly body. He filled the entire door frame.

"No, I'm glad to see you. I wondered if Chief Meyers decided I didn't need extra protection."

"She did not." Officer Downs's lips turned down.

"I need to run over to Hotel Vierter Stock."

"Then I'll be with you." He motioned for me to pass him, waving at two other uniformed officers, who followed me to the hotel. The garden seating area was buzzing with tourists who had had their return plans canceled. Guests had spread out grocery store picnics and were playing cornhole and bocce in the grass.

I spotted Vienna carrying a stack of towels to a room upstairs.

In the lobby I asked for Jay. The front desk clerk told me they would check to see if he was still on the premises. While I waited, Eleanor and Russ came into the cavernous lobby, holding hands. They didn't see me. Eleanor made a beeline to the front desk.

"I've had a break-in! Two cases of my most expensive wine and five hundred dollars cash is missing." She sounded irate. Russ stood next to her, his hand on the small of her back.

So I hadn't been wrong about their affair.

The front desk clerk tried to appease her. "I'm so sorry. Can you please fill out this report and then we can have staff and one of the police officers take a look at your room?"

"A piece of paper isn't going to help." Eleanor refused to take the report that the clerk offered her. "I don't know what kind of operation you're running here. My entire weekend has been a disaster. Sara's murder. The police swarming the building. Not being allowed to leave. And now, even with an army of cops around, my things were stolen. This is ridiculous."

Jay appeared in the lobby. His staff waved him over to help. I watched as he strolled over to Eleanor, who was becoming more vocal. Russ left her side and went to have a conversation with one of the officers posted at the front doors.

"How can I help?" Jay asked with smooth confidence.

"My room was broken into!" Eleanor yelled. A small group had gathered round to witness the scene. "Thousands of dollars of wine is missing, along with cash! This is completely unacceptable."

Jay snapped his fingers at the young staffer behind the desk. "Call the manager on duty. Let's take care of this."

"How are you going to take care of it?" Eleanor shot back. "We're not allowed to leave town. I was planning to curl up in my room tonight. Now I don't feel comfortable setting foot in there again. It's so disturbing to think that someone was in my private things and stole the most expensive cases of wine. Whoever did this knew what they were doing. You have a thief amongst your staff!" She was dressed in a slinky red skirt and low-cut tank top, not exactly curl-up-with-a-book attire.

Russ and one of the police officers joined Eleanor. "You're going to have a serious lawsuit on your hands," Russ threatened. "Obviously this hotel has no regard for guest security and safety."

Jay lost a little bit of his swagger. "Listen, we're going to do everything we can for you." He addressed the police officer. "My manager on duty is on his way to the room. Can you escort them back to their room to make sure it's secure and take an initial report? I'll notify Chief Meyers."

"You expect us to stay in a room that's been ransacked?" Eleanor reached for Russ's hand.

"Unfortunately, I don't have any other open rooms. With the highway shutdown, every room is booked. I wish there was more I could do for you. I can offer you a complimentary stay."

Eleanor glared at Jay. "I don't want a complimentary stay. I want to feel safe, and I want my money and wine back."

Jay gave her solemn nod. "I understand, and I assure you we're doing everything to get to the bottom of this."

"You're not doing enough," Russ added.

"Let's go take a look at the room and get a police report going," Jay suggested, motioning to the police officer.

Russ threw out his hand. "Not you. We'll go with him." His hand traveled to Eleanor's hip as they took off with the officer.

Jay whispered something to his front desk clerk before trying to smooth things over with the other guests who had gathered. "Sorry about that, folks. I assure you that we have everything under control. Please feel free to help yourself to complimentary snacks in the garden. Our kitchen staff has put together a Bavarian smorgasbord for you this evening— meats, cheeses, pickles, pretzels, mustards, and of course our signature Black Forest torte and red berry pudding. We've set out lawn games and have tons of movies, puzzles, and books for you."

Vienna entered the lobby balancing a tray of pastries. She stopped short at the sight of Jay.

He gave her a wicked grin that made the hair on my arms stand at attention. "Ah! Here's our beautiful housekeeping staff with dessert now. Vienna, why don't you take that outside? Everyone please go help yourselves and enjoy the fresh mountain air."

A few people followed after Vienna.

I continued to watch Jay, who worked the room like a

politician, shaking hands with guests and putting on an air that everything was fine.

It wasn't.

My theory that Sara had been responsible for the thefts at Hotel Vierter Stock had just been proven false by Eleanor. Sara was dead, and the guest room break-ins continued. That meant that her murder couldn't have been because she had gotten caught stealing. I couldn't blame Eleanor for being upset, and I was inclined to agree with her. Whoever had been breaking into rooms must be on staff. That meant that Vienna was the most likely culprit. Had I made a mistake in feeling sorry for her? Could she be a killer?

CHAPTER
TWENTY-FOUR

JAY FINISHED WORKING THE room and noticed me. "Hi, Sloan, to what do I owe the pleasure? Two visits in two days?" He sounded casual, as if nothing had happened.

"Can we talk somewhere more private?" I glanced around at the crowd of guests still milling about after Eleanor's explosion. "It seems like people are bit on edge."

He bristled, but quickly recovered. "Sure, let's go sit over here."

Jay flipped on the golden chandelier and pointed to a chair on the opposite side of the impressive conference table. "Have a seat. What can I do for you?"

"It's about Sara's murder." I got right to the point.

He stood and walked over to a buffet near the book-shelves. There was a large assortment of travel books and hiking, snowshoeing, hunting, and fishing guides. A silver pitcher of water and a stack of clear glasses sat on the buffet. "Do you want a glass of water?"

"No thanks. I'm fine."

He poured himself a drink, but didn't return to the table. "What about Sara's murder?"

"I've heard from more than one source that you may have been involved." I decided I had nothing to lose at this point.

Jay nearly dropped the glass on the table. Water spilled from its top like a tsunami. He didn't bother to wipe it up. "Who? Who's been saying that?"

"Everything that I've learned has been in confidence. I'm not going to tell you who I heard it from, but the rumor is circulating through the village. It's not just one person." I tried to gauge his reaction as I pressed on. "I know it's none of my business, but I'm sure you heard about my son Alex's abduction earlier. It's personal now."

"Sorry about your kid. They got him back, though, didn't they?"

"Yes." I tried not to replay the memory of April rushing into Nitro to tell me Alex was missing. "There's a chance that Sara's murder is connected. I don't know what Chief Meyers has told you. That's why I wanted to come straight to you and not get caught up in rumors."

He picked a book on backcountry trails off the shelf and leafed through it. "You know, I don't even know what books we have in here. I ordered a crate of used books to fill these shelves when I bought the place. I don't know if anyone reads them."

Was he stalling?

"Look, I'll tell you the truth." He returned the book to its spot, with the spine facing inward. I wanted to go fix it. "I have an idea how those rumors started."

"How?" I was surprised that it was going to be this easy to get him to talk.

"Sara was upset with me. She threatened a lawsuit, actually."

This was huge news. Jay was admitting that Sara had confronted him—why?

"She claimed that I was being inappropriate with some of the women on staff. You can't joke about anything these days. Everything is taken out of context. I'm not always the most politically correct boss, but I wasn't doing anything out of line." His movements were sharp and stiff, like he was trying to contain his frustration.

"How did the lawsuit come into play?" I remained seated.

"She told me I had to stop flirting with the staff. What's the big deal? She apparently was documenting my 'behavior,' as she called it. I told her it was illegal for her to be taking pictures of me without my knowledge. She told me it was illegal to pat one of the girls on the butt or rub their shoulders. Total crap, if you ask me. She was trying to get more money out of me, that's all."

"Did other staff members know about the lawsuit?"

He shrugged. "I don't know. I know that she had been trying to rally my team behind my back. She had been having private meetings with everyone on staff, taking notes, trying to build a case against me."

This didn't sound good for Jay.

"I had to get my lawyers involved. Do you know how expensive it is just to get them to review some basic documents?" He didn't wait for my answer. "They made it clear that I could lose a potential suit, so I wrote up a formal apology letter and had to have HR enact some new policies.

It was no big deal. Sara was fine with the outcome, or at least that's what she said to my face. I know that she and Vienna were working together behind my back to keep the suit moving forward. They were in it for the money."

I couldn't believe he was telling me this.

"Renovating this property took my entire savings. I didn't have the cash for a lengthy legal battle, so I gave her what she wanted." He ran his finger along the bookshelf, finally landing on a guide for hunting elk that apparently captivated his attention more than our conversation because he opened the book and slowly turned page after page, not bothering to look at me.

"What?" I finally asked.

"A raise. A bonus and profit sharing. I set Sara up. We made a deal. She would give up the lawsuit, and I would make sure she was taken care of." He continued to leaf through the book as he responded.

"Did she agree?"

"Of course she agreed." Jay gave me an incredulous look. "Like I told you, she was in it for the money. She tried to claim that she cared about the young staff, but she didn't. She knew that a sexual harassment suit was her ticket to retirement. I've found that people's moral compasses tend to go haywire when you start to involve money. So that's what I did. I offered her a better position, a raise, and she took it without blinking."

"When was this?"

"A few days before she was killed." Jay picked up his water and wiped his hands on his pants. "Sara was my ally. Part of our agreement included her making sure to stomp out any employee uprising. She and I came to a mutual understanding and respect."

A knock sounded on the door, and the front desk clerk peered inside. "Jay, there's a call for you."

"Excuse me, I have to take this." He tossed the elk hunting book on the table. "Feel free to tell your friendly neighborhood gossips the truth." He gave me a once-over, ran his tongue over his lips seductively, and left the library.

I sat in silence for a minute, shaking off the grossness of his lecherous behavior and trying to make sense of what he had said. If he was telling the truth, then what motive would he have had for killing Sara? Unless he didn't want to continue paying her a higher salary or splitting the hotel's profits.

On the other hand, if Sara had agreed to be his insider when it came to employee relations, killing her made no sense.

After a few minutes, I left the library. I wanted to talk to Vienna and hear her side of the story. Did she know about Sara and Jay's agreement? If she could corroborate Jay's story, then suddenly it became much more likely that Marianne might have been involved in the housekeeper's murder.

CHAPTER

TWENTY-FIVE

HAD I COMPLETELY MISREAD the situation? Had I been helping a killer these past couple of days? The more I learned, the more likely it seemed that Marianne was *not* looking after my best interests and, worse, could have killed Sara. The question was why? Had the housekeeper caught her lurking around the hotel grounds? Or could Marianne have left plans to kidnap Alex in her room? Scenarios swam in my head. What if Sara had discovered paperwork spelling out Marianne's intentions while cleaning her room? She could have confronted Marianne and ended up dead. Marianne had definitely proven that she wasn't reliable. Maybe she hadn't meant to kill Sara. It could have been an accident. Or it could have been premeditated. What if she'd seen Sara with photos of Alex or me or sensitive documents? Could that explain why multiple people had claimed they had seen Marianne sneaking around the hotel? Maybe Marianne had plotted to kill Sara and silence her for good.

I shuddered at the thought and pushed away visions of Alex gagged and blindfolded as I returned to the lobby and asked whether Vienna was working the evening shift. The clerk told me he had seen her in the garden a few minutes earlier, so I made my way outside.

A pink dusky light fell over the ambrosial enclosed garden. The calming hum of the gurgling water fountain and the scent of sweet jasmine made me pause and take a long, slow breath. *Remember, Alex is safe.*

I followed the cobblestone path that cut through the patio tables. A few guests lingered beneath green and cream umbrellas snacking on slices of cake and sipping tea and coffee. Solar lanterns flickered on, casting shimmering yellow light on my footsteps. Vienna was on the far side of the garden, pushing a supply cart along the narrow pathway between the guest rooms.

"Vienna!" I called, waving to her.

She didn't acknowledge me. She pushed the cart onward toward the supply room.

I hurried after her.

When I finally caught up to her, I realized the reason she hadn't responded. She had earbuds tucked into both ears and was swaying to music that I couldn't hear.

I tapped her shoulder, causing her to jump.

She whipped her head around and yanked her feather duster from her apron, ready to use it as a weapon.

"Sorry, I didn't mean to startle you," I apologized, and took a step backward.

Her face softened when she realized it was me. "I didn't hear you. You scared me." She removed the earbud from her left ear.

"Sorry," I repeated. "I was hoping to ask you something. I called out to you, but you must not have heard."

She removed the other earbud, tucked them both in her apron pocket, and unlocked the supply closet. "What did you want to ask?"

"Did you hear anything about Sara trying to put together legal action against Jay?"

Vienna glanced around us. She motioned for me to come closer. "How did you hear about that?"

"It's going around the village," I lied.

"The last I heard, Sara had dropped it." Vienna kept her voice low. She restocked the cleaning cart as she continued, filling it with hand soap wrapped in monogrammed tissue paper, travel-sized bottles of shampoo, conditioner, and hand lotion, and individual grooming kits. "It's weird, because a few weeks ago she had been talking about it twenty-four/seven. She asked for my help to talk to some of the other younger members of the housekeeping staff. She told me to keep it a secret. That's why I didn't say anything to you about it earlier. She said that if Jay caught wind that we were banding together to sue, we would lose our shot. She was secretly filming him, you know."

"Wow, really?" I pretended this was news to me.

Vienna stepped farther into the supply closet. She hung her feather duster on a hook before continuing. "She told me to try to get him to make a move. She wanted me to be around him as much as possible so that she could catch him in the act. She wanted to trap him and record it."

"Then what happened?"

"I don't know. It was so weird. All of a sudden, she told

me the lawsuit was off the table. That we couldn't win. That we didn't have a case. She told me that she would watch my back and keep an eye on me. She said not to worry about Jay. She would take care of him, but that we weren't going to be able to sue him. I was bummed out. I thought we had a good shot. He was—is—constantly crossing the line." She tugged on her ruffled green skirt, as if she half expected him to swoop in and try to grab her ass again.

I glanced to the courtyard to make sure he hadn't snuck up on us. There was no sign of Jay, only Officer Downs, who stood near the garden gate. He reminded me of one of the queen's soldiers with his straight spine and severe stare. "Did she say why she didn't think you could win?"

"No. That's the weirdest part. She was convinced. It was her idea to put together the suit. She'd been talking with lawyers, HR, other hotel management people, and then suddenly it was done." Vienna snapped. "Poof. Over. She refused to talk about it and then she was killed. To tell you the truth, the whole thing creeps me out. I've been wondering if Jay found out. Maybe he threatened her and that's why she dropped it? Do you think he could have killed her?"

I didn't answer right away.

"If Jay wanted to put a stop to the lawsuit, that was a way to make it happen, right? I keep wondering if he threatened her and that's why she had such a quick change of heart. It makes sense, doesn't it?" She took off her apron, making sure to grab her earbuds from the front pocket. Then she tossed it in a hamper and locked the supply closet.

Vienna raised a good point. But then again, I wondered why she hadn't mentioned anything about a potential lawsuit or Sara secretly filming Jay earlier, especially when I had told her how important it was for her to share her harassment experiences with Chief Meyers.

"She was acting really weird for a few days before she died," Vienna continued.

"Weird how?"

"I don't know how to explain it exactly—skittish, I guess. She was on edge. I thought she was stressed about getting everything ready for Maifest, but what if I was wrong? What if Jay had threatened to kill her? She kept looking over her shoulder, she was short with staff, she was super jumpy. I just wonder if there was more to it. If Jay threatened her after she brought the lawsuit forward, it would explain her behavior." Vienna's face turned ashen at the thought.

"That's definitely a possibility," I agreed. "Have you shared this with Chief Meyers?"

"She knows about the lawsuit." Vienna didn't expand. Instead she checked the handle to make sure the supply closet was locked and started to move toward the lobby. "I need to go clock out. I've worked a fourteen-hour day, and I'm wiped out. I just want to go home and binge Netflix."

"Sure. Thanks for your input. It's been very helpful." I smiled.

"You don't happen to have any jobs open at the brewery or know of anyone else in town hiring, do you?" Her eyes drifted toward the lobby. "I don't want to hang around with Jay much longer, especially now that Sara is dead. I don't trust him."

"We're not hiring at Nitro, but Der Keller is always looking for help. I'll see what I can do, okay?"

"Cool. Thanks." She walked along the paved pathway.

I followed after her, aware of Officer Downs's steely eyes watching my every move.

"Vienna, before you go, can I ask you one more thing?"

"Go ahead." She folded her arms across her chest.

"It's about Marianne, the guest staying here. Did you notice anything unusual about her?"

Vienna nodded and flared out one nostril. "Uh, yeah. Where do you want me to start? She's super eccentric and pretty kooky, if you ask me. I caught her sneaking around the garden and hiding behind the vending machines more than once. She creeped me and the rest of the housekeeping staff out. Every time I'd turn a corner, she'd be lurking there, like she was spying on me or something. It was super weird."

"Did you happen to confront her about that?"

"It's not up to me to decide what guests do or don't do. Jay has strict rules about allowing guests the run of the place. They're not supposed to go in areas like this." She pointed to the supplies. "Or the kitchen, but otherwise they're free to go wherever they want, even if that means hiding behind the ice machine."

Vienna sounded truthful, but what about the argument? I pressed her. "Did you and Marianne fight?"

"Fight? No. Why? I didn't even know her."

"I had heard that there was an argument between you and her earlier. It could be important. I'm not sure if you've been in the gossip loop, but the police are looking for her."

"A fight? Me?" Vienna scrunched her face. "Are you sure you heard that right?"

"Yeah, that's what I was told. I don't care if you had a disagreement with her. That's your business. It's more about what you may have seen. She's in some serious trouble."

"I didn't see anything. What I told you. She's been sneaking around the entire weekend, like she's Sherlock Holmes or something, but I didn't have an argument with her. Whoever told you that is wrong."

"Okay." I dropped it and left her to clock out. The pink sunset had given way to a deep purple sky with a touch of haziness, much like our New England–style IPAs. Vienna's revelation left me stumped. There were two possibilities. Jay was telling the truth and had worked out a deal with Sara to stop her from pursuing legal action. Or Vienna was correct in her suspicion that Jay had threatened Sara. Had Sara refused to drop the suit? Maybe she told Vienna that to throw Jay off her trail, when in reality she intended to go through with it. If that was the case, then Jay definitely had a strong motive to kill her.

The bigger question was how did Marianne work into the situation? Vienna had been adamant that they hadn't been fighting. In fact she made it sound like they had very little interaction. Could she be lying? She seemed young and naive. So much so that I was considering brainstorming possible employment options with Garrett. She was in a bad situation at Hotel Vierter Stock with a boss who had no business exploiting her. Nitro was continuing to expand. Maybe we could hire her to clean the guest rooms and help with breakfast. That would free Kat for more marketing work, among other things, but I wasn't about to pursue that angle until I had a solid sense of whether Vienna was as innocent as she appeared. There was another possibility that I couldn't rule out, which was that Vienna could have killed Sara. The fact remained that Sara had threatened to fire Vienna. That was a very substantial motive for murder.

It felt like I was so close to figuring out who had killed Sara and at the same time miles away from any solution. My mind kept returning to Marianne. Had she been truthful since the beginning? What if she was right that Sara had simply been in the wrong place at the wrong time? Could Marianne have been the intended target?

But then why would she have kidnapped Alex?

Nothing made sense.

More people than normal for a Sunday evening were out and about on the sidewalks and at outdoor cafés. The road-block had kept the vast majority of tourists in town for another night. The mood was more subdued than last night. I wasn't sure if it was due to the added police presence and the buzz of a continued search, or if tourists had imbibed late into the night at the Festhalle and were slightly hungover. Either way, it was good see my fellow business owners taking in extra cash.

Every table was taken at Der Keller's patio, and a line snaked down Front Street. Shopkeepers had extended their hours, propping open their front doors and beckoning tourists with sidewalk sales and special pretzel and mustard tastings.

I took the back route to Nitro, passing the art gallery where ceramic pottery and watercolor paintings of the Enchantments and Blackbird Island were on display. Officer Downs's heavy footsteps thudded behind me. His radio crackled every now and again, reminding me not only of his constant watchful eye but that an investigation to find Marianne and Forest was still going strong.

I wondered if Chief Meyers had made any headway in tracking them down. Was Marianne working with Forest, or was she in danger? Both seemed completely plausible.

What didn't make sense was kidnapping Alex. If she had really wanted to harm him, she had had the opportunity.

Did she actually think she was protecting him? Or was my initial read on her correct—that she was in desperate need of mental health help?

I couldn't stop the questions and theories from cycling through my brain. I tried to push the thoughts away, but they kept returning, especially because I was acutely aware of Officer Downs breathing on the back of my neck.

I probably should have been concentrating on my own footing and where I was going, because as I rounded the corner toward Nitro, a hand reached out from the alleyway and grabbed me.

CHAPTER
TWENTY-SIX

THE HAND CLAMPED OVER my mouth as I tried to scream and break free. Adrenaline pulsed through my body. I struggled, trying to fight my way out from the forceful arms holding me. Where was Officer Downs? I thought he had been right behind me.

My assailant yanked my ponytail, dragging me farther away from the sidewalk.

Where was my police protection? How had Downs lost me?

I tried to wiggle free.

My muffled screams went unanswered.

The next thing I knew, my body was being slammed against the brick wall. Pain seared through my back and hips.

"I didn't want to have to do this," a vaguely familiar man's voice shouted. "You should have stayed out of it."

He released his grip on my head and mouth and clasped my wrists so tightly I thought they might snap from the pressure. I fought to turn around to face whoever had me in a neck lock.

"Bozeman?" I blinked hard. "What are you doing? I have no idea what you're talking about."

"You know. Don't pretend like you don't." He kept my wrists glued to the wall above my head with one hand. With the other, he yanked a large hunting knife from his pocket. "You scream, and I slit your throat. Got it?"

I nodded. "I'm not going to scream, but I swear I have no idea what you're talking about."

"I just saw you at the hotel, talking to Jay. Talking to Vienna. You've been asking questions all weekend. Too many questions." I could smell stale alcohol on his breath. Was he drunk?

"No, no. You don't understand. It doesn't have anything to do with you." I tried to reason with him. "I've been asking about Marianne. Like I told you earlier, she took my son. I'm trying to find her, that's all."

A brief look of remorse flashed on his face, but it quickly disappeared. "No, I heard you asking about Sara, too. I know that you're working with the police."

"I am. To find Marianne," I insisted. The alleyway hit a dead end about twenty yards down from us. I could see the brick exterior of the building that housed the Nutcracker Shoppe on the first floor and a tapas bar upstairs. Trying to break free and running that way would get me nowhere. My only choice was to wrangle out of his clutches and make a break for the street. There were dozens of police officers patrolling the village, not to mention Officer Downs, who had been my shadow. How had no one seen Bozeman drag me into the alley? For the last two days, I had had constant protection, and now that I was actually in danger, they were nowhere to be found.

"She wasn't supposed to die," Bozeman spit out. "It was an accident. She wasn't supposed to be in the room. What was she doing there?"

It didn't sound like he wanted an answer.

"She shouldn't have been in there. I blame Jay. I think she caught him again and ducked into the guest room to try to get a photo. She'd been doing that, you know? Taking covert photos of Jay harassing the women on staff." His nails dug into my wrists.

"Yeah, I heard." I bit my bottom lip, trying not to let him see that I was in pain. I had to stay in control.

"The room was supposed to be empty. I only took things from empty rooms." He sounded like he was trying to convince himself, not me. "It wasn't a big deal. Nothing major. A few hundred bucks here and there. You don't know how hard it is to earn a living in a town like this. These rich tourists come in, and they don't even have any idea how much cash they have in their wallets. They aren't going to miss a couple hundred bucks."

So Bozeman had been responsible for the guest room thefts. I wondered if he had stolen Marianne's files, too. And had he just broken into Eleanor's room? That was brazen, given how many police officers were patrolling the hotel.

"The room should have been empty," he repeated. His face blotched with color. His body swayed. I was sure he was drunk. The smell of alcohol permeated the alley and made me sick to my stomach.

I tried to formulate an escape. He had me pinned to the wall. My arms were getting tired from being over my head, and my wrists burned with pain. If I got out of this alive I would have some nasty bruises and cuts. A trickle of blood dripped down my right hand. Bozeman's nails had cut through my skin. I guessed that I could get out of his clutches with a knee to the groin. The only issue was the hunting knife.

How quickly could I make my break?

And where the hell was Officer Downs?

"I didn't mean to do it. You have to believe me. It was an accident. I went into the room. It was dark, and she startled me. I grabbed the first thing I could find—a lamp—and hit her. I guess I hit her too hard. I didn't mean to kill her. I'm not a monster. I just reacted too fast. That's all. Mom always said I didn't know my own strength." His voice broke.

"Bozeman, you need to tell the police. If you explain your side of the story, Chief Meyers may be able to offer you some leniency." Maybe if I could reason with him, I could get out of this.

"No way. I'll still go to jail." He shifted his body weight and squeezed my wrists harder.

I winced. "Probably, but this is going to make it worse. As of now, you can confess to accidentally killing Sara. But killing me is going to be premeditated. Any chance of working a deal will be gone."

His cheeks were drawn. The blotchiness spread to his thick neck.

"What's your endgame here, Bozeman?" I asked, catching a glimpse of a flashlight on the sidewalk. "There are police officers throughout the village. You're not going to get away with this, and you're going to make things much, much worse for yourself. Let's go find Chief Meyers together."

"Why would you do that?"

Was it my imagination, or were those flashlights coming toward us?

I had to keep him calm. "Because that's what we do for each other in Leavenworth. I can't promise that everything's going to be fine, but I can tell you that your chances of not spending the rest of your life in prison will be greatly improved if we go find the chief now."

I could tell that he was shifting. He looked younger, like Alex or the twins.

"Chief Meyers is going to arrest me."

"Yeah." I nodded. "And won't that be a relief? You won't have to hold on to this any longer. You can work toward forgiveness. Forgiveness for yourself and forgiveness from Sara's family."

He dropped the knife and released my hands. "It was an accident."

"I know."

He crumpled on the pavement and broke down. "I didn't mean to kill her. I can't believe she's dead. It was just a couple hundred bucks. A couple hundred bucks."

I placed my hand on his shoulder.

He sobbed.

Everything happened in a blur. Light blinded me as Officer Downs and a troop of police rushed toward us.

"Hands in the air! Hands in the air!" Officer Downs shouted. His gun was drawn and pointed at Bozeman.

"Don't shoot him!" I yelled in reply, removing my hand from Bozeman's shoulder. There was no danger of him hurting me. He was hurting. I didn't condone what he had done, but I did believe him that he hadn't intended to kill Sara.

Downs kept his gun targeted at Bozeman while the other officers surrounded him and within seconds had him hand-cuffed and on his feet.

"You okay, Mrs. Krause?" Downs returned his gun to his holster and shined his flashlight in my face.

I shielded my eyes from the light. "I'm fine."

"Let's go," Downs commanded. He directed the officers to remove Bozeman, and then took my arm.

As we departed the alley, I felt a sense of relief that one of the mysteries looming over the village had been solved. Bozeman had killed Sara. Not because of a lawsuit or anything to do with Marianne or Forest, but because she'd been in the room when he had snuck in to steal Marianne's cash.

What a shame.

An innocent woman had been killed over a petty theft.

Bozeman was a big guy. It didn't surprise me that he had overpowered Sara and not realized how hard he had hit her.

His admission cleared Marianne. She hadn't been involved with the housekeeper's death. Could that mean she was the one in real danger now?

CHAPTER

TWENTY-SEVEN

A CROWD HAD GATHERED outside the alleyway. Between Alex's kidnapping earlier and now this, I had a sinking suspicion I was going to be the talk of the village for weeks to come. Officer Downs made way for the police to shuttle Bozeman to the station. April pushed her way to the front of the small audience made up of shop owners, a handful of tourists who had noticed the commotion, and the small army of police officers surrounding us.

"Sloan! Over here!" She waved with both hands, jumping up and down in her skimpy barmaid dress.

"You want me to stop her?" Downs asked with a tiny sparkle of sarcasm in his eyes.

I chuckled. "No. It's fine, but I do appreciate the offer."

He allowed April to come forward. Then he addressed everyone who had gathered. "Okay, folks, let's move along. Go about your business as usual. We've got things handled here."

April practically tackled me in a hug. She stepped back and gaped at me. "My God, Sloan, you're gushing blood. Someone should get you medical attention."

I glanced at the nail marks on my wrists. Gushing was an overstatement to say the least, but I wiped the blood on my shorts. "I'm fine."

"Fine? Fine? You look terrible, Sloan. Awful." Leave it to April to make me feel better.

"I'm fine," I insisted.

April's garish makeup—bright orange lipstick and daisy yellow eye shadow—made her look like a comic book villain under the glow of police flashlights. "Was that Bozeman? What happened? It looked like he was being handcuffed and taken to Chief Meyers's office. What did he do? Is he responsible for kidnapping Alex?" She assaulted me with questions.

I threw my hands up. "April, you should talk to the police. Not me."

She flared her nostrils. "Sloan, don't start with me. You know how imperative it is for me to disseminate important information throughout the village. People depend on me. Did his arrest have anything to do with Alex's kidnapping? Villagers want to know. They need to know that our Bavaria is safe and crime free."

I wasn't about to be the cause of new rumors circulating through town. "Like I said, April. You'll need to talk to Chief Meyers."

"Some help you are, Sloan Krause. I've been sick with worry about you and your family, and this is the thanks I get?" She huffed. "This is going to be the last time I come to you for information. And I'll remember this the next time you want to know what's happening in the village."

If only that wish could come true.

"Would you like to comment?" April looked to Downs.

He remained silent.

"Fine." She let out another long sigh. "Since you're both going to stay tight-lipped, I need to make my way over to the police station."

"Good luck." I gave her a breezy wave, knowing full well that it would infuriate her even more, before continuing on to Nitro, followed closely by Officer Downs.

"Where did you go?" I asked as he continued to move bystanders out of the way. "I thought you were right behind me. I heard your footsteps and breathing, or so I thought."

"A call came through from dispatch," he replied. Even with my long legs, it was an effort to keep up with his giant stride. "I stopped for less than a minute to take the call, and you vanished. I can't believe that drunk kid got to you. After I escort you to Nitro, I intend to resign immediately."

"What?" I couldn't tell if he was being serious.

"Absolutely. I neglected my one and only duty. I don't deserve the badge."

He wasn't kidding.

"No way. I'm not letting you do that, and I'm sure Chief Meyers or your supervisors in Seattle will agree. It happened in a flash, and to tell you the truth, I don't think Bozeman wanted to hurt me." My wrists stung. They would need some attention, but nothing a little antiseptic and Band-Aids wouldn't fix. Otherwise I was unscathed.

Officer Downs didn't share my sentiment. He stopped at Nitro's patio. "I'll be out here. I need to call dispatch."

"Please don't resign on my account," I pleaded. "I'm fine." It was true. In fact, in some ways, I felt better than I had since

Marianne's arrival in Leavenworth. Maybe I had needed something like Bozeman's attack to shake me from the utter panic I'd felt with Alex's disappearance. I could handle myself. What I couldn't handle was anything happening to Alex.

I was more forthcoming with Garrett and Kat when I went into the pub and gave them the rundown on what had happened. Kat was stacking chairs on the tabletops, and Garrett was polishing the tap handles. The tasting room was deserted. It smelled like the lemon polish we used to clean the distressed wood bar.

"You're back," Garrett said. His eyes immediately landed on my wrists. "And you're hurt." Without hesitating, he grabbed the first aid kit we kept at the bar and directed me to a barstool. "Sit!"

I knew it was futile trying to argue with him, and I had to admit that my wrists stung. Garrett gently cleaned my wounds with an antiseptic swab. Kat served as his nursing assistant, holding the garbage can for him to dispose of the cleansing cloths and finding tubes of antibiotic cream and bandages in the first aid kit.

"Who did this to you?" He applied pressure to ensure the bleeding had stopped.

"Bozeman." I flinched in pain as he wrapped my cuts with a gauze bandage. Then I proceeded to tell them about Bozeman yanking me into the alley, how he had confessed to Sara's murder and been arrested by Officer Downs.

"That's terribly sad," Kat said when I finished relaying what Bozeman had told me. "It sounds like the housekeeper's death was an accident, but it doesn't excuse him, and he never should have been stealing from guests in the first place."

"Exactly, and he didn't do himself any favors by lying about it." Garrett closed the first aid kit and returned it to the bar. "If he had called the police right away and stayed at the scene, I think I might have more sympathy for him." He caught my eye. "I don't like what he did to you, Sloan, regardless of whether he felt bad about his crime or was drunk."

"True." Kat sighed. "He's so young, though. He's my age. Can you even imagine? He has his whole life ahead of him, and now he's going to spend it behind bars."

"I don't know about his whole life, but yes, I'm sure he'll be in prison for many years to come, accident or not." Garrett poured himself a half pint of Lemon Kiss. "Anyone else need a nightcap?"

Kat and I declined.

We were quiet for a moment, reflecting on the sober reality that a woman had been murdered and a young life ruined.

"No word from Chief Meyers yet." Garrett wasn't asking a question, rather confirming what I already knew.

"Nope." I shook my head. "I sort of wondered if she might stop by, but I bet she's busy with Bozeman's arrest."

"You calling it a night, Sloan?" he asked, swirling the buttery yellow IPA in his glass.

"I'm leaning that way. I promised Alex, Mac, and Hans that I wouldn't leave until they met me here, but I'm not sure how long they were planning on staying at Der Keller."

My first thought was that I didn't want to bother them. Old habits die hard. Then I realized I should check in with them. I pulled out my phone and shot off a quick text letting them know I was ready to head home and that if they weren't ready I could meet them at the cottage.

Alex responded right away with a thumbs–up emoji: "ON OUR WAY."

"You don't need to come in early," Kat said. "Jack and I already prepped your German sausage casserole for the morning. Garrett and I talked about it. We'll cover breakfast. Jack said he's happy to come in early."

"I wonder why?" Garrett teased. "He's a morning person, right? Or could it have something to do with getting to spend more time with you?"

Kat's jaw dropped open. "What? No. We're just friends."

"Sure. I'm glad my staff is getting along so well." He winked.

Kat's dimples sunk into her rosy cheeks. "We're just friends," she repeated to Garrett. To me she said, "Seriously, Sloan, we've got the morning covered, so don't sweat it. You've been through enough this weekend. You should sleep in and relax."

Again, I was about to resist, but I stopped myself. The new me embraced the idea that my friends and family wanted to support me as much as I wanted to support them.

"Okay. That sounds good. I'll come later."

Garrett let out a long whistle. "Wait, did I hear that correctly? Did Sloan just tell us that she'll come in late?" He turned to Kat.

Kat grinned. "We've finally broken her!"

She and Garrett gave each other a high five.

Mac and Alex arrived shortly to escort me home. Not surprisingly, they had already heard the news on Bozeman. I had a guess who had been circulating the news of his arrest in the village—April. Needless to say, her version of events involved her arriving on the scene before the police. I gave them the real rundown of what had gone down with me and Bozeman.

When we arrived at the cottage, Mac went straight to the kitchen to warm up the teakettle. Alex went to take a shower. I plopped down on the couch. For the first time in weeks, I thought I might be able to sleep through the night.

Mac poured me a steaming mug of chamomile tea and brought it to me on the couch. "How you doing, Sloan?" His eyes were filled with concern.

"Fine." I cradled the warm mug and stared at the fireplace.

He sat down next to me, propping a throw pillow behind his back. "How are you really doing? It's me. I know you hate to admit this, but I do know you, Sloan Krause."

"No, really. I'm feeling better. I think knowing that Bozeman killed Sara brought me unexpected relief. Don't get me wrong, it's terrible on all accounts, but his confession means that Marianne wasn't involved."

"I never thought she was." He sipped his tea. "Alex told me more while we were working. He's sure that she wasn't going to hurt him. He's convinced that she was really scared and thought that she was helping him."

"I know, but why? I get hiding him at Hans's place if she thought that Forest was coming after him, but why tie him up? That part doesn't make sense."

"No." Mac was thoughtful for a moment. "You're right. That part doesn't make sense."

"Hopefully the chief will be able to tell us more. That is, if they ever find her."

"They'll find her." Mac sounded confident. He glanced down the hall and listened for the shower. "Sloan, what are we going to do?"

"What do you mean?"

"I mean about us." His eyes watered. He tried to fight tears back. "It's really over, isn't it?"

"Yeah, Mac. It is." I felt teary, too. I had loved him for my entire adult life. That wouldn't change. Mac would always hold a piece of my heart.

He forced a smile. "I figured. I kept thinking that maybe there was a way that we could salvage things, but the last few days have opened my eyes. You're different, Sloan. You're stronger and you're softer at the same time. It's good to see." His smile was a mix of sadness and pride.

"Thanks." I reached over and squeezed his hand. "You, too."

He kissed the top of my palm, careful not to touch my injured wrists. Then he let my hand go. "I guess this means we should move forward with the divorce?"

"It does." I nodded as I took a long drink of tea. The hot herbal liquid warmed my body. I hadn't expected that our conversation would take this turn, but it was good. Everything that I had been bottling up for months—for years—had bubbled to the surface this weekend. Otto and Ursula's past, Marianne, Mac and me. It was time to release it. To let it go. It was time to accept what was next, and embrace the new.

"Are you going to change your name? It's weird thinking about my folks—they created new identities for themselves when they moved here. It's hard to believe, isn't it?"

I'd had longer to sit with the news of the Krauses' past. "Yeah, but also such a testament to who they are and how much they love you and Hans."

His question brought up something I had been ruminating on for a while—my name. Marianne had said that my family name was DuPont, but I didn't feel a connection with that name. I didn't want to give up being a Krause. It was the name I had identified with for decades. The name that had given me a family. A purpose. "Would it be okay if I didn't?" I asked Mac. "If it's not weird for you, I'd like to stay a Krause."

"I'd love that." Mac cleared his throat. "I'll talk to our Der Keller lawyers tomorrow and get a referral for a good attorney."

"That would be great. I appreciate it." I paused for a minute. Had the shower stopped? No. The steady sound of water continued. It wasn't a surprise. Alex lived in the shower. He had gone from refusing to take showers or baths in elementary school to showering twice a day.

"You know that I will always love you and do anything for you, right?" Mac's voice was thick with emotion again.

I moved next to him and leaned against his broad shoulders. "Same for me."

We sat together in silence. I suspected that, like me, he was remembering happier times and the many years we spent raising Alex together and building a life here in Leavenworth. Something had shifted. My anger at him was fading. I was seeing him in a new light. Our separation had been good for him, too. He had stepped into himself in a way that I had never seen before. His confidence was palpable and not in a sleazy way. It was subtle. It was internal.

Our growth was parallel, although different. Maybe our time together had made us too comfortable. We didn't have to become the best of ourselves, because we'd had each other. Losing that stability had pushed us to change and evolve. If you had asked me on the day that I'd caught him with the beer wench, I never would have imagined we would be here now.

I felt good about where we were going. I knew that Mac would always be family, and not only because of Alex. Because I did love him. How could I not? We had spent nearly three decades together. He was a part of my past, and he was going to be part of my future. For the first time since everything had fallen apart, I felt a renewed sense of comfort. I had no doubt that our divorce would change things yet again, but I also knew that we would find a way forward as co-parents and friends.

Alex emerged from the shower and joined us for tea, packages of raspberry Linzer cookies, and popcorn. Mac lit a fire, which cracked and burned amber flames as we spent hours reminiscing and joking. It was easy and natural.

This is a glimpse into what's next, I told myself after fighting to keep my eyes open and heading to bed. *Alex and Mac are your family.* I drifted off to sleep content with the knowledge that I was loved.

CHAPTER

TWENTY-EIGHT

THE NEXT FEW WEEKS were relatively uneventful. Bozeman's arrest was top news in the village, as was his hearing. He had been transferred to Spokane to await trial. Chief Meyers was pushing for manslaughter, but it would be up to a jury to decide Bozeman's fate.

Police activity lingered in the village for days after Marianne's disappearance, but there were no further leads, and eventually the teams returned to their respective cities. Officer Downs did not end up turning in his resignation, but after an additional week of duty, he, too, returned to Seattle.

One afternoon in mid-June, nearly six weeks after the dreadful events of Maifest, Chief Meyers called me to her office. We were between festivals, and it was still too early for throngs of summer tourists to arrive for rafting trips on the Wenatchee and backpacking trips in the Cascade Range, since school was in session for another week. The village was aglow with brilliant arctic blue skies and a warm early summer sun. If possible, the Maifest flowers had bloomed bigger and brighter. An angelic calm washed over the village as I strolled from Nitro to the police station.

There was an easy lull about Front Street. Shopkeepers chatted with one another. The cobblestone sidewalks were empty. A local preschool class had free rein of the park. Kids rolled down the grassy hill and chased each other around the gazebo. I grinned and waved as I went past.

Chief Meyers was waiting for me when I arrived at the police station. She motioned me to the back with two fingers. "Come on in, Sloan, take a seat." She pointed to a padded folding chair next to her desk. The oak desk was covered with coffee stains and scratches. "I have a couple pieces of news."

My heart skipped a beat. "Okay."

"The first is regarding Hotel Vierter Stock. I'm sure this will be public soon, but I thought you would want to know that Jay has stepped down from management and put the property on the market."

"Really?"

"Staff complaints led to some serious allegations, which I believe you may be aware of?" She widened her eyes.

"I may have heard some rumors." I thought of Vienna, who had just started at Der Keller. I had convinced Mac (not that he needed much convincing) to hire her as a waitress. Garrett and I had also been penciling out the cost of sending Kat and one of the twins to some regional beer festivals this summer. If we were able to make it work, I had promised Vienna I would be in touch about some extra part-time work at Nitro, cleaning the guest rooms upstairs and helping with breakfast prep.

"Funny thing about rumors in the village. Sometimes they end up true," Chief Meyers philosophized.

"Honestly, I had kind of hoped that Jay was the killer because that would have fed two birds with one scone, so to speak." I used Garrett's favorite reworking of the old adage. "For a while there, I suspected Vienna, too, and Eleanor."

"They were on our list as well," she confirmed. "We were able to recover Eleanor's case of wine along with quite the stash of other personal belongings from a number of recent guests from Bozeman's property. He had everything stored in an old barn on his parents' farm. Most of the cash had already been spent, but I take some relief in being able to return valuables to their original owners."

"That's good," I agreed. "Do you think it was an accident?" I wanted to believe that he hadn't killed Sara in cold blood.

"He's sticking to that story. It will be up to a judge and jury now." She frowned. "There is more news." She pushed a file folder toward me. It contained a police report about a suspicious death. A body had been discovered by the train tracks in Walla Walla, Washington. The photos were horrific. A freight train had collided with a car at top speed, instantaneously killing the driver. It had taken a while to identify the body, but DNA tests had come up with a match.

I stared at the name—Forest.

"He's dead?"

"It appears that way."

"What about Marianne?"

She shook her head. "There's no sign of her. Forest was the only person in the car. Although if you read on, you'll note that there were high levels of sedatives in his system."

"What does that mean?"

"It could mean a lot of things. It could mean he took a

bunch of pills and got behind the wheel." She shrugged and tilted her head from side to side as if weighing her words.

I took a moment to digest her meaning. "But that's not what you think?"

She shook her head, again, deliberately, slowly.

"What do you think?" I leaned in.

"I think that someone could have sedated him, put him in the driver's seat, and sent him on a one-way collision course with a freight train." She picked up a pencil from a canister on her tidy desk. Each yellow number two pencil had been sharpened to a perfect pointy tip that reminded me of the alps surrounding the village. She doodled on a notepad.

I stared at the dated office. Posters from previous Oktoberfests and Christmas markets hung on the walls along with notices of safety procedures and a large map of Leavenworth and the surrounding lakes, rivers, and mountain ranges. "Marianne?"

"It adds up, don't you think?" She drew a squiggly line on the paper.

I did, but I still had so many questions.

"You think she killed him?" I asked out loud.

"I don't have any proof, but the circumstances surrounding his death are suspect, to say the very least."

"Are you still searching for her?"

"You bet. That's never stopped." Her eyes drifted to the map, where a variety of primary-colored pushpins had been stuck in different locations.

"Does this mean that I'm out of danger?"

"Probably. That is, if we're to believe Marianne's story." She returned the pencil to its stack.

"Do you believe it?"

"I do, Sloan. I did from the start. It matches what we know from Sally and your time in the foster care system. It matches what you learned from the Krauses. She had every opportunity to harm you and your family, and she didn't. That tells me something."

"But why kidnap Alex? I'm so confused about her behavior."

She nodded. "I understand, and I wish I had answers for you. I'm not sure that we'll get any until we're able to locate her. And I have to warn you that she spent decades underground. I can't guarantee that we'll ever find her, but I'm not going to stop trying."

"I appreciate that."

"We have been able to find proof of your mother's murder. I have that file for you, too." Her tone changed. She glanced around us to make sure that none of her staff were listening. "I made copies because I thought you might want to look it over on your own. There are a few things that might help shed some light on Marianne in here."

"Thank you."

She handed me the file. "You take care of yourself, Sloan. If you hear anything from Marianne, you let me know, okay?"

"Okay."

I left the station in a daze. Front Street Park glowed green under the warm June sun. The spindly leaves of the weeping willow tree quaked as passed I beneath it. One of the restaurants across the street had opened its balcony windows and piped out Mozart. I could smell roasted chicken and summer sausages grilling, along with the scent of blooming wild roses. The preschool class had returned to school, leaving the park deserted. The same was true for the gazebo, where banners hung touting upcoming activities—wine tours, stand-up paddleboarding, horseback riding, fishing, cycling, and kayaking. Our quaint remote alpine village would soon become an adventurer's playground.

I walked to an empty bench near the gazebo and leafed through the file Chief Meyers had given me. It was good that Front Street Park was empty, because what I read in the paperwork sent my head spinning and tears pouring down my face. I didn't care whether anyone saw me crying as I studied pages and pages of my past.

My mother hadn't simply been murdered by Forest. She had been a federal agent, deep undercover. Claire DuPont had been recruited by the FBI after graduating from college. She had followed in her sister Marianne's footsteps. Both had been assigned to the Seattle office. Her initial cases involved tracking a neo-Nazi group responsible for a number of hate crimes against small businesses. She quickly rose through the ranks. Notes from her supervisors praised her work ethic and ability to separate her emotions. A skill I had obviously inherited from her.

She had taken a short leave of absence after giving birth to me. There was no mention of my birth father.

When she'd been assigned Forest's case, something had shifted. At first there were logs of her tracking his movements. She'd done extensive surveillance on him before going deep undercover, pretending to be an unwed mother desperate for cash to feed her young daughter. She'd spent two years living a dual life, inserting herself into Forest's circle and all the while maintaining meticulous notes and careful contact with her handler in Seattle.

The evidence she had collected on Forest and his shady dealings was pages thick. Theft, racketeering, assault and battery, and multiple cases of suspected homicide without enough evidence to officially issue a warrant for his arrest. According to her notes, my mother had suspected that Forest might have associates within the criminal justice system, but she hadn't been able to prove it.

She had been close to getting him on terrorism charges. Her wiretaps and notes documented his plans to blow up a downtown Seattle coffeehouse run by immigrants. The bombing was stopped, but Forest must have figured out that Claire was the informant and ordered her assassination, because the last pages in the file were dedicated to her unsolved murder and the ongoing search for her killer.

Flashes of memories flooded my brain. Her deep laugh. Her ebony hair and soft skin. The scent of apples, and listening to Billy Joel blasting on high in the car with the windows rolled down. I remembered her.

I sobbed harder as I ran my finger across grainy photos of her rocking me as an infant and pushing me on the swings at the playground.

I recognized the undeniable look of love and adoration in her eye when she smiled at the camera while holding me in her arms. I had been loved. That wasn't a lie.

So many talks in Sally's office came flooding back, too. Sally insisting that my family had loved me enough to let me go. To make sure that I was well cared for. That had been true, too.

The one thing I had no memory of was my mother's actual death. I skimmed over crime scene photos, not wanting to embed images of her lifeless body in my head.

My fingers quaked as I read on.

After her death, Marianne stepped in. She, too, had been

trained as an FBI agent; only, her sister's death changed her. According to notes and reports from her supervisors, she had ignored orders to follow protocol and procedure and gone rogue. She decided to take justice into her own hands and try to avenge my mother's death. Sally's theory had been right about her, too.

She'd spent nearly thirty-five years tracking Forest's every known associate. There were dozens of pages of her extensive notes on his potential criminal ring which included high-profile members of the mafia and even a few career politicians.

There were even more notes on me. She had amassed years' worth of research on me. Seeing my old files from foster care and photos of me playing at the park and walking to school gave me pause. She hadn't been exaggerating when she said that she watched me grow up.

She had—literally.

I broke down after reviewing the files. Ursula was right, Marianne really had had my best interests at heart. She had spent her entire life protecting me and trying to avenge her sister's death. For what? A life spent in the shadows? Living alone?

I felt a deep sense of gratitude for Leavenworth and the life I had made here.

CHAPTER

TWENTY-NINE

AFTER I COMPOSED MYSELF, I took the file home and tucked it away for later. At some point, I would sit down with Alex and tell him everything I could about his great-aunt and grandmother. Then I called Sally to invite her to come stay in one of our guest rooms at Nitro and spend a long weekend with me and Alex. There was much to tell her and to share, but that could be done in person over hoppy pints and summer salads on my back deck. Sally had been an integral part of my formative years, and I was looking forward to rekindling our friendship without the angst of my past lingering over every conversation.

"Sloan, I would love to come. How's next weekend? I have to admit that I'm eager to hear the whole story, and so relieved to know that you're safe and that you finally have some much deserved resolution." I could hear the smile in her voice. "Plus, I have a gift for Alex. I remember you mentioned that he's a big Sounders fan. My neighbors' son is the team captain. I hope you don't mind, but I was bragging about what an amazing kid you've raised, and she told her son. He dropped off a signed jersey and a bunch of posters for Alex and his soccer team."

"That's so thoughtful of you. He's going to lose his mind." I could picture him throwing on the jersey and running to the pitch to share the posters with his team.

"It's a date. I'll book a train ticket right now."

When we hung up, I thought of how lucky Alex was not only to have the Krause family and the village looking after him, but Sally, too. It was incredible to think about how much my circle had expanded since coming to Leavenworth. The thought brought happy tears to my eyes.

I brushed them aside and focused. For the moment, there were other pressing issues. Like a keg tapping. I was due at Der Keller for a celebration of our newest beer—a special collaboration between Nitro and Der Keller. It had been Mac's idea. A peace offering of sorts. He and Garrett had worked exclusively on the project, not allowing me anywhere near the brewery.

"Think of it as our gift to you, Sloan," Mac had said. "It will be like your beer worlds colliding, but you have to promise not to peek until it's ready. I remember how you used to sneak around the farmhouse, checking closets and the attic for your Christmas gifts."

I had agreed to stay away from Der Keller while he and Garrett crafted their special brew. It had been fine; there was plenty to do at Nitro. Our summer line was nearly ready to tap, the guest rooms had been prepped for longer stays, and Kat and I had been focused on decking out the back patio. It had been such a success during Maifest that we decided to keep it open for the summer, adding more seating and a pergola custom built by Hans. I had planted fast-growing wisteria that had already started to snake and climb up the wooden structure.

Soon Leavenworth will be bustling with tourists, but for now, I'm glad to have our village to myself, I thought, as I changed into a knee-length white lacy skirt and thin gray T-shirt for the keg tapping. I tied my hair into a ponytail and finished my celebratory outfit with a funky beaded necklace and matching earrings that Alex had found for me at the Maifest markets. At Der Keller I was greeted by familiar faces—Hans, Otto, Ursula, Mac, Alex, Garrett, Kat, Jack, Casey, many friends from the village, and even April Ablin, who, true to form, wore an elaborate red plaid barmaid frock with navy blue trim and lacing across the bust. Her dyed orange hair had been twisted into a tight braid wrapped with a matching plaid ribbon.

The patio doors and each of the wooden shutters had been propped open, allowing the ambrosial June air inside. Waitstaff circulated through the cheery room with platters of smoked trout, beef brisket sandwiches, potato fritters, and mason jars filled to the brim with Bavarian vanilla cream and wild raspberries.

German polka music played overhead. The atmosphere was upbeat and electric; everyone was happy to be together to celebrate and raise a pint before the rush of the summer season brought droves of tourists to our beloved village.

Der Keller's wall of tap handles was a sight to behold. There was something on tap for every beer drinker, from a light summery pilsner to a Dunkel heavy with notes of caramel and malt. But the reason we were all together was to tap the newest creation—a Reuben IPA. Brewed with—you guessed it—sauerkraut. It was Garrett's idea (he had secretly spilled the brew details to me one night a week or two earlier when we had been closing up Nitro. I may or may not have pressured him for specifics).

Garrett had said that when he suggested the unconventional ingredient, Mac had jumped on board immediately to brew the unique sour beer in the style of a Gose. Garrett promised the collaboration was tart and slightly salty, but they had balanced it by adding natural sweetness from strawberries and rhubarb. I couldn't wait to try it.

I found a spot next to Alex in front of the bar. Alex was dressed in his uniform, ready for another day on the job. He'd been working extra hours leading up to the festival weekend, and I hoped it wasn't going to impact his schoolwork.

"Hey, Mom. The necklace looks great." He let me kiss his cheek. I'd noticed since the abduction that he'd been more affectionate. Otherwise he seemed unscathed. I'd been checking in relentlessly, so much so that Hans and Ursula had both suggested that maybe a better approach would be to give him space to come to me when or if he was ready for help outside of our family.

"Someone has good taste." I ran my fingers along the dainty frost, indigo, and charcoal glass beads. "How was your lunch shift?"

"Easy. Dad had me help in bottling because the dining room was pretty dead."

"Help? Don't let him sell himself short, he was running the bottling plant." Hans had come up behind us. He ruffled Alex's hair, while paying him the compliment. "I think the future of Der Keller is in good hands with this one."

"*Ja, ja,*" Otto seconded. He and Ursula beamed with pride at their grandson. "It has always been our dream zat ze family business will continue, and, Sloan, I must tell you zat I zink Alex has ze nose, too!"

Alex's cheeks reddened. "Opa, stop."

"No, it is true. We were testing our new batch of sodas for ze summer, and Alex, he has created ze best flavor. Did you tell her?"

"No." Alex shook his head.

Ursula called one of the waitstaff over and asked them to go pour a glass of Alex's creation.

"You didn't tell me you've been experimenting with soda flavors," I said while we waited for the drink to arrive.

"I wasn't sure how it was going to turn out. I wanted to make sure it was good first."

"See! Ziz is what I am saying. He has ze nose," Otto insisted.

The waiter brought us each a small glass of Alex's soda. It was as clear as the glass beads on my necklace. I fell in love with the drink at first sip. Tiny lemon effervescent bubbles exploded on my tongue followed by a tropical pineapple and mint finish with lingering notes of summer berries.

"Alex, this is amazing." No wonder Otto thought he had inherited the nose. The soda was like nothing I'd ever tasted. It was sophisticated yet approachable. I could picture it being served in a swanky downtown Seattle restaurant.

The blush on his cheeks spread and turned blotchy. That was a trait he had gotten from Mac. "It's no big deal. It's just a soda."

"It is ze best Der Keller soda ever!" Ursula patted his wrist. "Otto has found a competition to submit your soda into, so now you must come up with a name for it, *ja*?"

"Really? Cool." I could tell from the way Alex held his shoulders higher he was pleased with this news. "Okay, I'll think about a name."

"*Ja*, it is cool. Our grandson, he is already on his way to being famous." Ursula shared a knowing look with me.

Mac broke into our conversation by tapping a stein with the edge of a spoon. "Welcome, welcome, everyone. Please gather round." He took his favorite position in front of the wall of shiny tap handles. Garrett hung to the side of the bar. "We're so thrilled to invite you to the first ever co-brew with our friends at Nitro." He motioned for Garrett to join him.

I was struck by how different they were. Mac looked almost corporate. He'd recently trimmed his hair short and wore a pair of slacks and a collared Der Keller black T-shirt. Garrett wore a pair of khaki shorts and a beer chemistry T-shirt. His wavy hair fell over one eye. His style was closer to surfer than anything resembling a corporation.

"We're hoping this will be the first of many future collaborations." Mac clapped Garrett on the back.

They took turns roasting each other in good fun. Garrett teasing about selling out to the man, and Mac joking about Nitro brewing on a kid's chemistry set. I was happy to see that they had formed a mutual respect as brewers, if nothing else. I didn't anticipate that they would ever be fast friends, but that was fine with me. Leavenworth was a small town, and there was no need for enemies or challenging relationships.

In that spirit, I moved closer to April and offered her an olive branch. "Did you hear the news?" I whispered as Mac touted the fact that the collaboration had the very best hops in the Pacific Northwest.

"No, what?" She immediately perked up.

"Rumor has it that there's a new romance in town."

April scanned the crowd. "Who? Mac?"

"No." I scowled. "Do you really think I'm keeping tabs on my ex-husband's love life?"

"I would." She shot a glance at Mac that lingered a moment too long.

That I didn't doubt.

"No, think young love." I nodded toward Kat. I knew she wouldn't mind me breaking the news that she and Jack had recently become an item. Neither Garrett nor I were surprised when Jack had asked her out. They'd been nearly inseparable ever since.

"Ohhh." April clapped. "I absolutely adore young love. I'll have to cozy up to the new couple and get the scoop. *Die Zeitung* could use a good puff piece. They'll make for a wonderful cover story for the next issue. We can do a photo shoot at Nitro. The place where it all began. I can see it now, an adorable Bavarian couple—lederhosen, the dress I loaned Kat, overflowing beer steins. It's perfection!" She scurried over to talk to them.

I mouthed "sorry" to Kat, who leaned against Jack's shoulder. She shot me a teasing glare.

Mac jumped onto the top of a table. His signature move. "Who's ready to tap this beauty?"

Everyone cheered.

"Okay, let's do it. We named this beer the Brewin' Reuben, and we can't wait for you to try it!" He nodded to Garrett. "Go ahead and do the honors, my friend."

Garrett tapped the keg and poured the flowing beer into huge pewter steins for him and Mac. Then he raised his stein and said, "To collaborations and bright futures."

He caught my eye, letting his gaze lock with mine for a moment before smiling and turning to Mac.

"To collaborations and bright futures," Mac repeated. They clinked glasses and then poured pints for the crowd.

I found myself overcome with emotion. Collaborations and bright futures sounded like exactly what I needed. Scratch that. Collaborations and bright futures were exactly what lay ahead for me. I could definitely raise a glass to that.

I took a pint from one of the waitstaff, held it high, and said a silent thanks to the universe for my friends, my family, and my beloved village.

Garrett worked his way over to me after frothy pints were passed around the room. "Hey, brew partner, be honest. What do you think?" He studied me as I tasted the beer.

"A Reuben, really? Are you sure Mac didn't talk you into this? It's more his style." I teased.

His eyes twinkled. "Nah, I wanted to push the envelope. That's science, right? And if it's terrible, Der Keller can take the blame."

I anticipated the beer would have a punch-you-in-the-face sour quality. To my surprise, it had a touch of sourness, but a delicate level of fruitiness that balanced out the sauerkraut, much like a traditional Gose, which was known for its lemon sourness. The style originated in Goslar, Germany, where it was fermented with salt and coriander.

"It's amazing." I took another sip, letting the flavors settle on my tongue. "You know, this actually makes sense. The saltiness of the sauerkraut really works."

Garrett beamed. "Thanks. That's good to hear. I was hoping to impress you." He leaned closer and whispered in my ear. "You're hard to impress, you know."

"Am I?" I clutched the pint glass in an attempt to gain control of the tingling sensation flooding my body.

"You are, Sloan Krause, you are. But I'm going to make it my mission to keep finding ways to impress you." He moved back slightly but held my gaze, staring at me as if we were the only people in the room. "For starters, what do you say we take a road trip to Wenatchee later this week? There's a brewery doing farm-to-table dinners. Five courses, beer pairings, you and me under the stars. What do you say?"

"Strictly for research purposes, of course?" I tilted my head to the side.

"I don't think I said anything about this being a research dinner. That is, unless you want to keep things *strictly* professional." He gave me a half grin.

"Dinner sounds nice." I left it at that as he got caught up in a conversation with an admirer who had already fallen for his beer.

I wasn't sure where things were headed with us, but these last few weeks had taught me a valuable lesson on keeping my heart open. I'd learned so much about my own shortcomings from my breakup with Mac. I wasn't ready to dive headfirst into a new relationship with Garrett yet, but I was ready to dip my feet into the pool, and I felt confident that our friendship and mutual trust would provide a stable foundation for whatever came next.

Later that night, I strolled home to my cottage, feeling contented and more at peace than I'd been in years. Spring had given way to the early days of summer. Sunlight lingered as solstice loomed nearer. The cobblestone sidewalks were packed with people waiting in line for fudge and marzipans at the chocolate shop and clapping along to oompah music on bar balconies. I grinned as I passed by. These halcyon days were meant to be savored. I had learned that in almost losing Alex. It was time to live in the now. My past was my past, and whatever the future held, I knew I could handle it.

A small white envelope was taped to my front door. My name was written on the front, but there was no return address or other identifying information. I yanked the envelope free and went inside.

Since the evening was still warm, I took the envelope outside and flicked on the Edison-style lights strung around my back porch. I sat in the latest addition to my ever-expanding outdoor area—a wooden rocking chair that Hans had delivered the other day. It creaked ever so slightly as I rocked back and forth, and still held the faintest aroma of wood stain.

I opened the envelope to find a handwritten note addressed to me. I recognized the cursive writing.

My dearest Sloan,

It is with great sadness that I write this. I'm sure you have questions. I have some answers, but not all.

Before I get to that, please let me apologize for taking Alex. I never intended to harm him. I thought it was the only way to get through to you. I realize now that I probably did more damage than good. However, he is your son, which means he's strong and resilient, and while he might carry a scar or two, he will recover.

Forest is dead. He won't be bothering you or anyone you love ever again. I've made sure of that. When I realized that he was already in Leavenworth, I had to act fast. I could tell that you weren't going to budge. You weren't going to run. I understand. I don't blame you, but that's why I had to use Alex. It pulled attention away from me and gave me a chance to get Forest out of town—far, far from you and your family.

I'm sure you've seen the police files and the footage from the hotel. I went willingly with Forest, promising to deliver Alex to him. A friend on the force helped me plot my escape. Once I knew Forest was nowhere within reach of you, I was able to convince him that I had Alex hidden in an abandoned train depot. I'll let you fill in any details from there.

You might not approve of my tactics, but I promise you that everything I've done over the years has been for you and for Claire. My greatest regret is not getting to be a part of your life. I had hoped maybe that could change, but now it can't. You won't hear from me again. You're probably happy to know that. I just wish I could have shared more about Claire with you. She would be so proud of you. Of who you've become. Of how you've raised your son. You are your mother exemplified. Even getting to spend a few days with you has brought me more joy than you'll ever know. You gave me the gift of seeing my sister again through your eyes. It's a memory I'll cherish and carry with me wherever I go.

On that note, I'm going away. Not that that's anything new for you. I've watched you from afar, and now I must let you go for good. You are the daughter I never had, Sloan. I wish so many things. I wish I could have been with you to braid your hair when you were young. I wish I could have stood next to you when you married Mac or held your hand when you delivered Alex, but fate had other plans. You may not believe it, but I have loved you from before you were born. I will love you until the day you die. The love that Claire had for you ties us together. I see how loved you are by your family in Leavenworth. This brings me comfort. Embrace that love, Sloan. You have so much more to offer the world.

With deepest love and affection,
Your aunt, Marianne

I clasped the letter to my chest when I finished reading. Tears didn't flow, rather a profound sense of warmth and comfort flooded my body. Everything Marianne had told me was true. I had been and *was* loved by her and my mother. She had made the greatest sacrifice for me, her own happiness for mine. I wasn't sure if or how I could ever repay her for that. But I knew one thing—I would spend the rest of my life trying to live up to her legacy of love, with Alex and surrounded by my family and friends in my own Bavaria.